The Cow Shed

ALSO BY EMMY ELLIS

DETECTIVE ANNA JAMES
Book 1: The Pig Pen
Book 2: The Lion's Den
Book 3: The Copy Cat
Book 4: The Cow Shed

DI BETHANY SMITH
Book 1: The Cold Call Killer
Book 2: The Creepy-Crawly Killer
Book 3: The Screwdriver Killer
Book 4: The Scorched Skin Killer
Book 5: The Street Party Killer
Book 6: The Candy Cane Killer
Book 6.5: The Secret Santa Killer
Book 7: The Meat Hook Killer
Book 8: The Blade Killer
Book 9: The Sledgehammer Killer

DETECTIVE CAROL WREN MYSTERIES
Book 1: Spite Your Face
Book 2: Hold Your Breath
Book 3: Guilt Burns Holes
Book 4: Best Served Cold
Book 5: Blood Runs Deep

DETECTIVE TRACY COLLIER
Book 1: Gutted
Book 2: Crushed
Book 3: Skinned
Book 4: Grabbed
Book 5: Sunk
Book 6: Cracked

MORGAN YEOMAN
Book 1: Dead in the Dirt
Book 2: Dead End
Book 3: Dead Secrets
Book 4: Dead Reckoning

THE
COW
SHED

EMMY ELLIS

JOFFE BOOKS

Joffe Books, London
www.joffebooks.com

First published in Great Britain in 2025

© Emmy Ellis 2025

This book is a work of fiction. Names, characters, businesses, organisations, places and events are either the product of the author's imagination or are used fictitiously. Any resemblance to actual persons, living or dead, events or locales is entirely coincidental. The spelling used is British English except where fidelity to the author's rendering of accent or dialect supersedes this. The right of Cath Staincliffe to be identified as author of this work has been asserted in accordance with the Copyright, Designs and Patents Act 1988.

No part of this book may be used or reproduced in any manner for the purpose of training artificial intelligence technologies or systems. In accordance with Article 4(3) of the Digital Single Market Directive 2019/790, Joffe Books expressly reserves this work from the text and data mining exception.

Cover art by Dee Dee Book Covers

ISBN: 978-1-80573-218-1

PROLOGUE

2004

Effie Workington stopped in the darkness of Cooper's Crossing to listen for the sound again. She was sure it had been the shuffle of grass. Another noise now — the sole of a shoe on the path just behind where she stood. She turned, ready to have a go at Shannon, wanting to tell her to bugger off and leave her alone. Her cousin had followed her from the pub but had gone the other way just as they'd reached the Crossing. She'd embarrassed Effie in the Plough, kicking up a fuss, and Effie needed some time to calm down.

Typical Shannon, coming after her for another go.

A shape stood in the murk, and the breath catching in Effie's throat dried it out. She coughed, then swallowed, her heart beating hard. Even if it was Shannon, it was still unnerving to find someone there.

"Shannon?"

No response. Was it someone she didn't know?

"Oh God," she said, annoyed that her voice was trembling. Her dad had taught her never to show fear because it let your opponent know they had the upper hand, but how could she not be spooked? "What do you want?"

The person didn't answer.

"Look, Shannon, if that's you playing games, then for God's sake just leave me alone for a couple of days, all right? You've pissed me off, and all because you don't want me to have a boyfriend."

That was about the sum of it. Shannon had never been one to have full-blown relationships, so could never understand. Maybe the odd one-night stand, never anything serious. She'd never fitted in with men, or even women. Effie was her only real friend, which made it awkward when Effie had a fella. Trying to juggle her time between a bloke and her cousin was exhausting.

"I know how you feel, I really do, but it's unfair of you to try and run my life. I had something really good going there, and you messed it up tonight — interfering, telling me to break it off with him. He's not going to want to have anything to do with me now, but that was the plan, wasn't it? What is it about *him* in particular? Why didn't you do that with all the other men?"

Still the person didn't speak. Why were they just standing there listening? Were they trying to formulate an answer? Oh no, had Shannon found out about . . . about when Effie was little? It would make sense then, why she'd butted in tonight, but Shannon would never understand that kind of bond with another person.

The figure breathed heavily. A pinch of fear twisted Effie's stomach — was this person a weirdo? Mum and Dad had warned her about Cooper's Crossing, the patch of land dividing the housing estate. You never walked through there at night, but she'd been so upset, not thinking straight, she'd done it anyway.

She stared beyond the figure at the lights coming from the houses, the sky partially lit by a sun that had long set, but as it was summer still gave off a grey-peach glow on the horizon. Behind her, a little alleyway led to another street. It was so close, yet far enough away that, if she turned to run and the person chased her, they'd catch her before she got there.

She remembered something else Dad had told her and took off her shoes. She held one in each hand as weapons. The heels would do some damage if they jabbed into someone's eye. She almost laughed at how ridiculous she was being, then her mind whispered that she could be in trouble here, this *wasn't Shannon*, so maybe it wasn't so ridiculous after all.

She backed away slowly so the figure wouldn't get the idea that she wanted to create distance, enough that she could run. The skirt of her above-the-knee white dress swung with her movement. "If you're not Shannon, who are you?"

With no reaction and her heartbeat speeding, Effie had the awful feeling something horrible was about to happen if she didn't get herself away from here. Would anyone hear her if she screamed? Probably, but this estate was renowned for people screeching and being daft.

Shenanigans. And no one would do anything.

She continued to back away and squinted ahead. As far as she could make out, the person hadn't stepped forward to follow her. Was it one of those drug dealers people had been going on about? A rash of them had set up shop on the estate, peddling on the street corners. Maybe they were just acting menacing so she'd piss off and leave them to it.

"Look, I never saw anything. I'm not going to tell anyone you were here, all right?" She sounded confident enough now, thank goodness, and to add to her fake bravado she turned and casually walked towards the alley.

It still seemed so far away.

She'd made it five long strides when the slap of footsteps came from behind her, then a shove to her back sent her sprawling onto the path. Bits of tarmac dug into her bare knees and, reeling from shock, she scrambled to figure out what to do. She managed to get back to her feet, still clutching her shoes, and spun to face the bastard. She lashed out, swiping one of her heels through the air, but it met with nothing. The weirdo grunted, and the sound of it chilled Effie to the bone — they were angry. She swiped again and met with nothing again, and pressure on her chest sent her staggering backwards to land on her side. Pain lanced through her hip, and her eyes stung with tears of panic.

"Please, just let me go home."

They were down on the ground with her, punching her temple so the other side of Effie's head whacked onto the path. She struck out with one of her shoes, and this time it met with softness, maybe an arm? Hauled over onto her front, she registered what she thought was a knee pressing into her back. She flailed her shoes around in the hope she'd hurt whoever this was, but something cold and silky touched her throat, then drew tight. Was it a scarf?

The tension against her windpipe increased, and she gulped in a huge breath, her chest inflating painfully. The scarf tightened some more, and a waft of movement in front of her eyes gave her the idea that the weirdo had wrapped the material around again. More tightening, then the fumbling of perhaps a knot being tied at the nape of her neck. The knee on her back hurt, and her attacker yanked on the scarf so Effie's head and torso rose. Stars dotted her vision, and she tried to gulp more air in, but only managed a useless sip that did nothing to ease her burning lungs.

It was at that moment she knew she was going to die. She fought it, throwing her arms around ineffectually. Laughter rippled. She recognised it as belonging to someone she knew — and she understood why they were killing her now. Effie should never have taunted them. She shouldn't have acted so smug.

She tried to buck them off, but it was pointless. Her head and torso were pulled back even more until it felt like the scarf would cut through her skin. Just as her vision gave out, she received another blow to the head. Her shoes were placed on her feet, and there was the floaty sensation of being lifted and carried along the path.

Then nothing.

CHAPTER ONE

At five past eleven on a nippy October night, Mina Isherwood left her favourite pub, the Dagger Point, and headed towards home on the Rowan Estate. She tottered left towards the kerb, ready to cross the road, then remembered she didn't live that way anymore. She'd recently moved from a flat to a house, and a lot of her old neighbours were giving her gyp — she didn't have kids or a husband, so why had the council handed her better and larger accommodation? She wasn't about to tell them she had health issues and her flat had been riddled with mould. It was none of their business.

Regaining her bearings, she stumbled across the road to the right, a bit worse for wear. All those gins that man kept buying for her were giving her loose legs. Mind you, she wasn't about to complain. She was skint and had only popped into the Dagger for a swift half after work, but here she was, hours later, three sheets to the wind.

Her ankle turned, and a spike of pain shot up her leg.

"Bloody hell. Shouldn't have worn these chuffing shoes."

She hobbled onto the grass verge beside the pavement and bent over to check for any damage. She couldn't see too well in the dark, but the pain had receded.

She continued walking, readying herself to whip past the mouth of an alley that always gave her the creeps. The front was lit by the glow of a nearby lamp post, but at a quick glance, the stretch of tarmac looked like a dark tunnel with nothing at the end of it. Fathomless. In reality there was a play park, the usual swings and roundabouts, and a large field. It would be quicker to go that way — her house was only on the other side of it beyond the border of trees — but she wasn't brave or stupid enough to do it alone.

Only one more step and she'd be at the edge of the alley. She hesitated in taking it, then told herself to sprint and not look down there. She got the sprint part right but not the looking. She peered to her left and wished she hadn't. Someone stood just beyond the splash of light: white dress, long blonde hair, creepy pale face. Was it that ghost people spoke about? Mina screamed, dashing forward, only for the sound of footsteps to chase her. Whoever had been in that alley shot past her, giving her a nudge with her elbow, then raced ahead into a ginnel down the way between two houses that stood in darkness, the residents likely in bed.

A ghost can't touch you, but I definitely felt something.

Shuddering, Mina stopped, pressing a hand to her chest, taking a moment to decide which way to go. If she continued onwards, that weird woman could rush out at her again, and she didn't need another scare like that. But if she went back to the alley . . . So much for thinking she wasn't stupid enough to go down there alone. She actually contemplated it.

She checked the nearby houses, looking for one with lights on she could run to for help. She could go back to the Dagger and order a taxi, but that seemed daft when her house wasn't that far away, and anyway she couldn't afford it. She retraced her steps, pausing at the mouth of the alley and staring into the darkness, daring herself to be brave and face her fears. If she squinted hard enough, it wasn't as black as she'd thought — the sky was a lighter shade, and the faint silhouettes of roofs materialised. If she focused on those and not her fear, and if she used the torch on her phone, she'd be all right to go that way, wouldn't she?

"Don't be so bloody silly."

She abandoned that idea and walked the original route, taking a deep breath and staring down the ginnel. Whoever that woman had been wasn't there. It could have been that odd lady, the one people said wasn't really missing, but wasn't she too young? Mum said her disappearance was twenty or so years ago.

Maybe it's someone mucking about near Halloween.

Mina put on a spurt of speed and made it to the end of the street, checking over her shoulder every now and again to make sure the woman wasn't following. She turned left at the corner, onto a road leading to the other side of the park. Glad of the lights on inside the houses here, she quickened her pace even more, ignoring the slight twinge in her ankle. She veered left again and crossed the road to her house on the other side. She entered her front garden via the picket gate and secured the little metal latch. Eager to get inside, she spun round, ready to rush up the path, but a flash of white caught her attention down the side of her house by the wheelie bins. Was it that bloody woman again? Did she have *ballet* slippers on?

Heart hammering and breath stalling, Mina headed for her front door, scrambling to get her key out of her handbag. She shoved it in the slot, hand shaking, and twisted it, pushing inside and slamming the door behind her. Slipping the chain on and drawing the top and bottom bolts across had her feeling a little less frightened, although her tight chest had other ideas about that, and another frisson of panic sluiced through her.

She kicked her high heels off, leaving them at the bottom of the stairs, and hung her pink leather jacket on the newel post. In the kitchen, she didn't part the slats of the Venetian blind over the window at the sink. Instead, she moved across to the dining area. The back door had two windows either side, the whole lot thankfully covered by closed curtains. She sidestepped to the far edge and peeled one back a little, enough of a gap that she could see out into her garden.

The automatic security light had snapped on. The ghost woman stood by the rotary washing line, strands of her hair pegged to it as though she'd been hung there to dry. It *had* to be a myth, this silly ghost story, because she looked too real, and she was *definitely* too young to be . . . what was her name? Effie, that was it.

Mina laid a hand on her ever-tightening chest, then let go of the curtain and scuttled over to her table. She sat with a thud, and ferreted in her bag for her phone. She'd ring the police and tell them some nutter had pegged herself up in the garden. Christ, how weird was *that* going to sound?

A tap on the back door had her shrieking before she could rein the sound in, and she tossed her phone in fright. She registered it falling to the floor, the clatter — had the screen smashed? The tapping changed to banging, as if a fist was smacking the glass. She let out another shriek, then slapped a hand over her mouth and lunged for her phone. Another big bang, and she darted to the edge of the curtain again to peer out. The creepy cow had unpegged herself from the washing line, and stood in front of the back door. She must have caught a glimpse of Mina because she looked to the side and they made eye contact.

"I've phoned the police," Mina shouted. "So you'd better fuck off before they get here."

What was she doing, warning her? Truth be told, she just wanted her to go away. The woman took two steps back, then forward, both palms raised as if she intended to smash through the pane. Thinking quickly, Mina let the curtain go and snatched her phone and keys up, then ran down the hallway to the front door. If she could exit this way, she might get help before the mad bitch caught up with her.

The banging started up again, so she drew the bolts across as well as the safety chain. Another bang from the back of the house and she opened the front door and pelted outside barefoot. The cold of the ground seeping into her feet, she legged it across the street to the only neighbour who'd spoken to her since she'd moved in, and pounded on the door.

No one answered and, panicking, she turned to run, intending to go to the next house along, but a smudge of white flickered in the corner of her vision. *Oh God, no . . .* She faced her house. The woman stood in the front garden, ballet dancing her way down the path in ethereal swirls. She opened the gate and pranced out onto the pavement, did a pirouette, and then ran hell for leather down the street and around the corner.

Mina stared that way, momentarily stunned into staying where she was, but the thought of the freak coming back propelled her into her house. She locked up again and sat on the bottom stair, kicking her shoes to one side so she could warm her chilled feet on the carpet. The shock of everything hit her, and she trembled all over, finding it difficult to keep her finger still enough to press the icon to ring her mother.

"Everything all right, love?" Mum asked. "Has something happened? You're ringing me ever so late."

Mina blurted it all out, hot tears falling, turning cold when they reached her jawline. She dashed them away.

Mum sighed. "There's no way it can be Effie Workington, darling, if she was as young as you're saying. Personally, I've always said Effie wouldn't have disappeared the way she did without telling anyone, so I don't believe she's still alive anyway. Whoever keeps pretending to be her is sick in the head. Do you need me to drive round and stay the night? Or I'll pick you up to come to mine?"

"No, I'll be all right."

"Are you sure?"

"Yeah, it's just someone dicking about."

Mina said goodnight, ended the call, and remained on the step, staring at the mottled glass panels in the front door — at the shape coming closer, blurry and white. That pale face hovered close to the glass, breath creating a circle of condensation.

It wasn't a ghost, it bloody wasn't.

Mina lifted her phone to call the police, but the woman retreated. Mina couldn't see from where she sat, but had the crazy cow gone round the back again? Would the banging start up? She rose and edged across the hallway, then darted into the living room so she could part the curtains a bit and look out.

The woman stood directly in front of her on the other side.

Mina screamed, but anger surged this time — she didn't *need* the bloody police, she could deal with this on her own. Who the hell did this nutjob think she was, scaring her like that? Or was it a kid in a mask? Whatever, she wasn't going to put up with it. She marched to the hallway, undid the bolts and chain, wrenched the door open and stepped out to give the bitch what for.

The woman was gone.

Mina crept to the left and went down the alley beside her house.

No one there.

Letting out a long, unsteady breath, she scuttled inside and locked up. She drew the curtain across on the front door and clutched her phone. If her visitor came back, she was dialling 999. She turned to go and make a cup of tea.

The woman stood in the kitchen doorway.

CHAPTER TWO

The Cow Catcher stood in the Cow Shed. Irritation flickered. Catcher had experienced that before, and it hadn't ended well then either. Jealousy played a part. It was difficult to rein in the emotions when they gripped you so hard. Catcher had promised not to do it again, but the inevitable had happened. Mina should have stayed in her lane. Tonight had been the last straw after watching her for several nights.

Still, she'd paid the price, and now it was a waiting game. Waiting and watching to see what the police made of things. They'd been crap in the past and Catcher had got away with it, but that might not be the case now. Forensics had come on in leaps and bounds, and, while Catcher had worn the disguise, it didn't mean clues wouldn't lead straight to the front door. Like touching pegs from the washing line without wearing gloves.

You know better. You should have taken the pegs with you.

The mask hung on a hook, the skin dried out twenty years ago and fashioned onto a cast of Effie's face. Her hair had been cut and attached to a cream-coloured woollen hat stuck to the mask, and Catcher usually put it on to venture out into the night and dice with danger.

People saw Catcher on those expeditions in the darkness. It gave a giddy thrill to be so exposed yet hidden at the same time. The short white dress Effie had worn on the night of her death hung in the cupboard, the ballet shoes with their long ribbons on the base beneath — those weren't Effie's. Her high-heeled shoes took pride of place on a podium inside a glass case next to the dress, ones she'd used to try to hurt Catcher. They'd become hard weapons, but the soft scarf had been the victor.

Effie now resided underground, rotted after all these years, her skeleton nestling in the mud along with her handbag and its contents — a lipstick, a tampon, a packet of sweets. And a purse with a fiver, a few copper coins, and a bank card in it. The police had searched endlessly for the bag, and one of them had whinged about how someone must know where it was.

Catcher stroked the mask. It was surely covered in DNA by now. Effie's face could get Catcher in so much trouble.

And those pegs.

Did Mina have the potential to do the same?

Time would tell.

CHAPTER THREE

Shannon Workington tromped across her large back garden towards the allotments at the bottom, two of which she rented out to other people, giving her a little extra income. She had vegetables to pull before the frost ruined them. A large wicker basket, the handle in the crook of her arm, banged against her skinny thigh with every step, and she plotted the rest of her day in her head. She'd clean and chop the carrots, and freeze most of them. Then there was the beetroot to pickle and, joy of joys, she had her first pumpkins to pick. They wouldn't win any prizes — to be honest, they wouldn't even make very good jack-o'-lanterns — but she was proud all the same and intended to make an open flan with the flesh.

She wound her scarf around her neck three times, and tucked the ends into the collar of her thick padded coat. She could be out here a while, especially if one of the renters came by later. They'd likely want to talk. Shannon didn't mind, even if she gave the impression she did. She lived alone, and, if she didn't have the gardeners to speak to, drinkers in the Dagger, or her next-door neighbours, she'd live a pretty lonely existence.

She reached the top edge of her patch and got down on her knees to start on the carrots, but a hump-like shape in Mr Daltrey's part of the garden had her frowning and back up on her feet quicker than she'd like. Her head went giddy, something she'd noticed it did of late.

She placed her basket down and stared over there, squinting to determine what, exactly, it was. Definitely a person. Dark jeans or trousers. A black coat. A hat. Oh God, had Mr Daltrey fallen over when he'd come here yesterday evening and stayed outside all night? He'd be so cold by now.

He could even be dead.

Spurred on by adrenaline, she tromped over there, moving around the lump for a better look. But what she saw wasn't Mr Daltrey. It was a woman, one she'd seen a lot in the Dagger, mainly at the bar talking to Old Tanner, the creep always eyeing up the younger women. Bloody pervert.

She recalled something else she knew about him and shivered.

"Mina?" Shannon called. "Are you all right, love?"

Blue eyes open, Mina stared at nothing, her cheeks so pale, her lips without their usual candyfloss-pink colour. A tinge of blue surrounded them, but that wasn't surprising, considering how cold it was. Shannon stepped forward, ignoring her instinct to run indoors and get a blanket to cover her with. She had to check whether she was alive first. Shannon was a practical woman, a realist. She bent over and pressed two fingers to the side of Mina's neck.

The skin was cool enough, even through her glove, to confirm that this young lady was no longer alive. Shannon straightened and took a moment to process the information.

A dead body on Mr Daltrey's allotment patch.

A bruise ring around Mina's neck.

"Oh, sodding heck!"

The enormity of it sank in. Shannon staggered backwards, distancing herself. The thought flickered through her mind that someone might accuse *her* of being responsible for this, but she was fifty-one and didn't run in Mina's twenty-something circles. She had no beef with Mina, so why would anyone point the finger at her?

Because of Effie . . .

"The police. I need to phone the police."

She lurched away, back up the narrow patio-slab pathway between her plot and Mr Daltrey's. Perhaps meanly, she thought about the number of police boots that would ruin the ground and how her crop would be lost if she didn't get the chance to pull it up.

She checked the backs of the houses either side of hers. It had always been just this trio of homes on this edge of Marlford. Shannon and the other two residents owned the land out the back of their gardens and refused to sell it to developers. The farmer, whose land abutted either side of theirs and beyond that at the back, had also dug his heels in on that score. Would he have seen anyone coming here? Would Shannon's neighbour Yvette, who never slept too well? She'd gone to work earlier, so Shannon didn't have to worry about her snooping at what she planned to do next, but Tuesdays were her other neighbour Nancy's days off. When Shannon had drunk her morning coffee at the living room window earlier, she hadn't seen her leaving her house on her bicycle. Not that she was the nosy type or anything, she just liked knowing what was what. It paid to be vigilant, living out in the sticks, and Mina's body proved it.

Instead of going inside and finding her phone, Shannon nipped around to the front of the houses and knocked on Nancy's door. With no answer and no sign of movement behind any of the windows, she reckoned she must have missed Nancy going out when she'd been in the shower. Satisfied no one would see her, she returned to her plot and quickly pulled up the vegetables, bunging them in the basket. She'd make out she hadn't seen the body until she'd finished. It wasn't as if Mina was going anywhere, was it? So there was no rush for the police to get here. Dead was dead, no reviving her.

Annoyed her day was going to be shot to pieces, what with officers on her property, she took her loaded basket indoors, then collected the pumpkins, one under each arm.

"Like two heads."

Shannon chortled, despite the severity of the situation. Back indoors, she acted out what she was going to tell the police. She placed the basket and pumpkins on the draining board, stared out of the kitchen window as if to admire the view, and shrieked at the sight of what was undoubtedly a body.

"Oh my God!" She nodded to herself. "Yep, that's a good response."

She rushed outside and down to Mr Daltrey's plot, once again checking for a pulse in case Nancy *was* indoors and just happened to look out at this precise moment. Finding nothing, she moved quickly back into her house and locked herself in, only now thinking that the killer could be lurking behind one of the trees beyond the rear gardens, ready to murder *her*.

"Christ alive!" She shuddered. "Bugger, what if they've killed Nancy?"

She found her phone on the little side table next to her favourite chair in the living room, and with a shaking hand dialled 999. After the man had answered and asked her which service she required, she gasped out, "Police. There's a dead woman in my back garden."

* * *

It didn't take long for the police to arrive. Shannon spied on them from her favourite chair. Two uniformed officers in a patrol car got out of the vehicle and surveyed the street, although they wouldn't exactly see much apart from three houses, three front gardens, fields opposite, and a lane that led to the outskirts of Rowan. It was a ten-minute walk to the Dagger; she no longer owned a car. Shannon would definitely be going for a stiff drink later.

One of the coppers opened the white-painted gate and approached the front door. It was Julia Parsons's son, who'd been a little shit as a kid but had clearly sorted himself out. What was his name again? Ah, Maddox. The other officer followed him, a red-haired woman of about twenty who Shannon didn't recognise.

She waited for the doorbell to ring before she bothered getting up. She took her bunch of keys from the bowl on the radiator cover in the hallway and slipped them in her pocket. She didn't want those two traipsing through her house, and she wasn't prepared to leave the door open, not in this weather. It'd let all the heat out. She stepped outside, flapping her hand to indicate to Maddox that she needed him to step away, then she closed the door.

"She's round the back," she said. "Come on."

She led the way across the patio and the big expanse of grass, towards the three plots at the bottom, all of it cut off from Nancy's and Yvette's gardens by high wooden fences.

"My veg patch is on the right, Mr Daltrey's is in the middle, and Vaughn Bates's is to the left. I'll give you their addresses if need be, but I can't see either of those two bumping anyone off." She pointed to each plot as she spoke, dipping down the patio-slab path between hers and Mr Daltrey's. "She's there, look, can you see her?"

"If you could just stay here and let us deal with it, Miss Worthington," Maddox said.

Shannon had never liked being told what to do, but as it was a policeman asking she thought she'd better do as he said, even if she *did* have a few stories she could shame him with from when he was a naughty nipper. It'd be fun to watch him blush, but now wasn't the time. She stopped so abruptly he bumped into her back, as was her intention, and she smiled at his *oof*.

"Steady on." She turned to face him. "You'll do yourself some damage if you're not careful."

She liked the way his eyes narrowed, as if he was trying to work out whether what she'd said was sinister or not. She did enjoy winding people up, getting them guessing, although she'd promised herself she'd stop doing that when Effie had gone missing. Back then, she'd been a suspect in her disappearance, and she'd been warned that some people couldn't hack a joke and that her weird way of saying things could be taken the wrong way.

Shannon shrugged off the memory and jerked her head towards the body. "It's Mina Isherwood. I know her mum; she's got a fabric stall down the market. I've got her number if you'd like me to go and get it for you — there's times she has to ring me when a bolt of cloth's come in. The one I want, like. I expect a cup of tea would go down nicely an' all. I'll bring one out to you."

Shannon retraced her steps, unlocking the back door and rushing into her kitchen so she didn't miss a thing. She filled the kettle while staring out of the window, judging when it was full by the sound. She popped it on the base by feel alone, still staring outside, imagining what those two were thinking as they gazed down at the body. The officers stepped back from Mina, and Ginger used her phone. Come to think of it, that was a bit rude. She hadn't introduced herself to Shannon. Maybe that was because Maddox knew her, but still . . . She'd make a point when she took the teas out and let her know she'd cocked up.

It wouldn't be long now until a load more coppers arrived, plus those ones in white overalls. There might even be a tent. Mr Daltrey wasn't going to be able to pull up his beetroots, so they might succumb to the frost.

It's all right, I'll share some of mine with him.

She found it odd that Maddox hadn't asked her any questions about the discovery of the body, but maybe their main priority was checking whether Mina was breathing. The questions would undoubtedly come soon.

I must remember to tell them Nancy might have copped it an' all.

She popped upstairs to nose out over the adjoining fence to make sure Nancy wasn't lying dead in her Japanese-themed garden with its pagoda thingies, the strange-looking trees, and the pea shingle paths. No one there, thank God, so she returned downstairs and got on with making the tea, then placed three mugs on a tray and went out the back, holding it with one hand and gesturing to them with the other.

"Tea's up," she shouted.

Ginger walked towards her. It took a while, what with the length of the garden, but she finally reached Shannon.

"You young people need to learn some manners," Shannon said. "I have no idea what your name is."

"Sorry, I should have introduced myself. PC Hawkins." She smiled. "Jayla."

"What kind of name is *that*?" Shannon blurted. "Are you taking the piss? You know, *jailer*, as in jail?" She handed over a mug of tea in her ugliest, most chipped mug. "I put two sugars in both. I don't hold with that sweetener muck, you don't know what's in it. If you don't take sugar, then that's tough."

Jayla smiled at her again. "Two sugars is perfect, thank you. I'll just nip this one down to Maddox and come back to take your statement."

Oh. I wanted her to have the ugly mug because I'm not fond of her so far. Mind you, I'm not fond of Maddox either, so . . .

"Are there going to be other officers coming to ask me the same questions? Detectives, like? Only, I don't want to be repeating myself umpteen times." *Like I had to with Effie.*

"If you could just tell me really quick so I can pass it on to whoever the senior officer will be, that'd be grand. They'll want to speak to you in depth."

"It'll be that Anna James who was on the news that time, I bet you."

Jayla flashed her teeth yet again and took the mug towards Maddox. Shannon watched her go, envying her youth and slim body. Shannon was slim but no longer toned, nor was she fit. Maybe she ought to do what her doctor had suggested after all and get herself down the gym. Age, he'd said, wasn't an excuse not to go. She sniffed, dismissing that idea as quickly as she had with him, and picked up her favourite mug.

She took a loud sip. Maybe it wouldn't be such a bad idea to have the police here today. She'd have something to watch as she washed and chopped her vegetables. She could make rounds of tea, be seen as someone useful rather than just the woman who propped the bar up in the Dagger a few nights a week. At one time she used to drink at the Plough on the other side of the estate, but that was before Effie had gone missing. People over there had made it clear she wasn't welcome anymore.

Jayla returned and took the final cup. "Thanks for this, it's really appreciated. Do you mind if we pop indoors to do the statement?"

"I do, as it happens. Your boots are filthy. I'd have to mop up after you."

"Officers are probably going to want to search your house anyway."

"What the hell for?"

"Whoever did that to Mina could have come inside while you were in bed."

Shannon shuddered at the thought. "And I suppose it's only right. I mean, you lot have to check if *I* killed her, too, which I bleedin' well didn't. Well, I'll tell you what happened out here anyway, but first you might want to nip next door. I have a key, but I'm worried about Nancy because she's usually home on Tuesdays and I didn't see her going out. If you're bothered about gaining entry without permission or whatever, I don't give a shit about getting told off. Wait there."

She ambled inside, put the tray on the table, and grabbed Nancy's spare key. Outside, Jayla followed her round the front, and Shannon let them in.

"Nancy?" she called. "Are you about?" She nudged Jayla, who spilled some of the tea she still held. "Go and have a gander upstairs while I check down here."

Before Jayla could protest, Shannon set off, wandering around and sipping her brew while she was at it. Nancy had left the place pristine, as usual — everything modern, the space airy and minimalistic, the same as Yvette's. Shannon preferred a house to appear lived-in herself. But there you go, it took all sorts.

In the hallway, she smiled up at Jayla, who came downstairs. "Nothing."

"Same here."

"I expect she's gone into town. I saw her bike's gone from the back garden."

Jayla walked outside. Shannon followed. She closed the door and took the lead in returning to her back garden, taking a deep breath ready to launch into her story. "You wanted to know what happened. Well, I'd just finished pulling up the last of my crop and taking it inside when I happened to glance out at Mr Daltrey's plot . . ."

CHAPTER FOUR

To: carebear@worldnet.com
From: thecowcatcher@worldnet.com

I've done it again — I know, I know, I said I wouldn't, but it was too difficult to fight the urge. You MUST act upset, like before. We won't discuss it in person, not yet. Remember, I hold all the cards and always did. If you even think about opening your mouth, you know what will happen. I'm not averse to doing it again, my little Care Bear.

PS, do not even THINK about responding to this email.

CHAPTER FIVE

In protective clothing, a mask pulled down by her chin, Detective Inspector Anna James stood to the rear of the three properties, the fences at the bottoms of the gardens to her back. A smattering of elderly oak trees stood directly in front of her. An expanse of scrubby grass came after, then a hedge border, a field beyond, a farmhouse, and then properties in the far distance in the village of Lower Reith.

Beside her stood DS Lenny Baldwin, and, close by, DC Oliver Watson, who'd been out in the field with them since he'd taken DC Peter Dove's place in the team. The trio had been going out and about together for a fair while now, and Anna was more than happy to send Oliver off with DCs Louise Golding and Rupert Cotter, two other new recruits to her little gang. Sadly, Sally Wiggins and Warren Yates were no longer a part of it.

"What do you reckon?" Anna said, knowing exactly what *she* thought about the body dump situation, but she wanted Oliver's take on it.

"None of the grass in front of us has been disturbed. Whoever brought the body came before the frost set in, because if you look left—" Oliver gestured from Shannon's back gate to past Nancy Rawlings's part of the shared grounds — "you can see where the grass has been trampled down in a line all the way to Rowan. The frost is still intact, so that came after the person had been and gone."

"It could also just be from an early dog walker," Lenny said — his role was to play devil's advocate with Oliver to get the DC to think outside the box.

Oliver smiled. "A dog walker who walked right up to Shannon's gate and didn't go any farther? It can't have been Shannon herself because there's another row of footprints where they must have left after they'd put the body in the garden. She'd have just gone into her house, surely."

Anna turned towards the fences. The photographs had already been taken, the grass here searched, but prior to any officers opening Shannon's gate and coming through to this side there had been an obvious trodden path from the gate to the patio slabs near where Mina had been placed. Anna glanced in the direction the person must have carried her from Rowan — there weren't enough impressions in the grass for Mina to have walked as well.

She thought about the body they had yet to view. A tent had been erected before they'd got here, and the pathologist, Herman Kuiper, was inside doing his thing. SOCOs crawled all over the allotment patches, the garden grass, and the patio, and some were inside Shannon Workington's house — much to her dismay, according to Jayla, who'd passed on the news that Shannon was a bit of a strange one. The woman currently sat in her living room, Jayla keeping her company in between making trays of tea for the officers.

"There's another angle, you know," Anna said. "Mina walked here and had an altercation with Shannon, maybe even Nancy Rawlings and the other neighbour, Yvette Danes, as well." There was an obvious flaw in that theory, but she'd offered it forward to see what Oliver said.

"What, all three of them?" Oliver asked.

"What's the matter with that?" Anna asked. "There's plenty of opportunities for joint enterprise when it comes to murder."

"If that's the case," Oliver said, "who made the other footprints going back the same way? What would be the point in doing that?"

Lenny sniffed, the end of his nose red from the cold. "Going by what Shannon told Jayla, those three women are in their fifties. Why would they have an issue with someone in their twenties?"

"That's something we'd need to find out," Anna said. "And much as I don't want to, we need to go and view the body, see what Herman has to say."

This was Anna's least favourite part, staring at the shell that remained of someone who'd once been alive and so vibrant. Shannon had informed Jayla that Mina drank in the Dagger Point most evenings and was a happy type who tended to laugh a lot. Who had she offended enough that she now lay lifeless on the cold ground? Or had this been a random kill as she'd walked home from the pub?

Anna led the way, entering the garden and turning right towards the slice of allotment tended to by a Mr Daltrey. Farther along was a patch rented by a Vaughn Bates. Louise and Rupert would be speaking to both this morning. Much as Anna liked interviewing everyone herself so she could gauge reactions, there was no way she could stretch herself so thin. She'd learned to delegate. Had it been Sally and Warren doing that job, she wouldn't have that weird itchy feeling about it at all; Louise wasn't as probing or intuitive as Sally, and, as for Rupert, he'd never quite fitted in from the minute he'd joined the team, so the jury was still out on him. Their former boss, Ron Placket, had also decided to permanently abandon the station, so now there was a new DCI, Isabella Edwards.

It had taken a while to get used to the changes, but, as Anna had discovered the hard way, if you created a fuss you just made more trouble for yourself. No, she wasn't fond of Louise and Rupert, but everyone did their best to make it work. Yes, it was odd without Placket, who understood Anna and her methods and left her to her job, whereas Isabella liked to be more hands-on. But it wasn't awful. It didn't make Anna want to leave, and for the most part she got on with any investigations without grumbling. Much.

She walked across the evidence steps leading up to the flap of the tent. "Is it okay to come in?"

"Fine by me," Herman said.

Anna entered, Lenny and Oliver following, and they each stood on a step with Mina facing away from them. She lay on her left side, knees bent, arms out a little, palms touching, as if she were asleep in bed. Dark jeans, a coat, and a beanie hat, so perhaps she *had* been accosted on her way home from the Dagger. They had yet to glean what she'd been wearing in the pub.

Uniforms would be at the Dagger to question the landlord and find out who'd been in there last night. If Anna had time later, she may well nip in there herself.

Herman took a deep breath and let it out slowly. "Going by my initial observation, she was strangled with what I predict is silky cloth, so maybe a tie or a scarf. Her neck will be swabbed for fibres, so I'll be able to give you a better idea on that over the coming days."

"How do you know the material is silky?"

"Okay, put it this way, it wasn't wool. Think of a tourniquet and how tight they are. Impressions from the material have been left behind on her skin. If you look closely at her throat, you'll see various lines in the bruising from the material being concertinaed, held taut enough that it's made marks."

"And she was brought here, not killed here," Anna confirmed.

"The ground hasn't been disturbed enough. She would have struggled while being strangled — unless, of course, she was knocked out beforehand. Whoever did this walked up the little path between the allotments and placed her at the edge on top of whatever's growing beneath. And they were strong."

Wayne, the photographer, popped his head inside. "Sorry, I was eavesdropping, but, just so you know, there are no footprints in the mud around the body — I've looked at close-ups of the images. Nothing was disturbed other than the beetroot underneath her."

"How the bloody hell do you know it's beetroot?" Anna asked.

"My granddad grows it. I recognise the leaves."

Anna glanced across. Going by the thick red stems, she'd have thought it was rhubarb. She toyed with the idea of the vegetable being significant. Stranger things had happened. "From what we could see out the back there, whoever it was walked close to the fences. There are some uniforms and SOCOs following the trail, but I'm not holding out much hope — maybe we'll get lucky with CCTV or witnesses. The trail curves, so I believe it'll stop at the edge of Rowan. Either the killer lives there, or they've used this route on purpose to throw us off to make us *think* they live there."

Lenny stared down at Mina. "I'm curious as to why the body was left here, in this particular garden. Why not just leave it out the back, propped against a tree with her facing the farm? No one would have discovered her for a while if she'd been positioned right — those trunks are wide. Did the killer want her found?"

"Hmm, they could be making a statement." Anna resisted rolling her eyes. How many criminals did that? How many had egos the size of houses, wanting to be seen, noticed, classed as important? Or was this a case of someone screaming out for help? All right, it was a bit of a drastic way to go about it, but some people's minds worked differently, so what made sense to them made no sense to anyone else.

Wayne's head disappeared, and Maddox's face took its place. "Sorry to interrupt, but I just wanted to let you know I've been over to Mina's mother's and told her the news. Family liaison are with her now."

"How did she take it?" Anna asked.

"She fainted."

"Oh shit, poor woman. We'll go and have a word with her at some point. Which FLO is it?"

"Katy Clark."

Anna nodded. "Good, she'll tease information out of her without making it obvious. What was your take on Shannon when you first arrived here?"

"She didn't seem shaken up or anything, but that doesn't surprise me at all. She knows my mum, used to come round ours for a cup of tea, and she's always been a bit . . . I don't know, rude? They talked a lot about some woman called Effie. She went missing. I think she was related to Shannon, but don't quote me on it. It's that ghost story that's been going about for years, you know the one?"

"Yep. Thanks for that." As a PC, Anna had worked on Effie's case, and it wasn't something she'd likely forget. "We really need to go and speak to Shannon now anyway."

Maddox withdrew his head from the tent, and Anna studied Mina. It wasn't a stretch to wonder if her body had been left here on purpose. Going by the last three major murder cases Anna had headed, it wouldn't surprise her in the slightest if this one stirred up the past. Then again, didn't the past play a part in aspects of the present anyway? Who people were, who they'd become, what they'd been through to be the people they were today. It was all relevant.

Oliver lifted a hand to get her attention. "Shall I go back to the station and look into this Effie?"

"That's not a bad shout. All we'll be doing here is talking to Shannon."

Oliver left the tent.

Herman's eyes crinkled over his face mask. "You did the right thing in encouraging him to become a DC."

"I'd like to think so." Anna gave Mina one last look. "Will you be doing the post-mortem today?"

"Not sure. We'll be here for a while yet."

"Okay, I'll see you when I see you, then." Anna exited and made her way over the evidence steps, bracing herself to speak to a rude woman who may well have all the answers Anna sought.

CHAPTER SIX

DC Louise Golding had big shoes to fill and sometimes got sick of trying. She felt like she wasn't up to scratch, although no one else in the team had ever said anything outright to her regarding her performance. Maybe it was something she imposed on herself, to prove she could be as good as or better than Sally, who'd moved away with her little boy, Ben. Studying the statements in the files from previous cases, Louise could see Sally was diligent and thorough, excelling especially in rooting out information.

We can't all be perfect.

With Rupert beside her on the way up Mr Daltrey's garden path in Westgate, close to Jubilee Lake, she sighed out the seemingly constant frustration and told herself to get her head in the game. If she kept thinking about what she could do wrong or what she might not pick up on, that meant she wasn't concentrating properly and wouldn't be classed as diligent anyway.

"Are you all right?" Rupert asked.

She liked him and didn't mind sharing her thoughts. "I will be when I get this monkey off my back."

"What monkey?"

"Anna. Me not fitting in. Feeling like I'm not good enough."

"I know how you feel, but Anna's never made it obvious she doesn't want us in the team. She's been professional. If you think about it, she had the same team for years and then all of a sudden it broke apart, including Placket going."

Louise hadn't thought of it from Anna's point of view, which wasn't unusual. She was self-centred and indulged in self-pity, as her mother had told her enough times. Charming that the one person who was supposed to completely have her back had a habit of pointing out her flaws, but Louise was used to it. Although her counsellor had told her she shouldn't *have* to be used to it and she should stand up for herself. Easier said than done when it meant having a go at your mother.

"Come on, let's dig in and see what's going on here, if anything." She raised her hand and knocked on the front door.

Mr Daltrey knew they were coming. She'd phoned ahead to save a wasted journey. Would Anna notice that forethought?

I doubt it. She'd say it was a given that I'd double-check he was going to be in.

The door opened to reveal a well-put-together Mr Daltrey, who matched his Facebook profile picture. Louise had looked him up earlier. Sixty-five, a widower of six years, and father to one child. Surprisingly, he didn't have that much grey in his brown hair, yet his neatly trimmed beard was full of it. Unless he didn't mind getting his nice clothes dirty, he clearly hadn't intended on going to his allotment today, although he could have changed once Louise had told him he had to stay away.

She held up her ID and introduced them.

"Come in, come in." He wafted a hand back and forth in a gesture that said he wanted them to hurry up, probably so the heat didn't escape. He turned and walked down the hallway, the hems of his pressed trousers trailing on the floor. He ran a finger around the collar of his shirt at the back and disappeared through a doorway at the end.

Louise followed him, leaving her colleague to close the door. Did that finger around the collar signify anything? Had

Mr Daltrey broken out in a sweat? Was he uncomfortable in their presence? She imagined those were the sort of questions Sally would have asked.

Stop comparing yourself to her.

She found him in the kitchen, where he poured coffee from a full carafe. She quickly glanced around to check the cleanliness of the place. There was no way she'd drink out of someone's cup if they didn't keep things hygienic and tidy. Everything looked to be in order, and at Mr Daltrey's urging she and Rupert sat at a white dining table. He brought the coffees over and placed them on coasters, collected a Christmas-themed biscuit tin from the worktop, then joined them.

He took the lid off. "Help yourselves."

Rupert dived in, the gannet, but Louise was watching her waistline so declined the offer, much to her chagrin. She really fancied a chocolate Hobnob.

"So what's this visit all about, then?" Mr Daltrey asked. "And please, call me Tate."

Louise cleared her throat. "The reason you're unable to go to your allotment at the moment is because a body has been found on your plot." She waited for his reaction.

"Um, I beg your pardon?" His mouth dropped open, and he flicked his gaze from her to Rupert and then back again. "Is it Shannon? Is she all right? Did she have a fall or something?"

He clearly hadn't registered that Louise had said *a body*. "It's not Shannon, no, she's fine, but I imagine she was shocked because she was the one to discover the deceased." As Louise and Rupert had received text confirmation that the next of kin had been spoken to, she had no qualms about revealing Mina's name when she felt the time was right. "I have to ask, when was the last time you went to your allotment?"

"Last Monday. I was meant to pull up the rest of my beetroot, but I got distracted because Shannon invited me in for a cuppa and some cake. I told myself I'd go back on the Tuesday, but then my daughter and two grandkids turned up — *that* was a surprise, I can tell you — and they only went back home this morning."

Alarm bells rang. Had his daughter done the deed and then hightailed it home? "Could we have your daughter's name and phone number so we can verify your movements?"

"Of course, yes."

He took a phone out of his trouser pocket and rattled off the number. Louise put it into her notes app along with the name. There had been no hesitation on Tate's part. Louise would check Rupert's take on it later. He was busy dunking biscuits into his coffee and didn't appear to be paying much attention. He did that often, giving a certain impression, when really he was listening and sizing people up.

"Who's the body?" Tate asked.

"Mina Isherwood. Do you know her?"

Tate shook his head. "Can't say I do, no, but I know the surname. There's an Elizabeth Isherwood who runs the fabric stall on the market of a Thursday and Friday. I know that because my wife used to get her cloth there. Maybe it's the same family — the surname's not exactly common, is it?"

Louise didn't need to write that down. She'd already discovered Elizabeth was Mina's mother prior to leaving the station. "Do you have any theories as to why a body would be placed on your particular allotment patch?"

Tate's eyes widened. "No bloody idea, love."

Louise's and Rupert's phones bleeped with the matching tones they'd assigned to Anna. There were times they bunked off for a cheeky cuppa or lunch so needed to know when the boss was on their arse.

"If you could excuse me for a second." She read the message, responded with an *okay*, and popped her phone back on the table. "Is there anything you can tell me about Effie Workington? She went missing twenty years ago."

Tate stared at the ceiling. He didn't seem fazed by the switch in topic. "I remember her being reported missing and people saying they didn't believe she'd gone off without telling anyone because she wasn't the type. I think she was in her thirties or something like that, wasn't married, didn't have any kids, and spent a lot of time in the Plough over on Northgate. The gossip was rife, that's how I know all these things. I used to live on Rowan with the wife before she died, see. I only moved over here to get away from the memories and to downsize. Pointless having a big house when it's just me. Anyway, what I'm saying is, I didn't know Effie personally, just of her."

"So what was the general consensus?"

"That she disappeared one day without a by-your-leave and no one's seen her since. Well, that might not be true. She's been seen often enough on Rowan, although it can't be her because she doesn't look any older than the day she went missing. Some say it's her ghost and others reckon it's kids mucking about, trying to get a legend going, or a myth, whatever you want to call it. Dressing up as her, you know?"

Louise glanced at Rupert. Not once had anyone told her about a local ghost. "That's the first I've heard of it."

Rupert stopped munching on his biscuit and checked his phone, likely reading Anna's message. "I've actually seen the ghost myself, or whatever it really is. She wears a white dress and ballet shoes. When I spotted her, I was on my way home from a mate's house late at night, and she popped out from an alley. She danced around in front of me and then ran off. It was all a bit surreal to be honest, but I shrugged it off as, like you say, a kid mucking about."

Tate took a sip of his coffee. "There must be a reason why you're asking me about Effie, like there's some connection between her and Mina. The only one I can think of is Shannon, but I'm telling you, she's no murderer. She's weird, I'll give you that, a tad abrupt and doesn't know how to articulate herself sometimes, but she means well."

"How did it come about that you rented allotment space from her?" Louise asked. "Have you known Shannon a long time?"

"No. Shannon put a post up on the local Facebook group. Me and Vaughn just happened to be the first ones to reply. That's Vaughn Bates, by the way, and he lives over by the Plough. Nice fella, so he's not someone you ought to be looking at either."

Nice fellas kill, though.

Louise was about to tell him they'd have to speak to Vaughn all the same, but she stopped herself. She had to remember that not everything needed a response. Her habit of putting people right got on her own nerves. "I'm sure he is. So other than Shannon being a connection between Effie and Mina, is there anything else you can think of? Would your daughter know Mina?"

"No, my Charlene only had two friends the whole time she lived here, and the pair of them died in a car accident back in Charlene's thirties. She'd already left Marlford to go and live with her husband by then."

The daughter's visit played on Louise's mind. "Where does Charlene live now?"

"Liverpool."

"Was there any reason for the surprise visit?" *Could she have returned to kill Mina? Parents don't know everyone their child has a connection with.*

"She came to let me know she's left her husband — well, she kicked him out at any rate. The bastard . . . sorry, he decided to take his fist to her the last few months. Pressure from work is his excuse, but there's *no* excuse for it in my book. She came here for a few days to get away because he'd been pestering her at the house. She's got a restraining order out on him now so felt happy enough to go back. I'd rather she'd have stayed here, but that wasn't my decision."

Louise would look into that back in the office. They could have cooked up the story between them. Tate might be covering for his daughter. Louise had a penchant for letting her imagination run away with her, but she didn't think in this instance her thoughts would be seen as ridiculous. Still, she'd check the daughter regardless.

They chatted for a while, Tate reminiscing about life when his wife had been alive, how he missed her smile. Louise felt sorry for him and wished they could stay longer, but they had Vaughn to speak to. She left Tate reluctantly, asking that if he remembered anything of significance he give her a ring. She handed him a business card, got in the car and stuck her seat belt on.

Rupert flumped into the passenger seat. "What did you think?"

She started the engine and drew away from the kerb. "The daughter story . . ."

"Hmm. He's nothing but a lonely man, though, right?"

"Who knows, but I'm glad Anna's message said Ollie's dealing with the Effie angle, because it's probably going to be a big waste of time."

Rupert chuffed out a breath. "Not necessarily. Never rule anything out."

"God, you sound like Anna."

"It's true, though. Until we can strike this Effie business off the list, then it's something we need to consider. Maybe it's a big coincidence that Mina was left on Shannon's property. It seems pretty obvious to me that there's no connection with Mr Daltrey, but, again, we can't rule that out either until we can."

Louise drove on, humming to let him know she didn't want to talk anymore. Sometimes Rupert came across as being a bit self-righteous and a know-it-all. She'd caught Lenny rolling his eyes at him behind his back on more than one occasion, but she got the impression that, had Rupert been facing Lenny, he'd still have done it anyway. Lenny seemed an open and straight-up kind of bloke. She'd seen his profile on the dating app she was on but hadn't let him know. Why would she, when the photos she'd uploaded of herself were years old and looked nothing like she did now? Not to mention she'd opted for a username instead of her real one, as had he.

She continued humming, zoning out until they reached Vaughn's street.

CHAPTER SEVEN

Shannon had thawed towards Jayla, who didn't seem to take offence at her abrupt manner and some of the things she accidentally blurted out. But just as she'd *further* warmed to the young woman by another couple of degrees, the goalposts had moved. Anna James and a man called Lenny Baldwin had relieved Jayla of her duties, and they currently sat at the table in the dining side of Shannon's kitchen. The PC had been right. Police *had* come through the house.

I'm going to have to use that bloody mop.

Shannon had positioned herself so she could watch what was going on outside. People in white suits milled around, or they knelt to inspect the grass. Two leaned over Shannon's vegetable patch, using tools of some kind to scrape away the earth. She personally felt her patch was too far away from where Mina lay to be of any significance, but she supposed there had to be a rhyme and a reason to their movements. Maybe they thought she'd hidden something when she'd pulled up her veg.

A white marquee covered the body, so there was no longer anything to see there. She didn't know what she expected to see anyway, just people peering down at Mina, taking photos, discussing what might have happened.

She drew her attention away from outside and stared across the table at Anna, who'd been quietly sipping her coffee, perhaps gathering herself after seeing the body, or maybe she was the type to remain silent so it unnerved people before she interviewed them. Everyone had tactics, didn't they?

"Firstly, I'd like to say I'm sorry you had the ordeal of finding Mina today." Anna put her mug down — the ugly chipped one. "If you need to talk to anyone about it, I have a few numbers you can ring, counsellors and the like."

"No, no, I've got people down the Dagger who'll chat to me later." She was almost one hundred per cent sure they would. People liked to gossip, and as she was the one who'd found Mina she had a fair few titbits she could pass on. It would be quite exciting. She might get people buying her drinks to steady her nerves and whatnot. The money her parents had left her when they'd died would only last so long, so she saved wherever she could.

"That's good, then." Anna smiled. "From what I understand, you don't really know Mina, other than through her mother, Elizabeth, who runs the fabric stall on the market."

"That's right, but she's in the pub a lot, the Dagger, propping up the bar of an evening. Some nights she stays a good while if she gets drinks bought for her, and others she only has a quick half a lager."

"So she's a regular there, then?"

Shannon tutted. "That's stating the obvious."

"I was just confirming." Anna smiled again, although it was a little tight this time.

Shannon hid a smile, chuffed she'd riled her, but maybe that wasn't the best thing to do in the circumstances. She didn't want them looking at her for this, especially because of the Effie business. "She seemed happy-go-lucky, full of chatter, although I never spoke to her."

"Do you know of any reason why someone would have chosen to leave her body on your property?"

"Not a bloody clue."

"What about Mr Daltrey's vegetable patch? Why would someone place the body there?"

"You'd have to ask him that question."

A message bleep sounded, and Anna checked her phone. She popped it back in her pocket, sipped more coffee, then placed the mug down again. "Can you give me a bit of background on Effie's disappearance?"

What did that text say? Have they been poking into me and seen my name in their files? "I wondered when that would come up. What are you going to do next, accuse me of killing Mina like I was supposed to have done to Effie?"

"I'm not about to do that at all, no. I'd just like you to tell me what you know, especially about the person going around as Effie."

Shannon eyed her. *Does she think I'm green?* "You've lived here all your life, so you must have heard about the ghost. How come you need me to tell you about it?"

"I'd like your perspective. I remember Effie going missing, I was a PC at the time."

Shannon's mind went back to the past. She recalled listening to a couple of coppers talking in the Plough. There had been no leads whatsoever, and people had been frustrated and confused as to how a woman could just vanish. Then came the first sighting the year after Effie had gone. A lot of police resources had been used to find her again, but nothing had come of it. Nothing had come of other sightings afterwards either.

"You'd have been up on those moors, then," Shannon said. "Looking for her."

"I was. Can you refresh my memory as to your relationship with her?"

Like she's even forgotten. That case was massive. Still, Shannon would keep that thought to herself and indulge her. "She was my cousin. Our dads were brothers. Both of them are dead now, and our mums. I'm the only one in the family left — unless, of course, Effie's taken herself off somewhere. But I'd like to think she'd come and see me if she were alive. Do you remember how I was a suspect, all because we left the pub at the same time? The thing was, at Cooper's Crossing, I went one way and she went the other, and I never saw her again after that, not even as the ghost. There've been times I've looked at people and wondered whether it was them who took her away. She had no reason to disappear and start again elsewhere, unless she was keeping secrets from me."

"People do, I'm afraid. Do you generally leave your back gate unlocked?"

The switch in subject threw Shannon, and she blinked several times to process the question. "I suppose I should have put a padlock on it. Now I come to think of it, that would have been ideal. Mina might not have been left in my garden then."

"Sadly, if people want to gain entry somewhere, they'll find a way, like going down the side of your house from the front. What were you doing last night?"

Shannon shivered. "I was up in my bedroom watching telly until two in the morning, and whoever brought her here might have seen the flickering behind my curtains because my room's at the back. It gives me the bloody creeps to think of them out there and me none the wiser." She paused for a moment. "Did Jayla tell you we went next door to Nancy's to check if she was all right?"

"Yes, she said Nancy wasn't in. Is that normal for a Tuesday?"

"It's her day off because she works Saturdays. I must have been in the shower when she went out. It's doing my head in not knowing where she is. I've tried phoning her and everything, and so has Jayla, but it keeps going to voicemail."

"Perhaps she went to do a bit of shopping? Her bike's gone from the garden, so that would make sense. Okay, what about Yvette?"

"She'll be at work, I saw her leave. She never has a day off unless she's at death's door."

"Where does she work?"

"She's a manager at Sainsbury's in Bridge End shopping centre. I thought you lot would have known that already."

"Uniforms will have been looking into it, yes. What's your take on Mr Daltrey and Mr Bates?"

Another swift subject change. Shannon panicked for a second or two and took deep breaths. This reminded her too much of the Effie interviews. What if she cocked up now like she did back then? "They're both lovely, and I doubt very much they'd have done that to Mina. Mr Daltrey's always been polite to me, and respectful. He was here last Monday actually, and we sat at this table having a chat. He was supposed to come back and get his beetroot on the Tuesday but didn't. It's all right, he can have some of mine."

"That's very kind of you. And Mr Bates?"

"He was here yesterday from ten until one. He'd already pulled up the last of his veg the week before and had come to rake the ground and measure up because he asked me if he could put one of those plastic greenhouses on half of his plot. I haven't got a problem with it and was thinking of doing the same myself. We had a natter about selling our excess veg at the bottom of the lane using an honesty box."

Anna smiled. "I get my eggs from one of those on the way to Upton-cum-Studley."

Shannon stared at Lenny, who so far hadn't said a word, even when she'd given him his coffee, which reminded her... "You didn't thank me for the coffee, Mr Baldwin. Like I said to Jayla earlier, some people have got no manners."

He blushed. "Sorry about that. Thank you. It's very kind of you. I should have said something at the time, but my mind was occupied with what was going on in the garden."

She studied him to see if he was taking the piss, but he appeared genuinely contrite. "I'll let you off, then. But only this time, mind."

"How long have you lived out here?" he asked her.

Wasn't that something they'd have already established before they'd come here? Or was he asking to see if he could catch her out in a lie? That other copper had done that, the one in charge of Effie's case.

"Up until I was about twenty, then I got a place on Rowan, then I moved back here," she said. "This house was left to me. Yvette was born in Marlford, too, although her mum and dad are still alive, she just stays in their house so they could go off and live in Spain. She's been here for over twenty years. And Nancy moved here years ago with her husband, but he snuffed it. Before that, she lived on Northgate."

"I don't suppose you get any traffic up the lane, considering it terminates just past Nancy's," Lenny said. "It's almost like a long private drive, all the way to the left edge of Rowan."

"That's right."

"So if any vehicles come up this way, it would be either to visit one of you three or it would be Yvette's car."

"Yes . . ."

"What I'm getting at is that it would stand out a mile if a car or motorbike came up here and it wasn't Yvette's or a guest's."

The penny dropped, and Shannon nodded. "I get what you're saying. Yes, if we were in our living rooms, we'd have noticed any headlights or the noise of an engine. It's so remote here that sound carries, but unfortunately I went to bed at eight for a TV marathon and took a flask of tea and some biscuits up so I didn't need to come back down again. With my room being at the back and the telly on loud, I didn't hear a car at all. Maybe Nancy or Yvette did."

"We'll ask them," Anna said.

"It's bothering me that Nancy's not answering her phone." Shannon picked at a hangnail. "What if she saw whoever it was leaving the body and they did something to her? I sleep with ear plugs in, so I wouldn't have heard a thing if it was after I switched the telly off at two." She felt the need to repeat what time she'd had the telly on until; she needed them to believe her. No way did she want to go through what she had during Effie's case.

"I'm sure we'll find her." Anna asked a few more questions, and, once she'd finished her coffee, she stood and took their mugs over to the sink. She washed them up in the bowl of soapy water and placed them upside down on the drainer beside umpteen others.

Shannon wished she hadn't given her the ugly chipped one now. She'd revised her opinion of Anna. "I'd best boil the kettle again. That lot out there must want more drinks by now." She bustled over. "I've got another kettle in the cupboard I keep for a spare. I'm probably better off boiling both."

"Would you like any help with that?" Anna offered.

You'll get the best mug next time. "No, thank you, you're all right. Get that Jayla back in here, unless she's busy elsewhere." Shannon waited for Anna to move out of the way, then she filled the kettle. "It wasn't me, you know. Effie or Mina. I wouldn't hurt anybody."

Anna laid a hand on the top of Shannon's arm. "Is there someone who can come and stay here with you for a little while? You must be unsettled, and the company might do you some good."

"Like I said, there's no family. It's okay, I've got Nancy and Yvette. Maybe we could all stay in one house together until the killer's been caught." Shannon put the kettle on the base and flicked the switch. She shivered again, looking outside. So many people in her garden. "When will Mina be gone?"

Anna checked her watch. "I'm not sure to be honest. There's a lot of ground out there to cover, especially around the body. Forensics will want to triple-check that before she's allowed to be removed."

"Right."

Anna said goodbye, and Lenny followed her down the hallway to the front door. She'd already explained they'd prefer to exit that way so they didn't have to put on another forensic suit. The front door closed behind them, and for a moment Shannon experienced such excruciating loneliness that tears stung her eyes. The creak of the back door opening soon brightened her up, though.

Jayla walked in after taking her paper booties off. "It's about time for another cuppa, isn't it?"

Shannon smiled. "That it is."

CHAPTER EIGHT

Catcher mulled over what could be going on. No whispers had filtered in, and checking social media and the news sites had proved fruitless. Catcher had two phones, one for contacting Care Bear. It would be foolish to use the personal one to browse the internet or to send intermittent reminders for Care Bear to behave. The second phone was a pay-as-you-go, something cheap and unregistered, although if it was found and inspected it would no doubt give the police Catcher's recent locations.

Catcher switched it off, slipped it into a pocket, and sat, trying to conjure up the fear of being caught, to experience what it must be like to be a normal person. Except there *was* no fear, and that could well be Catcher's downfall.

Maybe leaving Mina out in the open was a mistake. Maybe she should have been placed underground with Effie, but that hadn't been possible, not without attracting attention. Catcher begrudgingly acknowledged that Mina's death was a mistake, but she'd become a fly in the ointment.

If only I hadn't allowed her to annoy me.

CHAPTER NINE

To: carebear@worldnet.com
From: thecowcatcher@worldnet.com

Have you heard about it yet? Don't be stupid and answer me, it was a rhetorical question. Are you worrying about the Effie thing coming back to bite not only me but you? It's always good to remember it, our secret past, especially now this has happened. And to remember how much you owe me. I paid for your silence, never forget that, and I'll pay you again when everything's gone quiet. Think about what you could buy. I'm under no illusion that you secretly hate me, but I control you, and I hold the keys to your prison cell. One word from me, and your life will change. Never forget what I'm capable of, my little Care Bear.

CHAPTER TEN

Rupert was well aware he rubbed people up the wrong way, mainly his colleagues, but to be honest he didn't much care *what* they thought of him so long as they let him get the job done. Lenny was a little prickly, but Rupert put that down to trust issues. Anna and Lenny had put all their trust in Peter Dove, and look what he'd done to them.

It had come to light that he'd been an undercover gang member for the Northern Kings, joining the police force to get inside information. The gang had supposedly disbanded now, and to be honest there was no way of proving that. The Kings had always worked in the shadows and likely still did. But Dove's mistake was Rupert's gain. He'd put himself forward for the position on Anna's team, although he wished DCI Placket was still around. DCI Edwards was nice on the surface, but he had a feeling she was a bit of a bitch underneath. Her claws were sheathed, but he'd bet as soon as her feet were properly under the table they'd come out.

Rupert got on with Anna well enough, although he sensed she didn't like him much. She'd never said anything to give him that idea, it was just a feeling he had. He wasn't bothered whether she liked him or not. Unlike Louise, he didn't have a burning desire to overly prove himself to his seniors or to score points. He was there to help catch criminals, not to make friends. Saying that, he'd grown close with Louise, kind of, as they tended to be paired together. They had their little secret, the way they skived off and took a breather, something he'd suggest once they'd arrived at Vaughn's.

Irritatingly, Louise had been humming all the way there, something Rupert didn't think she was even aware she did. He likely had a quirk she wasn't fond of either. She pulled up outside what appeared to be an ex-council house and shut off the engine. She'd already phoned ahead to make sure Vaughn would be home.

"Ready, then?" He unclipped his seat belt.

She released hers and opened her door. "Yep."

"Do you want to go for a sneaky lunch after?"

She stared out of the windscreen. "Sod it, yes, why not? As for this visit, can you take the lead so I can observe this time?"

Rupert nodded. She might have one of her migraines coming on.

They approached the red front door. There was a flicker of movement to the right at the large window, then the net curtain swayed. Vaughn must have been watching out for them. The door opened, and a white-haired man no taller than five feet smiled at them, his eyes watery behind transparent-framed glasses. His lower lip had that look about it where he may not have bottom dentures in, and a red mottled effect marred his cheeks and nose. His skin spoke of too much sun.

"DC Rupert Cotter and DC Louise Golding." Rupert smiled and held his ID up.

Vaughn squinted and leaned forward to inspect it. "Right you are, come in." He stepped back for them to enter and closed the door, sliding the chain on. "Is it all right if my wife sits with us? I don't like to leave her alone for long, else she gets up to all sorts. She's been known to slip out of the house when I'm busy."

Rupert took that to be Alzheimer's or dementia, not that the wife was a prisoner here, and he smiled in sympathy. He'd test the waters in a bit to see where in her journey Mrs Bates was. "Of course, that's not a problem at all. She might well be a big help — we've got questions about the past."

"God, yes, she can tell you about the past, all right, but ask her what she had for breakfast and she won't remember. We're not at the stage where she doesn't know who I am yet, thank God. Dreading the bloody day." Vaughn ambled down the hallway, his slippers shuffling on the tiled floor.

Rupert allowed Louise to go first so he could poke his head into the living room. It was your average view, nothing untoward, so he walked into the kitchen.

"These are police officers, Flora love." Vaughn laid a palm on her shoulder as he sat, then he removed it to hold her hand, which she'd rested on the table. "They've come to ask us a few questions."

"I set out the tea things while you were gone," she said.

Vaughn said gently, "I told you not to. Remember last time when you scalded yourself?"

Rupert sat and eyed up the teapot spout poking out of the woolly cosy, a ribbon of steam curling upwards. "Would you like me to pour?"

Flora gave him a big smile, and Vaughn nodded, seeming relieved.

Rupert got on with that, filling the floral china cups. He prattled on about the weather and how it had taken a turn towards being cold lately.

"That's why I got my vegetables pulled up a few days ago," Vaughn said. "Then I raked the ground over yesterday, ready for winter."

"That's your patch at Shannon's, yes?"

Vaughn gave him a look. "You know it is, son. Don't be treating me daft now."

Rupert added milk to each cup. "When do you plan to go back?"

"Once my greenhouse is delivered there next week. I'll spend the day putting it up myself. It's plastic windows instead of glass, so it won't be a bother."

Rupert thought about Vaughn's small stature and couldn't imagine the bloke handling it by himself — nor could he imagine him carrying a body unless it was a child. "Will you be going with him, Flora?"

The woman appeared to be lost inside her mind, her eyes glassy.

"She'll go and sit with our daughter-in-law for the day. Naomi's a good girl like that, helps me out no end."

"It's always nice to have support, isn't it?" Rupert gestured to the cups. "I'll leave the sugar for everyone to sort out because I'm not sure who has what." He added one spoonful to his cup and took a sip. He smiled at Vaughn sorting out Flora's; he was clearly devoted to her. "Okay, Vaughn, I'll just come straight to the point and state why we're here, unless Tate Daltrey's already got hold of you."

"I've not heard from him, no. If we don't see each other at the plots, we have a weekly meet-up in the Plough on a Friday evening when Flora's at her memory club. What's gone on?" Vaughn appeared concerned, his eyebrows beetling, his gaze darting between Rupert and Louise, finally settling on Rupert.

"Do you know a Mina Isherwood?"

Vaughn frowned again. "The surname rings a bell."

"An Isherwood runs the fabric stall on the market," Flora said. "That family's had that stall for about eighty years. I remember going there with my mum to pick out the material for my summer dresses." Her glassy-eyed look had vanished, and she seemed bright and happy reliving the memory.

Rupert was sad that he'd have to draw the conversation away from where the woman seemed completely comfortable — back in the past. It felt almost criminal to wade in with this news, but it had to be done. "Mina's body was found on Mr Daltrey's plot this morning. Shannon discovered it after she'd pulled up her vegetables."

"Oh my God," Vaughn said. "Is Shannon all right?"

"As you can imagine, she's shocked."

Vaughn studied him. "You said a body. What happened? Did the poor girl collapse and die or something?"

"Unfortunately, it's looking like murder."

Vaughn gawped. "You don't think it was Shannon who killed her, do you?"

Flora tapped her fingernails on the table. "Some people said she killed Effie."

"That's nonsense," Vaughn said. "You know how people gossip."

"Who thought she killed Effie?" Rupert asked.

"The police and a few in the Plough." Flora became animated again. "They left the pub together, and Shannon said she went home by herself when they reached Cooper's Crossing, but she could have easily done away with Effie because of how dark it is there at night. She could have done something to her, then gone home to collect her car to pick the body up and dump it. She had a Fiesta, a blue one, and she sold it not long after. She didn't live up the lane at the time, she had a flat on Rowan. From the minute Shannon supposedly left Effie, that woman was never seen again."

"No one reported Shannon using her car that late, though," Vaughn said to her.

Flora had recounted it so easily and smoothly that Rupert was convinced it was a genuine recollection — whether it was true or not remained to be seen. As Vaughn said, people gossiped. "We'll be looking into that to see if there's a connection. Do you know of any link between Tate Daltrey, his late wife, his daughter, and the Isherwoods?"

"Not that I can remember," Flora said.

"I don't think so," Vaughn confirmed. "Why are you asking? Because Mina was left on his plot and not mine or Shannon's?"

"I'm afraid we have to look into every possible avenue. Did the Isherwoods have any skeletons in the closet that you know of?"

"Lovely family," Flora said, distracted by something on the ceiling. "They can't do enough for you."

Rupert went through some more questions and, satisfied with the answers, he glanced at Louise and raised his eyebrows to see if she had anything she'd like to ask. She shook her head and collected all the cups and saucers, then took them over to the worktop. Rupert stood and thanked the couple for their time.

"You're more than welcome," Vaughn said. "I'm just upset that it was a murder that brought you here. Should we be worried? I mean, could we be next? The only link we have to Shannon is the fact I pay her to rent land and I have the odd cuppa with her. And as for the Isherwoods, like Flora said, it was years ago when her mum used to buy fabric. I can't think why we would have a link to this in any way."

"As you can understand, we have to check. The fact that the body was left near your plot has to be investigated." As Rupert had already established Vaughn's and Flora's alibis, all he needed to do was phone the daughter-in-law to confirm she'd stayed here overnight because her husband had gone away for work and she didn't like staying in the house alone.

Back in the car, Rupert asked, "Shall we be *really* naughty and nip to that Italian on Southgate instead of going to the sandwich shop? Their new lunchtime takeaway menu is cones of carbonara or spaghetti Bolognese topped with garlic bread and grilled Parmesan for a fiver a pop. We can sit and eat in the car."

Louise nodded and pulled away from the kerb. She appeared distracted.

"What's the matter?" he asked, his patience wearing thin; she always seemed to have some issue or other, not that he'd let her know she got on his nerves with it. He couldn't think of one time they'd had a workday where she hadn't griped or become anxious.

She sighed. "I can't stop thinking about Flora."

"What about her?"

"That one day she's going to wake up and not know who Vaughn is. She might be scared. Her house could seem like it's a stranger's because she can't remember it." She blew out a long breath. "That's the one part of this job I hate. We're forced to face things we wouldn't otherwise know about."

"I expect there'll be more of that before this case is closed, so buckle up for the ride and get on with it." He had to distract her or she'd go on and on until they reached the Italian. "What are you having, carbonara or Bolognese?"

"Carbonara."

"Same." Rupert smiled and spent the rest of the journey imagining what his lunch was going to taste like. He couldn't allow himself to be like Louise and worry about Flora and Vaughn. There was nothing he could do, so what was the point in coiling himself up about it?

Louise started humming.

For fuck's sake . . .

CHAPTER ELEVEN

Anna had suggested Lenny take the lead when talking to Yvette in Sainsbury's. He didn't mind, but when they were together she usually preferred to ask all the questions. He liked to observe nuances in vocal tone, mannerisms, and expressions; having to think about what to ask next took his attention away from possibly catching a tell someone let slip.

They'd walked through the supermarket, and it had reminded him to pick up a bottle of wine after work. He had a third evening planned with someone from the dating app, which had progressed from meeting outside the pub to going round to hers for dinner tonight. He hoped he wouldn't have to call it off because of the murder, but, unless there was a drastic change later on, he didn't see any reason why they'd have to do overtime. Uniforms would be doing a lot of door-to-door enquiries on Rowan, and that freed the team up to talk to the main players.

A supervisor led them to the top floor, where a long line of offices stretched down a glass-walled corridor. She tapped on one and waved through a window at the woman inside. She let herself in and poked her head round. "There are two police officers here to see you."

"That's fine, send them in."

The supervisor gestured for them to enter. Anna went in first. Lenny closed the door and glanced at Yvette when she stood to shake their hands. Fifties. Blonde bob. Slender. When Anna had finished the introductions, they all sat.

Lenny took his notebook out; he preferred that over any of the electronic gadgets available. "Sorry to trouble you at work, but it couldn't wait until you got home. Can I just ask first, have you heard from your neighbours Nancy and Shannon yet today?"

Yvette frowned. "Oh God, has my drain overflowed again? I can't see why that would warrant a visit from the police, but you never know."

Strange thing to say. "Unfortunately, Shannon found a body in her garden this morning on one of the allotment plots, and we just need to know—"

"Hang on. A body?" She slapped a hand to her chest and fiddled with the pendant on a necklace, a ruby surrounded by diamonds.

"I'm afraid so," he said. "It's a young woman called Mina Isherwood. Do you know her?"

"Crikey. I don't, sorry. What on earth was she doing there?"

"We believe she was left there at some point during the night."

"Is Shannon okay?"

"Yes. She's worried about Nancy. Have you seen her at all today?"

"No, it's her day off, so she normally has a lie-in. Why, is she not at home?"

"No, and her bike is missing from the garden."

"Then maybe she went shopping — though not the supermarket, because she gets that delivered weekly. She could have taken herself out for breakfast, I suppose, she does that sometimes. Shall I try ringing her?"

"You can do, although it's going straight to voicemail when Shannon calls."

Yvette took a mobile out of a drawer and pressed the screen as she placed it down on the desk. It showed she'd put it on speakerphone. Was that a natural option for her or was she trying to tell them she was being open, no secrets to hide, when in actual fact she had plenty she didn't want them to know about? He hadn't been in her company for long enough to tell.

"Hello?" a woman said.

"The police are here with me at work. Where are you?" Yvette asked.

"I'm in town. I've just had my hair cut."

"A dead woman's been found in Shannon's garden — Mina Isherwood — and the police are asking me where you might be."

"Bloody hell!"

Yvette took a breath. "I think there might possibly have been a worry that you'd been hurt, too. Anyway, are you going home anytime soon because the police are going to want to speak to you."

"I'll go now."

"Okay, I'll see you later." Yvette swiped the screen and put her phone back in the drawer. "That's one mystery solved, then. As soon as she said she was having her hair cut, I remembered she'd told me that last week. Sorry."

Lenny smiled. "That's not a problem. Right, so if we can take your movements, say, from yesterday evening until now."

Yvette seemed startled. "Um, you can't think this was *me*, surely."

"Standard procedure to ask these things."

"Oh, right. Well, I was up until eleven doing the ironing."

"More power to you for doing that," Anna said, getting into her "matey" role as opposed to Lenny's questioner.

Yvette smiled, but it seemed forced, like she didn't want to *be* mates. "Hmm. I watched a couple of episodes of *Sherwood*. After that, I put all the washing away, then went to bed and watched another episode. I got up at seven, as usual, had a shower and my breakfast, then got in the car and arrived here about half past eight. There's CCTV, so you can check on my arrival or ask any of the staff members who were here at the same time."

Lenny wrote that down. "Thanks. While you were ironing, I take it you didn't hear any vehicles coming up the lane."

"No, I was in the living room and would've seen any headlights through the blinds because they don't shut completely. Everything was as silent as it usually is out there."

"So nothing was off at all?"

"No, didn't I just say that?"

A bit snippy there. "Carry on."

"I fell asleep quite quickly and didn't wake up until the morning."

"Lucky you," Anna said. "I'm up twice in the night for a wee."

Yvette smiled, and this time it appeared genuine. "Funny enough, same here. That was the first time I've gone straight through in years. I have insomnia."

Convenient? Lenny made a note of that. "Is your bedroom at the front or the back?"

"The front."

"Ah, so when you opened your curtains this morning, you wouldn't have seen anything out the back."

"No, obviously, because I was at the front." An eye-roll.

Lenny chose to ignore it. Once upon a time he'd have rushed to explain that there was a method to his questioning, but he didn't feel the need to do so these days. She could think what she liked. Her being salty concerned him, though. Perhaps she was nervous in the presence of the police, like so many people were, even when they were innocent. "Do you know a Mr Daltrey and a Mr Bates?"

"Only to nod to if I'm round Shannon's and they're on their plots. There were a couple of times in the summer we sat out on her patio while they were working at the bottom of the garden and they came up for a glass of lemonade, but they spoke among themselves about veg, not to us."

"Shannon said you've lived in Marlford all your life. Did you know Mr Daltrey and Mr Bates prior to them using the plots?"

"No, I don't tend to go out of an evening anymore, unless it's with Shannon and Nancy for a meal. I'm a bit of an introvert, prefer my own company, so there isn't anywhere I could really go where I'd bump into them other than at Shannon's."

She seemed sincere enough. Lenny glanced at Anna to check whether she wanted to add anything else.

"On the nights when you *do* get up to use the toilet," Anna said, "do you ever happen to look out of the window?"

"No, my main concern is getting into bed and going back to sleep. Why?"

"I'm just curious as to whether you saw or heard anything recently." Anna linked her fingers in her lap. "Anyone creeping about out the back, getting their ducks in a row for when it came time to leave the body."

Yvette stared in a way that said she wasn't about to repeat herself regarding not seeing anyone.

Lenny switched tack. "Do we have your permission to check the outside of your house for signs of an attempted break-in? This would also involve collecting fingerprints of any strangers. And if you wouldn't mind giving us your fingerprints so we know which ones are yours."

"I don't like the idea of having them on file."

"It's literally so we can eliminate you," he said. "As you can probably understand with a body found next door to your property, it would be easier for us if we had your prints so we know you aren't someone we need to be looking at. That way we won't be going down avenues that we don't need to go down." *But if she's involved and wore gloves when touching Mina, we're no farther forward.*

"But I don't want to get my fingers all black from the ink."

"We have an electronic device." He took it from his pocket.

Yvette didn't seem too happy, but she allowed him to take her prints. He understood some people baulked at having their prints in the database — that they saw it as authoritarian, and a violation of privacy — but wasn't it better that she removed herself from suspicion?

"Just to confirm, you consent to us checking the outside of your home while you're not there?" Lenny said.

"Yes, yes, whatever. You can even go inside if you like, but I'd want to be there for that."

"Okay, that's very helpful. Thanks for your time." Anna stood and leaned across the desk to shake Yvette's hand. "If we have any other questions, we'll get back to you."

Lenny popped the device and his notebook in his pocket and followed her out of the office, remaining silent until they sat in the car. He knew from experience that if Anna didn't immediately launch into a speculative chat after an interview, she needed a moment to process the situation, or she was desperate for some alone time. Anna could be a bit of an introvert, too.

"She sounded genuine enough, if a bit frosty," Anna said. "What was your take on her?"

"Same as yours."

"We'll go to the houses. Nancy might be back by the time we arrive." She started the engine and drove out of the staff car park. "Can you check the team chat group for me? My phone vibrated in my pocket while we were talking to Yvette."

Lenny took his out and opened the app. "Louise and Rupert have spoken to Mr Daltrey and Mr Bates. They're just going to the station now to check on alibis. There's a daughter and a daughter-in-law who can verify the men's whereabouts. There doesn't appear to be any link between Mina and those men or their families."

"Okay, but that doesn't mean a link doesn't exist, although, as we know, the simplest solution is usually the answer."

"In this case, the body was left on Shannon's land, so therefore that's where the link is."

"Despite Shannon not knowing of any link."

"That she's admitted to."

"Hmm. Hopefully Ollie should have got some notes up on Effie Workington by the time we go back to the station for a debrief. I remember the basics of that case, but there will be bits and bobs I wasn't aware of, since I was only a PC. We'll look at it with fresh eyes and maybe see a connection between Effie and Mina."

"Or not."

"Yeah, or not." Anna drove on, the set of her jaw saying she didn't want to chat anymore.

Lenny respected that and remained silent.

CHAPTER TWELVE

Anna took a left turn and estimated they had about three minutes before they reached the lane. "How did the date go? We didn't get a chance to dissect it this morning."

Lenny was her best friend, and they often chatted about his love life. The same couldn't be said for the other way around, though. Anna had strong feelings for a local ex-gang member, Joshua "Parole" Cribbins, ones she'd had to push down because dating a criminal wasn't exactly conducive to a career as a police officer. No matter how alluring the man was, she couldn't risk seeing him on the quiet.

She lived vicariously through Lenny, because there was no way she'd put herself in the dating pool when the one man she cared about was already out there waiting for her, even if he *was* off limits. Then again, *was* he still waiting? Would he be there like he'd said he would if she ever changed her mind? Surely not. Someone like him wouldn't be short of female attention, and no matter what he said she honestly couldn't see him remaining celibate for the rest of his life. Like her, he'd move on, only she'd likely remain partnerless.

She'd been single for a long while before crushing on him, and with her introverted nature she was better off without any romantic attachments. She managed to be an extrovert at work and appear like she was someone who enjoyed the company of others, the noise, the mayhem, when in reality she loved the silence of living alone, the peace of not speaking to anyone, and waking up in her own space all by herself.

Lenny gazed out of the window. "Date two went so well that I'm going to her house for dinner tonight — *if* work doesn't ruin it."

"Blimey, date three the night after date two? Wow. It isn't looking like work will muck it up at the moment. Is there a possibility of dessert after dinner?"

"Not the dessert you mean. I've told her I want to take this slowly. After all of the weird women I dated before, then having that break from the apps, it made me reassess what I wanted."

"Which is?"

"I'm probably asking for the moon, but I'd like a relationship, just not one that ties me down. I want to live separately, keep my own place, go out on dates or day trips, that sort of thing."

"Is this new woman aware of that?"

"As far as I can make out, she wants the same thing, but I don't want to go into this and find out later down the line that she's changed her mind. What if she goes all needy on me?"

"But what if you change *your* mind? What if you decide having a proper partner isn't that bad after all because you've got used to her and you end up loving her?"

"I doubt it, but then I suppose none of us know what the future holds. All I know is that I'm not ready to go all in at the moment."

"As long as you keep the communication up between you, I don't see there being a problem, but the minute you become unhappy, get out."

"Yes, boss."

She smiled and drove up the lane, taking stock of their surroundings more than she had the first time. Earlier, she'd just wanted to get to the scene and see what was going on. Trees lined either side of the road, but there was enough space between trunks to see into the distance. The faint white dots of SOCOs checking out the curved route back to Rowan blotted the landscape to her left. From what she could make out, a few PCs walked the land to the right, likely searching for any sign that the killer had been over there, too. Despite there being no tracks in the grass, it had to be gone over just the same.

"I wonder who the land belongs to either side of the women's property?" Lenny mused. "Shall I message the group to get one of them to check?"

"Maybe message the scene sergeant, see if he can help us out there. For all we know the landowner is the link, not Shannon. I'm betting it's the farmer who lives out the back."

Lenny typed on his phone, the message *whooshing* off just as Anna pulled up the handbrake. She'd parked behind Herman's sports car at the top of the lane, and they got out to walk towards Nancy's house. A woman stood at the front door, slim, short black hair, and an oval, elfin face. She waved at them as she came down her path and through her gate.

"Nancy Rawlings?" Anna glanced at Lenny to let him know she'd take the lead on this one.

He took his notebook out ready.

"Yes, Yvette and Shannon said you need to see me. I saw the tent and everything there. This is so awful. Mina was in the pub last night, the Dagger Point, and she was as happy as usual."

"Really?" *That might prove interesting.* "If we go inside then you can tell us about it." Anna nipped into the front garden.

Lenny gestured for them to go on ahead of him. Nancy sidled past Anna and pushed the door open, leading the way inside. Anna appreciated the minimal decor and furniture. It gave off show home vibes, not a thing out of place — or, she corrected herself, no knick-knacks or photos to even *be* out of place. She'd have sworn blind Nancy had only just moved in, but earlier Shannon had said Nancy had come here with her husband years ago. Maybe she couldn't bear to have anything on display that reminded her of him. She could have popped it all away once he'd died.

Or maybe she's the same as you and doesn't like clutter.

They congregated in the kitchen, Anna and Lenny sitting on stools at a black marble-topped island, the veins in white and grey. Nancy opened a double-wide larder cupboard and took out a coffeemaker. She plugged it in, filled a compartment with water, and selected some pods from a drawer. Anna spied a kettle, toaster, and microwave in the cupboard, too. There was being tidy, then there was having to lug stuff out each time you needed something. What a pain in the arse.

"I assume coffee is okay," Nancy said.

"That would be brilliant." Anna smiled. "So you said you saw Mina in the pub last night. What time was that?"

"Around quarter to six. I know that because I went there for my dinner after work."

"What is it you do?"

"I'm an assistant at the local paper."

"Was Mina talking to anyone at that time?"

"Yes, Old Tanner."

Lenny frowned. "Who's that?"

Nancy flapped a hand. "Sorry, everyone calls him that. His name's Arnold Tanner."

"Is he actually old?" Anna asked.

"He's in his eighties. Likes them young, if you know what I mean."

Anna's eyebrows drew together. "Has anything inappropriate ever happened? Not just with Mina, but with any woman?"

"You're better off asking him that, but I've seen him doing things that some would say makes for uncomfortable viewing."

In the day and age where everybody had to be careful what they said, Anna could understand why Nancy had erred on the side of caution — if she didn't grass him up, she couldn't get the blame for anything.

Anna took a coffee from her. "Thank you."

Lenny received his, and Anna wished they'd visited the toilets in Sainsbury's. Lenny nudged Anna's knee to let her know he needed to say something. She nodded at him when Nancy turned her back to collect her coffee cup.

Lenny waited for the woman to face them. "Are you okay with allowing officers to look around your house to make sure nothing untoward has gone on during the night? It's just a precaution."

"What will they do?"

"Check for any prints that may have been transferred that don't belong to you or anybody you're aware of being here."

"Is that something that would usually happen? People get found murdered in houses all the time, but you don't hear about the whole street having their homes checked over."

"It was a decision I made this morning, to ask you three if we could do inside as well as outside," Anna said. "Granted, it's unusual, but as all of you live alone, in a remote location, I'm concerned for your safety. If we discover your back door has been jemmied and someone came into your house, for example, we can advise you to move elsewhere for the time being."

"Then you'll need to take my prints for elimination purposes?"

"Yes, but we don't need to use ink, we have an electronic device."

"I was told Shannon and a police officer were in here already this morning. Couldn't prints have been taken then? From the handles, I mean."

"We can't do it without your permission or a warrant." Anna sipped some coffee. "And Shannon made the decision to come in here earlier, not the police."

"Fair enough." Nancy perched on a stool opposite.

"What do you know, if anything, about the disappearance of Effie Workington?" Anna clocked only a minuscule lift of Nancy's eyebrow.

"Me and George — that was my husband, he's dead now — we used to drink at the Plough, but after she went missing it felt odd to go there, as if the place was tainted. I suppose it was all the police presence and everyone being suspicious of everyone else. Then there was that row between Shannon and Old Tanner after Effie had gone missing."

Anna hadn't heard about that. "What row?"

"He accused her of bumping Effie off on their way home from the pub. A lot of people had been saying the same privately, but he was the first to get it out in the open. Even the police thought it was her at one point, but then you might already know that."

Anna nodded. "I was a PC but wouldn't have got to hear about all the little details. I *will* go and read up on the case now, though." Especially because Effie had gone missing on a walk home from the pub. "So what was Shannon's reaction to the accusation?"

"She had a right go at him and told him to get his facts straight and that she was sick of everyone thinking it was her."

"Did you?"

"It's natural to wonder, isn't it? I knew her because she'd come and visit her mum and dad when they lived next door. As we're the same age, we sometimes chatted over the garden fence or whenever me and George were in the Plough."

"Going back to Mina being in the Dagger last night, what time did you leave to come home?"

"Not long after I'd finished my dinner. I can't recall the exact time."

"Did you see anyone loitering around the lane or your houses when you arrived?"

"No, otherwise I'd have phoned the police. It's scary out here sometimes. I felt safer when George was alive, but since he's gone, even though Shannon and Yvette are only ten seconds away, I still get jittery."

"And what did you do once you came inside?"

"I watched the telly until ten. I know that because the news came on after my programme had finished. I had a shower and went to bed. I think I dropped off pretty quickly as I was tired. I didn't hear anything going on during the night at all. Slept straight through."

"Is your bedroom at the front or the back?"

"The front."

Anna switched the topic again. "Other than your concerns about Mina being with Old Tanner, how was her general demeanour?"

"She was laughing and joking with him. He patted her lower back at one point, which I thought was a bit too familiar. She didn't seem to mind, though. She leaned over and put her head on his shoulder."

"Perhaps she saw him as a granddad type?"

Nancy blinked. "Are you asking me or assuming?"

"Musing out loud, to be honest. Not to worry, we'll soon find out what was what between them. Back to Effie. What was your relationship with her, if any?" Anna waited for a sign that the constant switches in topic were getting on Nancy's nerves, but she appeared to be taking them in her stride.

"I knew her as a child, but we lost contact for a long while. When we were older, I saw her a couple of times up here when she'd come to see Shannon's parents. I smiled if I happened to see her in the Plough, and once or twice she and Shannon came to sit with us, although she didn't do much other than eye up the men. She wasn't interested in anything we had to say. Effie liked being looked at and having drinks bought for her. She enjoyed being the centre of attention. She had an affair with Old Tanner behind his wife's back. He'd have been in his sixties then, she was in her thirties like me. There was never any visual evidence of them being an item, though — they never acted any differently towards each other in public. Then Shannon brought it up on the night Effie went missing, exposing the truth to everyone in the pub. Since then, I've had the theory that Effie stepped on someone's toes and that's why she's no longer around."

"What, she was threatened and had to leave?"

"Maybe. Her body's never been found, so there's no proof she's dead. I think that's why they left Shannon alone in the end. The police, I mean. No one had seen her go home to her flat to collect her car. No one had heard the engine. That was the biggest rumour, you know, that she'd done away with Effie at Cooper's Crossing, left her hidden somewhere, then went back for her and took her God knows where."

"I remember everything petering out, the investigation, the chatter. It was as if, after the initial flurry of searches, no one seemed to be bothered about Effie anymore, until that first sighting a year later." All Anna had been told was that every avenue had been investigated and there was nothing but dead ends. The consensus was that either Effie had removed herself from Marlford and the lives of everyone who knew her, she was living with someone in secret, or she was dead. "Maybe this time round we can find out what happened to her."

Nancy frowned. "Shouldn't you be concentrating on Mina?"

"Yes, but we can also investigate Effie at the same time. Did you by any chance happen to overhear any of the conversation Mina had with Old Tanner?"

"I'm sorry, no. I was too far away. I sat by the jukebox."

Anna finished her coffee in three swallows as it was cooler now. She stood and held her hand out to Nancy. "Thanks for speaking to us today. Your information has been really helpful. If you think of anything else, could you please get hold of me?" She took out a business card and placed it on the island.

Lenny stood and also shook her hand. "If you're still feeling vulnerable out here at night, have you considered putting in CCTV?"

Nancy nodded. "I will now."

Anna and Lenny said their goodbyes and, out the front, they approached Steven Timpson, the lead SOCO.

He glanced at his watch. "I was going to say good morning, but it's afternoon now. I'll just give you a quick update.

Officers are still out looking at the footprint curve, going over the grass again, but absolutely nothing of import has been picked up so far, not even a chewing gum wrapper, which surprised me. The scene sarge sent a couple of officers over to the farmhouse because several clumps of animal droppings were found." He took out a notebook and flipped one of the pages. "The farmer's name's Frank Quinlan, and he owns the land either side of the lane, including where the curve is. Apparently, he asked the women if he could buy the land directly behind these houses, but they refused. Back in the day, the rear gardens used to be that much longer, going all the way to the hedge. Somewhere along the line, fences were put up."

"So if any of the women fancy it, they can just extend their gardens?"

"It appears so. Mr Quinlan said they'd told him they didn't have the time or energy to mow that amount of grass, hence those bottom fences going up and them letting him put his sheep on there to graze."

"We've heard somewhere along the way that they refused to sell the land because developers want to get their hands on it."

"Hmm, Mr Quinlan feels that they don't trust him not to sell it on if he bought it. The PCs believed him when he said he wanted it for his animals, nothing more."

"But he's got the better end of the deal anyway. He doesn't have to fork out for the land and the animals use it regardless."

"That's what I said. Anyhow, Mr Quinlan was in bed with his wife and didn't hear or see anything last night."

"Thanks for that. Anything else we need to know?"

"It might be advisable to get Mr Daltrey's and Mr Bates's fingerprints if they haven't been collected already. I'm just about to swab Nancy's door handles and check the interior of her property now — she gave us permission?"

"Yep."

"Good. I'm also hoping she won't mind me snooping around her back garden. Shannon said it's got a Japanese theme with pea shingle and has quite a bit of foliage around the tree trunks. I want to see if anyone stood by the greenery and left footprints."

"I'm sure she'll let you do that. What about at Yvette's?"

"There are no fingerprints on her back door or the handle at all, which I find odd. It's like they've been wiped clean, top to bottom."

Anna narrowed her eyes. "Well, *that* doesn't sound suspicious, does it?"

"She might not necessarily have cleaned it, though," Steven said. "Could have been someone else. Maybe the killer did try to enter her home and changed their mind, then they wiped everything over. Oh, Yvette and Nancy both have padlocks on their back gates on the outside."

"I noticed that. But Shannon's doesn't."

"Hmm. Each house has an alleyway in between. Nancy and Yvette both have gates at the end of them that lead to their rear gardens, but Shannon's is just open access. Had there not been clear footprint marks in the grass at the back, I'd have said the body was brought in down the side of Shannon's house, and someone used a vehicle to transport it up the lane, but that could still be the case. An accomplice could have come on foot and made the marks in the back grass, then met them in the garden."

"If there was a car, then none of the women heard it," Anna said. "Or so they say. I'm inclined to believe whoever brought Mina here carried her. Unless the residents here are lying."

Lenny pinched his chin. "Sorry to butt in when you're speculating, but we should really go to the Plough and speak to Arnold Tanner."

Anna nodded. "Bugger, yes. If you get anything else you think we need to know, Steve, give me a bell, and I'll do the same for you."

"We're going to be here for a good while yet, at least until the light starts fading."

Anna waved to him and walked towards the lane with Lenny. "What did you think of Nancy?"

"She was amenable and didn't mind answering questions. She didn't get flustered when you switched subjects."

Anna opened the driver's door. Lenny got in the passenger seat. Anna was eager to get to Rowan and empty her bladder, then find out exactly what Mina had been doing last night with Old Tanner.

CHAPTER THIRTEEN

Yvette couldn't stop thinking about the police visit. Several times she'd wondered whether she should go home. Her nerves kept spiking, and she'd found herself snapping at several employees. In the end, she'd locked herself in her office and drawn the blinds so no one could see her through the glass. She needed a moment to get her head together. The issue was the police were going to find no prints whatsoever on the back door, and that might pose a problem. She was probably going to be questioned about it because, to be fair, it *was* odd. What could she say that would sound plausible? Believable?

The truth, that I washed it.

She'd lied about sleeping through; she'd stood in her back garden in the night having a sneaky cigarette. She'd given up years ago but occasionally gave in to the urge. After lighting up, in the glow coming from her kitchen she'd spotted dirty marks on the bottom of her back door. It looked like an animal had scraped its muddy paws down it as if trying to get in. She'd bet it was the farmer's bloody cat. She'd dashed inside to get a cloth and some spray, and got rid of the marks, cleaning from top to bottom. Maybe she could tell the police she regularly washed the outside of her house and yesterday just happened to be the day for the back — that wasn't a lie. She was obsessed with housework. She could make out she was supposed to do the front after work today.

That excuse would have to be enough.

She cradled her forehead in her hands, elbows propped on the desk. It was frustrating not to be at home, standing at the top window and watching the goings-on. Maybe she should call the other manager in, say she didn't feel well and needed to go home.

She did that and slipped her arms into her thick coat and drew her gloves on. She left work, got into her car and shivered at the chill in the air. She wasn't ready to drive away yet so sat and stared at the wall ahead in the staff car park, her mind going ten to the dozen. Should she admit she'd been in her garden last night? No, it might get her in trouble later down the line. She was better off keeping her mouth shut.

She drove home in a daze, having to scoot over to the other side of the lane because of the numerous police vehicles parked there. She nosed her Saab out into the tiny area of her street, and an officer came towards her, his palm up.

She wound down her window. "I'm Yvette Danes, I live just there."

"Can I see some identification, please?"

She fished in her bag for her driver's licence and raised it for him to check. He nodded for her to continue on her way, and she parked bang outside her house like she usually did. She got out, and just as she was about to open her garden gate Shannon appeared at her front door.

"The kettle's just boiled if you want a brew," she called, then whispered, "There's a copper in here, mind."

"Why would I care if there was?" Yvette barked, and she regretted it. "Sorry, it's just been difficult hearing about what's going on. I didn't mean to take it out on you."

"It's all right. It's been pretty tense here all day."

Yvette followed Shannon into the house. In the hallway, she whispered, "Did they swab your door handles or whatever it is they do?"

"Yes, and they came through my house to have a look round, just in case the person who killed Mina has got a problem with me and they broke in while I was asleep."

"A problem?"

"Because she was left in *my* garden. They took fingerprints from various places, but they'll not find anyone's except mine, yours, and Nancy's. Oh, and maybe Vaughn's and Tate's. They're the only people who've been in here other than the police."

"Who's in here with you now?"

"She's called Jayla. She came with that Maddox — you know, *Julia Parsons'* son."

Yvette had heard Shannon rant about the woman enough times. Julia and Shannon had been good friends for a couple of years up until the time they'd had a falling-out at the Dagger five years ago. "Good job this Jayla's here instead of him, then."

"That's what I thought, but he's been quite nice to me, actually."

"I suppose he has to. It's his job."

"Charming. So you're saying if he wasn't a copper he'd be nasty to me, sticking up for his mum?"

It seemed Yvette was on a collision course to saying the wrong thing today. She had to be careful. *So* careful. "Ignore me. I didn't mean anything by it."

Shannon trotted into the kitchen. Yvette followed and put her game face on. She smiled tentatively at a ginger woman sitting at the table, who was squeezing a teabag in one of many cups on a tray. Yvette had always ribbed Shannon about the number of mugs she had in her cupboard, but they were coming into their own now.

"Do you need any help with that?" Yvette asked.

"You could add the milk for me, if you don't mind," Jayla said.

Shannon jerked a thumb. "This is Yvette from next door. I meant to ask, did you come home because you're poorly? Only, it's not like you to not be at work."

Yvette shrugged her coat off and hung it on the back of a chair, a little grossed out that the hem touched Shannon's floor. She popped her gloves in the pockets. "I couldn't settle once I'd heard what had happened." She picked up a carton of milk and began pouring.

"One of our officers wanted to speak to you, Yvette," Jayla said. "Nothing alarming, it's just something about your back door that he needs clarifying, that's all, plus they'll want to nip through your house to check no one got in last night."

Yvette's hand shook. She put the carton down so Jayla wouldn't notice. "Shall I go and speak to them now?"

Jayla smiled. "I'll tell him to come in when I take the first round of teas out."

Yvette continued with the milk, forcing her hand to remain steady. She couldn't get in trouble for washing her back door, she had to remember that. Yes, it might look odd, and yes, it might look convenient in the circumstances that there were no fingerprints, but she wasn't prepared to backtrack now and say she'd been outside during the night. She wished she'd been honest from the start, but if she changed what she'd said they might wonder what else she'd lied about or hidden from them.

There were plenty of secrets stashed away in her mind. It was just unfortunate that she couldn't pass them along in order to get out of the mess she'd found herself in.

Not when it meant spending time in prison.

CHAPTER FOURTEEN

Nancy stood at a window and stared down. A man came out of the tent in a white forensic suit and used some black steps that led to the little patio-slab walkway between Mr Daltrey's and Shannon's patches. He strode up to a PC in uniform, who offered him a cup of tea off a tray. Tea in hand and lowering his face mask, he moved to the grassed area and stood talking to someone else in the same forensic outfit.

She switched her attention to beyond the gardens, staring ahead at Frank Quinlan's farmhouse. Had he seen anything going on during the night? She knew from a chat she'd had with him once that he was in bed by eight in the evening as he had to be up at four.

She should have brought a coffee up here so she could nose in comfort. Thirst lured her downstairs. She boiled the kettle and made a drink and a sandwich, then returned to her lofty perch. It was dark up there, and unless someone glanced skywards no one would even notice her.

She should have dinner at the Dagger later, maybe get Shannon and Yvette to go with her. The police would have been there by then, and Nancy could glean more information, plus there'd be speculation, something she'd like to hear.

Many a thread of truth had come out of a gossip's mouth.

She leaned against the wall and ate one half of her sandwich, watching the officers as they worked. Would they find anything, a lead, something to send the investigation in the direction they needed it to go? Or would it peter out, like it had with Effie? The close-knit, sometimes suffocating community would dine out on this for weeks, throwing theories into the mix, and as for social media . . . She'd bet a pound to a penny the armchair detectives were out in force by now. She recalled it well from when Effie had disappeared, all those people suddenly piping up with something to say.

Nancy continued to observe.

CHAPTER FIFTEEN

Anna entered the Dagger and immediately checked where the bar was — to the left — then scoured the area for the jukebox. It was attached to the wall opposite the bar and a row of six stools. Nancy would have had a decent view of Mina sitting there, providing not too many people had filled the space between. Anna clocked an older man sitting on one of the stools — Arnold Tanner? She approached the bar and asked to speak to the manager.

"I *am* the manager," the young woman said, full of self-importance and with one of those faces you wanted to slap for no reason. Blonde, twenty-something, and she'd got the tattoo bug if her arms were anything to go by. Both had sleeves of black-and-white art.

They reminded Anna of Parole's, and the image of his tattooed face came to mind, an inky mask he hid behind. She hadn't heard what he was up to lately and assumed he still lived in his posh apartment beside Jubilee Lake on Westgate. She shook the image away and smiled at the manager, despite the bad vibes radiating off her.

Holding up her ID, she introduced herself and Lenny. "And your name is?"

The woman puffed out what could only be described as a derisive laugh. "The copper we had in here earlier already knew my name. He read it off the sign above the door."

Bully for him. Anna hadn't even thought to do that, and she wasn't sure what point the manager was making — implying that Anna wasn't exactly copper of the year? Annoyed but hiding it, she repeated, "And your name is?"

A tut, followed by, "Zoe Usher."

"Okay, Zoe, while I understand it may be irritating for you to repeat a few things to us, I *am* going to be asking you some questions. I would rather we did that in private, though."

Zoe glanced across at two other people working behind the bar. She lifted a hatch, gesturing for Anna and Lenny to follow her, the hand signal resembling the middle finger. They walked down the back wall to a door on the left marked *private*. She took them into a tidy office with art on the walls, various monochrome Banksy prints. She sat behind a metal-framed desk, a slab of wood on top, pushed her chair away from it, stuck her feet out and crossed her ankles. She didn't offer them a seat. Something about Zoe pissed Anna off more than it should — the general rude air about her — and she sensed scorn, maybe a general dislike for police officers.

Lenny took his notebook out and cleared his throat.

"We don't want a seat, that's okay," Anna said, sarcasm heavy.

"Good. Wouldn't want you to get comfortable."

"Why's that?"

"My customers aren't fond of pigs."

"I take it you're not either — but that's neither here nor there and no interest to me whatsoever. All I want from you is information and to get out of your hair as quickly as possible. What can you tell me about Mina Isherwood?"

"Like I told the PC, she was in here last night. I can't remember the exact time she walked in, but it was after five. She said she was only staying for half a pint because she was skint but ended up being here until eleven or so."

"Any CCTV?"

"No."

"Who did Mina spend the evening with, if anyone?"

"She chatted to Old Tanner — that's Arnold, the man sitting at the bar when you came in. He's here every single day, and no, he didn't leave after Mina did. He stayed on after I shut the pub. He likes to wrap the cutlery in napkins for me while me and the staff tidy up. Personally, I think he's lonely but he'd never admit it. I dropped him home about quarter past one, then went home myself."

"You live upstairs?"

"No, that's rented out to an eighteen-year-old artist whose mum and dad have got more money than sense. He's taking a year out to paint to his heart's content while they fund him. The copper from earlier on's already spoken to him, and to Tanner."

"What was Mina wearing?"

"I wrote it down in case someone else came in asking questions." Zoe planted her feet on the floor. She scooted the chair closer to the desk and flicked a spiral notebook towards them.

Lenny stepped forward to take it, and showed Anna a list on the top page.

Red high-heeled shoes. Dark-blue skirt. A white blouse, tucked in. Light-pink leather jacket.

Anna looked at Lenny, who'd clearly spotted the same as she had. That outfit was not the clothing they'd found Mina in. So, what, she'd walked home and then got changed? Why not get straight into her pyjamas? Had something made her go out again, meaning she'd put on the jeans, coat, and hat?

Anna took her phone out to snap a picture of the page. "Did she put a hat on when she left?"

"If I'd seen a hat then it'd be on the list."

Anna didn't care for her attitude, and it riled her that she needed this woman, otherwise she'd have just turned her back and walked out with no explanation, a silent "fuck you". She was too old to play games — well, being in her forties wasn't old, but she bloody well felt like it sometimes, what with perimenopause symptoms showing their smarmy faces. Anyone who had a mind to fuck her about for the fun of it never made it onto her Christmas card list.

She made a mental note to never come here and give Zoe her custom. "Is there anything else you could tell me about the time Mina spent here last night?"

"She accepted a fair few drinks off Tanner, so much so she was drunk when she left. What I call weaving drunk. She couldn't quite control the way she was walking."

"What was her mood?"

"Happy as ever. I very rarely saw her upset."

"What can you tell me about Tanner?"

"He's all right, just a bit misunderstood."

"In what way?"

"Some people take his tendency to pat you on the bum, for example, as something perverted, when I just think he's of the older generation and doesn't realise that some people feel unrequested touches are inappropriate."

"How touchy-feely is he?"

"Enough that people have commented."

"What are their names, please?"

"I can't remember."

Whatever. "Was he like that with Mina?"

"I only saw him lay a hand on her back last night. She was the one leaning into him with her head on his shoulder, and she shifted her stool across at one point so she could hug him around the waist. She had her cheek on his chest and told him he was the best friend she'd ever had."

"Do you know what else they talked about — and not just last night, at any time?"

"Last night it was too busy for me to be listening to conversations because we had a quiz at seven, but on quieter evenings she told him about her health problems, how she lived by herself."

"So Tanner provided a listening ear, did he?"

"That's it, as far as I'm aware."

"Thank you for your time." Anna walked out of the office and waited for Lenny at the bar, then she lifted her ID and introduced them to Tanner.

"Fucking hell," he said, "are you going to ask me to go through it all again?"

"I'm afraid so." Anna smiled. Recognition sparked inside her. It was the man's eyes, a really light blue, but she wasn't sure where she knew him from.

He held up one finger and poked it in the air towards her. "I remember you from when Effie went missing. You were out on the moors the same time as I was, when everyone from the estate got together and went out on that search for her. You haven't changed much."

Now he'd reminded her where she'd seen him before, she smiled. "Yes, I remember." She braced herself to perhaps go a little bit below the belt, considering she only had gossip to go on. "You were the one accused of having an affair with Effie."

He shook his head. "Bloody hell, and they say elephants never forget. You coppers have got memories like I don't know what."

"Were you seeing Mina?"

He picked up his half a lager and directed the top edge of the glass at her like he had his finger. "I don't know where you think you're going with this line of questioning, but I don't appreciate it. You can get that filthy rubbish out of your head."

"What did you do after Zoe dropped you home?"

"What normal people do. I got undressed and went to bed."

"Where do you live, sir?"

He sighed. "Cedar Avenue, and before you say it, yes, it's five doors down from Mina, and no, I didn't hear anything going on in the street. Short of a bomb going off, I was too rat-arsed to have been woken up."

This was the kind of information Anna needed to be told *before* she spoke to people. But she was to blame there, because she should have looked up his address herself. She leaned against the bar and faced the jukebox. "Did you ever see or speak to Mina in either of your houses?"

"No, never. We only ever chatted in here. I'm barely at home anyway, bar an hour or two for a nap in the afternoon. This pub's my second home."

"What sort of thing did you talk about last night?"

"This and that. Stuff on the telly. Listen, if you're thinking of framing me for this, then swivel that head of yours and look a different way because it wasn't me, and I'll say it before you do — just like I had nothing to do with Effie. It's a coincidence, that's all it is, and anyway, no one ever found a body, so for all we know she could have just swanned off and started again somewhere else."

"Not using her name, she didn't."

"She could have changed it." He sipped his lager and scooted round on the stool so he was side on to her. "I miss Effie, and I'll bloody well miss Mina."

"What's your response to those who feel your touches are inappropriate?"

He *tsked* and appeared offended she'd asked such a thing. "I'd say they need to get their minds out of the gutter. That's the problem these days, everyone sees things that aren't there. Wave at a kiddie while you're on the bus and you're a nonce. Use a machete to cut your front hedge and you're a killer. I could give you more examples, but you get the gist. I'm no pervert."

Anna was getting the ick. Pervert or not, there was something about him that didn't sit right. "Thank you for your time."

She moved away from him to the end of the bar closest to the front door. Lenny joined her, and they quietly agreed to take a section of the pub each and question the customers and the other two bar staff.

Unfortunately, nobody knew who Mina was, nor had anyone remembered seeing her. Anna and Lenny left the pub and headed for the station, but then Anna's phone rang in the cup holder, and she gave Lenny permission to answer it.

"It's Karen," he said. "I'm going to muck about and make out I don't know who she is."

"You're a sod."

He swiped the screen and put it on speakerphone. "DI Anna James's phone, DS Lenny Baldwin here. Anna's driving. Who are you?"

"Eh? It's me, Karen from the front desk."

"Hello, Karen from the front desk. Nice to meet you."

She laughed. "Pack it in, Lenny, this is important. Katy Clark's relief just asked me to get hold of you. Another FLO's taken her place at Mina's mother's house on account of Katy having to go to the dentist — she's got to have a crown fitted and couldn't put it off, something like that. Anyway, the FLO's new and apparently hasn't got your numbers. I offered to give them to him, but he asked that I pass this on."

"Okay . . ."

"The mother said she's remembered something."

Anna perked up. "What's that, then?"

"Mina phoned her last night."

Astounded, Anna said, "What the bloody hell's going on? Why the chuff didn't she remember this sooner? How is this something you'd forget?"

"The shock, maybe?" Karen asked.

Anna had to rein in her temper, because Karen was right. The poor woman *had* been shocked, her only child killed and discarded like so much rubbish, but by God, Anna wanted to scream. "What time was the phone call?"

"After Mina had got home from the pub."

"Shit, so she *did* get home. What was the call about?"

"Effie Workington's ghost had been trying to get into Mina's house."

Anna blinked. "What?"

"I know. Insane, isn't it?"

Anna turned right so she could head towards the mother's place. "We're on the way to speak to her now."

"Thought you might. The new FLO is called Xavier Braithwaite, just so you know."

"Sounds posh."

"Hmm, but don't hold it against him. He's a nice lad."

Karen, Anna, and Lenny usually shared station gossip, sometimes going to the Horse's Hoof pub down the road after work. There had been a fair few times that Anna had to keep things to herself, though, especially regarding Peter Dove, the Northern Kings, and Parole. While Karen understood she wasn't allowed to be privy to everything going on, she still chanced her arm and pushed for information. She was a lovely woman, and her jokes kept Anna smiling on the days when her lips were downturned.

"I'll be my most professional," Anna said. "Where did he come from, and how long has he been with us?"

"Chelsea, and this is his first week."

Anna smiled, imagining Xavier's reaction to what he may well think of as rough northern folk. "Okay, let him know we'll be there in five minutes."

"Will do. Toodle-pip!"

"Bloody hell, is he rubbing off on you *that* quickly?"

Karen's burbling laughter filled the car until a swipe of Lenny's finger cut her off.

Anna shook her head and smiled. "That woman . . ."

Lenny nodded. "We wouldn't be without her, though."

Anna couldn't argue with that.

CHAPTER SIXTEEN

To: carebear@worldnet.com
From: thecowcatcher@worldnet.com

Has the news brought everything back? I've been thinking about the past and how, if you hadn't been so nosy, you'd be none the wiser about me. You regret seeing what you saw, I know that, but you don't regret the payment I gave you. I've also been thinking of the little name I've got for you. Care Bear. Because you care too much. But you stopped caring once money was on the table, so what does that say about you? Oh, and we can't forget the fear of me doing the same to you — killing you, I mean. I wonder whether we all have that part inside us. Have you ever thought about killing me? I bet you have. If I wasn't here, your guilt would be guaranteed to remain a secret. But remember, I never washed the white dress, and who knows, your tears and snot might still be on it. Can they get DNA from that? Imagine if they found that dress . . .

* * *

To: thecowcatcher@worldnet.com
From: carebear@worldnet.com

You said I shouldn't respond, ever, but fuck this. If the dress is found, YOUR DNA will also be on it. Stop playing with me. I'm doing what you want. And I'm going to say it — the fact you put on that dress and Effie's face is sick. If you don't watch yourself, you're going to get caught. Killing Mina . . . I can guess why you did it, and I understand the pain Old Tanner makes you feel, but he doesn't give a shit about you, so becoming the "Cow Catcher" to catch the "cows" he gives his attention to is insane. You're killing for no reason because HE HAS NO CLUE THE DEATHS ARE LINKED TO HIM.

* * *

To: carebear@worldnet.com
From: thecowcatcher@worldnet.com

How can you be so cruel? You know what he's done to me.

* * *

To: thecowcatcher@worldnet.com
From: carebear@worldnet.com

Men like Tanner go from one little kid to the next, convinced those children won't tell anyone what they do to them because of their threats, so he won't realise you were still so fixated on being "his" that you were prepared to commit murder as an adult. And don't you think it's STUPID to email me? If the police ever ask to look at my mobile, even though I delete whatever you send me, they'll be able to find them. They might be able to trace who you are. For your own sake, stop communicating this way.

CHAPTER SEVENTEEN

Elizabeth Isherwood looked exactly like the person she was — a mother broken by the news that her only child had been murdered. Her face showed she spent a lot of time outdoors, plus that she'd been crying for quite some time. The end of her nose was as red as her box-dyed hair and appeared sore where she must have kept wiping it with the scrunched-up tissue she held. Her fringe stood up as if she'd been running her fingers through it. The notes Anna had received on her stated Elizabeth was fifty-five, but she looked closer to seventy. Grief was a bastard the way it could ravage your features in seconds.

Anna sat on one of the armchairs, Lenny took the other, and Xavier sat beside Elizabeth with a box of tissues on his lap. His Adam's apple was the same shape as his nose, slightly pointed, and it bobbed where he was perhaps nervous of Anna and over-swallowing. Someone must have informed him she could be blunt.

She shifted forward to the edge of the chair and rested her hands on her knees. "Okay, Elizabeth, if you could let us know what the phone call was about."

"She never phones me late unless there's a problem, so I knew straight away something was wrong because it was after eleven. She said on her way home that stupid Effie ghost was down the alley over the road from the Dagger — not the one that goes between the houses, but the wider one that leads to the park. The pretend Effie ran past her and jabbed her with an elbow for whatever reason, then went down the ginnel. Mina carried on and went home, but that *thing* was down the side of her house. It was the usual sighting, the blonde hair, white dress, and the ballet slippers. To cut a long story short, Mina went in and looked out of the back door, and the thing had pegged its own hair to the washing line — I mean, who *does* that? — then banged on the back door. Mina ran out the front to get help from a neighbour, but no one answered. The thing danced her way from the side of Mina's house, then ran down the street. Mina went back indoors and locked herself in, then she phoned me."

Anna took a moment to digest what she'd just heard. Who the *fuck* pegged their own hair to a washing line? If Mina hadn't checked outside, she'd never have known, so what was the point in the Effie lookalike doing that without an audience? "That sounds exceptionally strange. And we can only assume it was someone pretending to be Effie."

"That's what I said on the phone to Mina because she'd said the person was about thirty. Well, Effie would be in her fifties by now. She wasn't the type to just go missing. She wouldn't have hidden herself only to pop out in the dark like this. Mina thought it must be kids mucking about, and I was inclined to agree, but now . . ." She let out a terrible wail and slapped a hand over her mouth. She lowered it and dabbed at her eyes. "I wish I'd gone anyway."

"What do you mean?"

"I asked her if she needed me to go over and stay the night or I could bring her back here. She said no. I did press and ask if she was sure, and that's when she said it must be someone dicking about."

"You weren't to know."

"No, but it was weird enough as it was, and I just left her in that house by herself."

Anna had to change the subject or Elizabeth could spiral. "I expect you've been asked this already, and I apologise for repeating anything, but do you know of anyone who'd want to play a trick on Mina like that? Perhaps to scare her and then go on to do what they did?"

"I know a few of her neighbours in her old block of flats were annoyed she'd been given her house, but it isn't something to *kill* her over."

"Was Mina the secretive type?"

"Well, there must have been some things she kept to herself because you don't tell your parents everything, do you? But as a whole, I think she shared most things with me. Why?"

"I'm just wondering if there was another reason why she wanted to leave the flats. Could someone there have been bullying her, for example?"

"She never said. It was just the usual gripes between neighbours. Maybe you ought to go and speak to Molly Griffin."

Molly was the self-proclaimed Queen of Northgate. She'd had a few run-ins with the police, mainly for fighting and arguing, and she had her nose in everyone's business.

"Okay, we'll do that. We're not going to take up any more of your time." Anna smiled across at the woman. "Is there anything you'd like to ask?"

"How did she die? And you don't need to go soft with me. I'd rather know the proper facts; I'll only be imagining all sorts anyway."

"Initial findings are that she was strangled, either with a tie or scarf."

Elizabeth flinched. "Did this happen where she was dumped, elsewhere, or at her house?"

"There were no signs of a struggle around the body, so we believe she was killed elsewhere, then carried to the site."

"How can you possibly know she was carried?"

"By the flattened trail left behind in the grass. It's obvious only one person walked that way."

"But what if *Mina* walked that way? What if someone phoned her? The meeting place could have been Shannon's garden. Why that garden, though? I mean, I realise there's a link with the Workingtons, what with that *thing* bothering Mina last night, but other than that it's not making any sense. As far as I know, Mina had nothing to do with Shannon."

"It's something we'll be looking into, but your information has made a huge difference in how we'll view this going forward."

Elizabeth dabbed the end of her nose with the tissue. "When will I be able to see her?"

"Someone will ring you, or Xavier here can deal with it for you. Whatever suits you best."

"Does she . . . has she got any marks on her? Did they hurt her on more than just her neck?" Elizabeth bit her lip as if to brace herself for the answer.

"Not that we could see at the scene. She had a coat and jeans on and a woollen hat. We're interested in whether she left her house after her phone call to you. From the information we've discovered so far, the clothes Mina has on are not the same ones she wore at the pub. Was she the type to change into a whole new outfit when she got home or would she have put her pyjamas on?"

"Pyjamas, definitely."

"That's what I thought. Okay, we'll leave you be now. If you think of anything else, please phone me direct." Anna handed her business card over.

"I'll just see you out."

"Please don't get up on our account." Anna smiled and left the room.

Lenny and Xavier followed her into the hallway, Xavier closing the door on Elizabeth. He squidged past to open the front door, then waited for them to step outside before joining them on the path.

"How's Elizabeth dealing with this?" Anna asked the FLO.

"One minute she's in floods of tears and the next she's trying to think of things that could help you with the investigation, hence her remembering the phone call. I expect she'll think of something else later on. She's been keeping busy by cleaning the kitchen. I offered to help but she told me to sit down."

"What's going on with her stall?"

"Her colleagues are taking it in turns to man it. Apparently that's what they all do, help each other out when someone's ill or on holiday."

"Well, at least she won't have her income to worry about while she's grieving. Okay, if you can get the conversation around to the fact that we'll be holding the body for as long as it takes. Be gentle with her because she might be thinking she can have her daughter back as soon as the post-mortem's done. By all means help her arrange the funeral, but the date will have to be undetermined for now."

Xavier nodded. "Is it all right if I get hold of you instead of going through Karen at the station?"

Anna nodded. "Are you staying here overnight?"

"Yes, until tomorrow, and then Katy's back. I'm happy to stay here and see it through to the end, though."

"Elizabeth might prefer you anyway. Put the feelers out and see what her thoughts are on that. Right, we need to get going. We're in desperate need of a debrief."

Anna smiled at the officer and walked away. In the car, she stuck her seat belt on and took a deep, cleansing breath. It had been a lot of speaking to people today, gathering information, and there was too much of it to keep it straight in her head. A chat with the team would do them good so they were all on the same page.

Lenny got in the car and buckled up. "Poor woman."

"I know."

"And what the fuck about that person pegging her hair to the washing line? I mean, how *weird* is that?"

"What's even weirder is there might not even be a reason for it."

Lenny puffed air out. "There's a bright side. If she was banging on Mina's back door, forensics might have picked up prints from the glass or even on the pegs."

"They're no good to us unless she's in the system."

"But once they *are* in the system, if that person cocks up again . . ."

Anna eased away from the kerb. "We can but hope."

CHAPTER EIGHTEEN

Molly Griffin stood in the Plough with a cob on. Not only was nobody spilling secrets about Mina Isherwood, but she was being stared at as though she was shit on some of this lot's shoes. She supposed it might well come across as rude of her to be asking so many questions in the circumstances, but it wasn't to have a gossip like they might think. She wanted to find whoever had killed the poor cow so justice was served.

She didn't appreciate being looked down on, especially with the amount of things she'd done for some of these people. If they wanted hooky gear then she'd get it for them. If there were any lorries with stuff being sold off the back of them, Molly would be driving them. She was all about helping the community save a few quid while lining her own pockets, and freely gave her time and information and made their lives easier. So why weren't they returning the favour? Of course, they could very well be telling the truth that they didn't know anything. It had always been the same when it came to Effie's ghost. Whoever ran around the town pretending to be her had never owned up to it.

Molly would be going over to the Dagger in a bit to see if she could get people talking. Her little boy could do with the fresh air anyway. Three-year-old Basil — no one dared take the piss out of his name in her earshot — currently sat in his buggy griping about wanting to get out. He was doing her nut in.

"We're not staying here for long," she said to him, "so pack it in whinging. I'll get you a cheese roll, all right?"

She approached the bar, and the landlord, Harry Wells, stared at her, pulling his long grey beard. They had a bit of rivalry going on — who knew the most about the residents. She'd swear *she* was the more knowledgeable, but today might be a different matter when it came to what had happened to Mina, and she was about to probe and find out.

"Can I have a cheese roll, please? A soft one for Basil, not one of those crusty fuckers you've been dishing out lately."

"I had a deal on those with the baker, but it's stopped now." Harry prodded at the screen of the till. "Does he want one of those kiddie drinks?"

"Only if you're paying."

"Yeah, I can stretch to a Fruit Shoot." He pressed a couple more icons. The money drawer opened, and he shut it again. "I'll stump up for the roll an' all."

She narrowed her eyes at him, suspicious. "What are you after?"

"Nothing, except I thought we might pool our resources on this one."

"'This one'? I don't know what you're talking about."

"Oh, come on, you know damn well. You've been asking my customers questions about Mina and Effie. Apparently, they know sod all."

"Hmm, that's what they told me, too. I've been asking around to see if anyone else saw Effie last night."

"Why are you poking into it?"

"Mina was all right, she was, and I want to help find whoever did this to her."

"What did you hear?"

"There's rumours she's been found dead up the lane. Candy, her next door to me, saw a load of police cars going up that way this morning when she was out in her car dropping her kids off at school."

"It's a shame the Kings aren't still around. They'd have found whoever did it."

She scoffed in derision. "Give over. There's been times they've said they'd solve shit and the police ended up doing it before them. I don't believe they've disbanded anyway, it's all a load of bollocks to throw the pigs off the scent."

"I heard there's still a small team of coppers watching the members."

"Then they're going to keep their noses clean, aren't they, until the team buggers off. I suppose I could ask Parole if he knows anything."

"I'd watch yourself with him if I were you. He's gone on the straight and narrow and works at the chocolate factory now. He won't appreciate anyone trying to drag him back to the dark side."

"I know. It's my business to find out this sort of thing because I like to know what's what on the estate. Word has it he's finally given in to the family pressure and will be taking the factory over, he's just got to learn the ropes first."

"Is this gossip or from the horse's mouth?"

"That I couldn't tell you." She liked to have an air of mystery about her.

A buzzer sounded, and Harry glanced to the side. "That'll be your lad's grub ready. Hang on a sec." He ambled off to a hatch at the back of the bar and returned with the roll on a plate. He placed it on the bar.

"Cheers." Molly leaned down and put the food in Basil's chubby hand. "So what do you propose we do? You listen in here and I go out there and gather information?"

Harry nodded. "Yeah. Give me your phone, and I'll put my number in it."

Molly took her mobile out of her bag hanging from the pushchair handles and held it below the bar so he couldn't see her putting in the PIN. She passed it over to him, and, while he did what he had to do, she gave the Plough one last sweep to see if there was anyone she'd missed talking to. The customers avoided her gaze. She was proud of how most people feared her. It had taken her a good couple of years to bully her way to the top around here, and she'd never take her crown off for anyone.

A phone rang, and Harry gave hers back. "It was just me ringing myself so I've got your number."

"Don't forget Basil's Fruit Shoot," she said.

"Orange or blackcurrant?"

She tutted.

Harry smiled. "Just testing you."

"What, as to whether I know the flavour my own kid prefers? On your bike." She checked Basil wasn't choking on the roll — he had a tendency to scoff his food — then took the bottle of drink from Harry. "Wish me luck, I'm off to the Dagger. Zoe does *not* like me. Is there anything you think I should know before I go?"

"There's plenty I could tell you about the Effie business, but I haven't exactly got the time to tell it. No more staff are in until later, and I'd rather discuss it in private."

"I could come back once the kids are home from school. They can look after Basil for me." Her teenage niece and nephew loved watching Basil and her girl, Polly, who was five and at primary. They were happy as Larry so long as she slung them a tenner each.

"Okay, get here about four," Harry said. "In the meantime, give us a bell if anything crops up."

Molly nodded, bent over to tuck the blanket around Basil's legs, stuck his bobble hat back on, then marched out into the street. Halfway to the Dagger, Basil threw the remainder of his roll onto the ground, so she stopped to use a wet wipe to clean his hands and put his mittens on. It was about time he had a kip, so she leaned the pushchair back into the reclining position and again tucked the blanket around him. She drew down the rain cover to keep the chilly air off, and he closed his eyes.

As she stood upright, a car pulled over to the kerb. Normally, she'd baulk at speaking to the police, but today it might prove useful. Plus, it was that Anna and Lenny, so it wasn't all bad. As coppers went, she didn't mind them at all, especially Anna, who spoke to her like a proper human being instead of Rowan scum.

The window sailed down, and Anna smiled. "Have you got time for a quick chat?"

Molly glanced at Basil. "He's only just dropped off, and if I get him out and put him in your car he's going to wake up. Then there'll be hell to pay because he doesn't like being disturbed. He'll scream the bloody place down."

"Shall we go to your house, then?"

"What, and have all my neighbours nosing out of their windows at me, thinking I'm a suspect? No thanks."

"Where, then?"

Molly pointed across the road to the parade of shops. "Round the back of there."

Anna drove away, and Molly crossed the street. She pushed the buggy behind the little Tesco and continued on until she got to the other end, where the newsagent had a bench his staff sat on during their breaks. It was surrounded by trees and bushes, an enclosed patch tucked away that the kids had made into a den. If she stood in there, and Anna and Lenny stood by the bench, no one watching would know who they were speaking to. Molly had a reputation to uphold, and she didn't want anyone getting the wrong idea, thinking she was in trouble with the police regarding Mina. If she was carted off for scrapping, fine, but she wasn't risking being accused of murder. She'd bragged about having the guts to kill someone, but she'd never actually do it. Maybe that was what the police wanted to talk to her about: someone could have blabbed.

She parked the buggy against the side of the shop and poked her head round so the coppers could see her. They must have parked at the front of the parade as they appeared at the top end by Tesco, strolling past the staff cars. Molly often wondered what her life would have been like if she hadn't skipped school. She'd wanted to be a copper, but look how that had turned out.

Anna and Lenny approached the bench but didn't sit.

"What do you want to speak to me about?" Molly asked, keeping her voice low.

"Did you hear about Mina Isherwood?"

"Of course I bloody did. This city's like a village the way news spreads."

"Do you know anything?"

"Sadly not, and if I did I'd have phoned you lot. I've been asking questions since I found out this morning, and nobody's saying a word. I genuinely don't think they know anything, because I can't see a reason why they'd keep things from me. Unless they're involved. Mina was a nice girl, never hurt anyone, so I reckon it must have been a case of mistaken identity or one of them random kills you see on those documentaries. She had to have been in the wrong place at the wrong time on her way home from the pub."

"She made it home," Anna said.

Fucking hell, that's news to me.

Anna continued, "Some information has just come to light regarding her movements. I was going to ask you if you'd heard anything . . ."

"I honestly wish I had. Harry Wells at the Plough hasn't been able to find anything out either. Do you want me to go and nose down Mina's street in a bit, see if anyone's prepared to talk?"

"It couldn't hurt as long as you make it look casual."

"I'm not stupid. If I hear anything I'll let you know."

Anna took a card out of her pocket and placed it on the bench. "Do you know anything about Effie Workington going missing? Before you bite my head off and say you were only young when it all went on, you must have heard something from your parents or whatever."

"All I know is she disappeared and it was a shock to everyone. Then she pops up every now and again. I heard she came out last night, but I don't know whether that's true or not."

Anna's eyebrows shot up. "Who told you that?"

"Candy next door to me."

Anna looked as if she'd tasted something sour. "Oh. Her. And you think she's telling the truth?"

"She told me about your lot going down the lane and that Mina was dead, so yeah. Harry said he'd tell me about what went on with Effie. I can't go to the Plough until four when his staff's come in, but I'll tell you whatever he tells me for fifty quid." Molly glanced behind her to check no one was listening from behind the bushes. "But I don't want anyone knowing. No one likes a grass."

"The whole point of a grass is that nobody knows about them, otherwise we'd never find out any gossip because no one would speak to them. It has to be information I can actually use, though."

"Fair enough. I'll talk to you later."

Molly watched them walk away and didn't come out until they'd turned the corner. She picked up the card and slipped it in her pocket, then pushed the buggy along the car park, heading in the direction of Cedar Avenue instead of the Dagger. She'd find something out today if it killed her.

CHAPTER NINETEEN

Candy Jacobs looked conflicted. On the one hand, she appeared glad she had the police on her doorstep — a bit of notoriety, the feeling of being important — but on the other, she seemed uneasy. Maybe she thought Anna and Lenny were there to tell her off for spreading gossip, but at this point in the day Anna would take anything that took her in the right direction, gossip or not.

Unfortunately, Candy had kept them on her doorstep. Those on Rowan didn't tend to allow police officers inside their homes; the majority were too paranoid in case they were accused of something without a witness, or, worse, were assaulted. Thanks to Peter Dove, rumours had spread about the number of rogues in Marlford police force. If there was one corrupt officer, there must be more. The rhetoric drove Anna up the wall.

"I just need to ask a couple of quick questions," she said.

"Go on, then." Candy folded her arms.

Anna studied her for a moment. Her blonde hair had been excessively dyed, and she seemed tired in that world-weary way that having limited money and stress for miles did to a person. Anna felt sorry for her, and, despite the risk of getting her head bitten off, she'd ask her if she needed some help at the end of this short chat.

"You've been telling people Mina Isherwood was found dead up the lane. How did you know that?"

"One, I was taking my kids to school and saw cop cars racing up there, and two, when I'd dropped the kids off and came back afterwards, I hung around and stopped another car that was going up there, asked what was going on. They said Mina was dead."

"Who's *they*?"

"Never seen them before. Whoever it was went up the lane but came back again and drove off. It was someone from the papers. Blue Mini, if that helps."

Someone at the station must have leaked it. "Thanks. We've also been informed that you saw someone impersonating Effie Workington last night."

"Yeah, I'd been to the Dagger to pick up a free takeaway. They've started doing those, did you know that? You go there near the end of the evening, round the back, and Zoe hands stuff out. It's on a need-to-know basis."

Anna stood stunned for a second. She hadn't expected Zoe to have a heart. Lenny nudged her as a prompt to pay attention.

Candy sniffed. "Anyway, I was on my way back, and I saw this blonde woman running towards the alley, the one that leads to the park. She was right in my headlights, so there's no way I made a mistake. The white dress, the ballet shoes. It gave me the bloody creeps and I was going to stop, but ended up carrying on in case she came for me. You don't know what these ghosts are capable of, do you?"

Oh dear. "So you believe it's a ghost?"

"It bloody well looked like one. Maybe it was someone dressing up, I don't care, I saw what I saw. Anything else?"

"How are things?"

Candy frowned. "What do you mean?"

"In general, how are you?"

"Why do *you* give a shit?"

"Because you look too tired for words. I wondered whether you needed any help."

"If you've got two grand knocking about to clear the debt my old man racked up, then yeah, I'll take it, but otherwise, fuck off."

"So you're struggling for money."

"Who isn't?"

"Did you hear about the new food bank? You go in, no questions asked."

Candy perked up. "Where's that, then?"

"It's on Southgate, down by the kebab van next to the Jacobean pub. If you're worried about anyone seeing you, it opens at five in the morning, so you could get down there quick, grab your stuff."

"Right. Cheers." Candy stared at her. "You're all right, you are." She stepped back and closed the door.

On her way back to the car, Anna blinked tears away. She'd love to be able to fix the world, but unfortunately that wasn't possible. If she could fix those in *her* world, it would have to be enough.

CHAPTER TWENTY

Finally at the station, Anna took a moment to make the team some tea and coffee and distributed it. She stood at the front of the main open-plan office. She'd grown used to using the interactive board but still preferred having the traditional whiteboard so she could see everything at a glance instead of flicking through virtual pages until she found what she needed. Pictures of Effie and Mina had been placed at the top.

"Because time's ticking on and unfortunately we're closer to the end of our working day than I'd like, I want to go over the information we've got so it's all straight in our heads for tomorrow morning. First I want to address what's already been written on the board — thanks for that, Louise, much appreciated — and chat through everything we've found out individually. So, here we go. We've spoken to Tate Daltrey's daughter, Charlene. What was your initial take on that scenario prior to her giving them both an alibi?"

While she was still getting to know the new team members, she liked to ask this sort of question to get an insight into their minds while they were out in the field.

Louise, sitting behind her desk, picked up her notepad. "To be honest with you, my suspicious mind went straight to

Charlene having come from her residence in Liverpool to kill Mina, and then buggering off home again. For her to be able to commit murder, she'd have needed someone to look after her two kids, who she'd brought with her, and what better person than their granddad? However, I poked into her, and what Mr Daltrey told us is the truth. There *is* a restraining order out on Charlene's husband, as well as a report on physical abuse and stalking. She came to Marlford to get away for a week, nothing sinister going on. She stated she would have known if her dad had gone out during the night because she was so on edge, waiting for her husband to turn up unexpectedly, that she'd barely slept."

"Vaughn Bates's daughter-in-law, Naomi. I see she's been crossed off the list, too."

Louise nodded. "She confirmed that she stayed overnight with Vaughn and Flora, his wife, as her husband had gone away for work and she doesn't like being home alone. She didn't sleep very well either and is a light sleeper in general whenever she's there because Flora has a tendency to wander. Naomi's always on alert in case her mother-in-law leaves the house and gets lost."

Rupert held a pencil up. "Just for perspective, Vaughn is not much over five foot and pretty slight. Comparing him to Mina, I'd say he would have struggled to carry her anywhere. The same goes for Flora."

"Thank you for that," Anna said. "The third point on the list is Mina's house, but there's no corresponding information for me to read. Where are we on that?"

Louise spoke again. "I literally just got an email from Tom Quant when you walked in. He's the scene sergeant at Cedar Avenue today. Although there's no glass smashed at either of the entry points, which suggests Mina let someone into her home, there are signs of a struggle. Going by the description of the clothing she had on in the Dagger, her shoes were at the bottom of the stairs. We're unable to establish whether she took them off herself or if they were placed there, or if they came off during the struggle. They've been logged as evidence, so we might get lucky and find prints that don't belong to Mina. It appears the struggle was limited to the hallway and the main bedroom. An occasional table had been knocked over in the hallway, and a vase of flowers smashed on the floor. Tom assumes Mina tried to escape upstairs to perhaps lock herself in the bedroom as there's a bolt on the inside of the door, but she'd clearly been followed."

"Poor girl."

Going by her frown, Louise appeared annoyed to have been interrupted. "The quilt was messed up, so it was as if there had been a fight or something of that nature on the bed. There was a pink silk scarf on the pillow, so the killer had taken the time to untie it after strangulation."

"How do we know that?" Lenny asked.

Louise smiled at him. It seemed she wasn't pissed off that *he'd* broken her stride. "There were kinks in the scarf that indicated it had been knotted. There are no clothes in the house that match the description of what Mina had on in the Dagger, just the shoes. I'm hoping there will be DNA on that scarf from the killer. Praying they didn't have gloves on. Something else interesting to note is that her other clothes had been thrown around the bedroom as if someone was searching for something. Did the killer dress her for the weather? Weird if they did; she wouldn't feel the cold because she's dead. Was that a subconscious thing? Or does this show a level of empathy for the killer to want her dressed weather appropriate?"

Anna pondered that. "I think if I was dressing a corpse, if that's even what happened, and I wanted to dispose of the body quickly, I'd just grab something easy like a dressing gown. What if the killer told Mina to change her clothes, then killed her afterwards? That would explain the clothing all over the place. She'd have been panicking and frightened, tossing things around if she was being instructed on what to choose. If you can write all that up on the board before you go home today, Louise, that'd be great. Okay, what else do we have regarding Cedar Avenue?"

"Tom's reported that the neighbours heard banging from the back of Mina's and then knocking over the other side of the street."

"That's where our part of the information comes in," Anna said. "Elizabeth Isherwood remembered a phone call she had with her daughter last night." She went on to explain it. "So what I'm curious to know is, what kind of people live in Cedar Avenue if they're ignoring banging and knocking late at night? We all know Rowan is rough as arseholes, but is Cedar the worst of the lot? Are people too afraid to get up and see what's going on or to intervene? Did anybody actually bother to at least look out of a window?".

"They all minded their own business," Louise said. "Or that's what they're telling the PCs anyway."

Anna tutted. "Ollie, go through what you've written on the board about Effie Workington, please."

"The basics are she went missing twenty years ago in the summer after a night out with her cousin Shannon. Shannon claims to have last seen Effie at Cooper's Crossing, where they went their separate ways. Shannon went home to bed, but Effie seems to have vanished. Someone resembling Effie has been seen out and about in the dark since then — blonde hair, white dress, ballet shoes."

"What's the general feeling in statements and files from back then?"

"Some people thought Effie was still alive, coming out for whatever reason, there one minute, gone the next. Residents have described it as a pale face in the darkness, at a window, or lingering down an alley, and, when chased by people calling out her name, she just disappeared. Later on, when people reported seeing her, especially more recently, they've said she hasn't changed a bit. But how could Effie look exactly the same as the day she'd gone missing?"

"What's with the ballet shoes? Is there any explanation for that?" Anna racked her brain. "The white dress, yes, she went missing in one, but I don't remember anything about her being a ballerina."

"There's nothing in the files," Oliver said. "I think we should look at Shannon a bit more closely regarding Effie's case in relation to Mina's. Shannon was the last person to see Effie alive, that we know of, and there were some inconsistencies in her statements. Shannon claimed to have been flustered and that she'd been answering questions for so long that she was tired and wasn't sure what she was saying. It happens, interview exhaustion. The SIO on the case, a DI Keith Norton, states that, whatever slip-ups Shannon made, there was no evidence they could send to the CPS in order to charge her."

"What were the inconsistencies?" Anna asked.

"Small things like the time they left the pub that night, then, when all the other statements came in and called her account into question, she was asked again and changed her answer. It's possible she could have been so drunk she'd got it wrong. Then there was the fact that she didn't tell the police about the argument she'd had with Effie in the Plough the evening of the disappearance. Harry Wells, the landlord, gave a statement about it, yet previous to that Shannon claimed they'd had a brilliant night with lots of laughing. Again, we could give her the benefit of the doubt — she may not have wanted the police to know they'd argued because then she might be a suspect. She ended up being one anyway because she omitted information."

"And if Harry Wells heard the argument, then you can bet a lot of other people did, too," Rupert said. "So how the hell did she think she was going to get away with it?"

"She might have panicked," Lenny suggested. "Her cousin goes missing, and she's the last person to see her. She knows everyone's going to be pointing the finger at her. She was drunk, she can't remember half of what she did or said, so maybe she filled in some gaps, telling the police what she thought they wanted to hear, what she thought would keep her out of the shit. She could have had a hangover. I mean, come on, if you haven't done anything but it seems like you did, you're bound to panic."

"Not everyone would, but I get what you mean," Anna said. "So what was the argument about?"

"Effie's affair with Arnold Tanner."

"Oh." Anna moved closer to the board and wrote down a new title: AFFAIR. "We've heard about that. Arnold Tanner is many years older than Effie and was married at the time. When we spoke to him today, I alluded to his handsy reputation. He claims he's not a pervert, but Nancy Rawlings feels otherwise. So was it an inappropriate type of affair between Arnold and Effie? Did his wandering hands make her think she had no choice but to have sex with him? This is just me throwing ideas out there. Do we know exactly why Effie and Shannon were arguing?"

"One reason was Shannon's concern that the wife would find out and hit the roof," Oliver said. "But with them having a row in a pub, she was bound to find out anyway, so Shannon was a bit short-sighted there. The wife's dead, by the way. She was called Helen. They didn't have any children, she was a bit of a high-flyer, a solicitor and then a judge, and in one of the statements Shannon mentioned Helen was so busy with her career that Arnold had turned to young women. There were rumours that Effie wasn't the only one he'd been sleeping with, another reason why Shannon had warned her off him, but no one recalls who the other ladies were. Effie told her to mind her own business, and after that she'd given Shannon the cold shoulder."

"Yet they still left the pub together," Rupert said.

"Yes."

"Did Helen ever find out about the affair?" Louise asked.

"Yes, and she left him shortly after. She'd been interviewed by Keith Norton. He'd obviously had to ask her where she was the night Effie had gone missing. Helen likely wanted an explanation as to why she was being questioned, and Keith told her about the affair."

"Ouch," Rupert said. "So what did Arnold have to say back then?"

"He had a solid alibi. He never left the pub until the next morning. Harry admitted to holding a poker night for friends, and Arnold joined in. He'd fallen asleep in one of the booths, and the game had gone on until six in the morning."

"So where was Helen?" Rupert asked.

"Away on a work conference. CCTV confirmed she was in Glasgow. She claimed to not have known about the affair until *after* Effie had gone missing."

Lenny scratched his forehead. "The only suspect remaining then was Shannon, yes?"

"I haven't had a chance to read every single statement," Oliver said. "There are a lot of them because of how packed the Plough was that night. There are also statements from drivers who were out and about on the route from the Plough to Cooper's Crossing."

"I can imagine," Anna said. "It was such a big case."

"I've spent a lot of my time this afternoon poking into Arnold." Oliver brought up a page on the interactive screen. "I'll put a printout of this on the whiteboard in a bit. Right, Arnold's eighty-one, born in 1943. In 1983, someone accused him of inappropriate behaviour, whereby he touched a ten-year-old girl's chest. It was the mother who told the police. Arnold and the girl denied it."

"Who's the girl?" Lenny asked. "Anyone we'd know from around here?"

"It doesn't actually say in the report."

"Bloody hell," Anna said. "Not exactly a thorough investigation, then?"

"I'm afraid not," Oliver said. "It hasn't even got the name of the police officer who took the mother's statement."

Anna closed her eyes for a moment and thought about this logically. "I am *not* going to go off on one about this because there could have been an issue with the digitisation of the statements. This station was also flooded in the mid-eighties and a lot of paperwork got damaged. What a nice turn of events for Arnold. His accuser and alleged victim don't exist on paper, and I suspect, if we ask him about it, he'll probably deny it happened."

"I watched a documentary the other week," Rupert said, "about this girl who was abducted and raped, and her body dumped. The perpetrator was her uncle, who'd seemingly been allowed to touch her without any repercussions from other family members. All that sitting on his lap business and stroking her leg. It happened a lot back then, so would it be surprising if a police officer in 1983 brushed the accusation against Arnold under the carpet?"

"It's bloody gross that it went on and no one batted an eyelid," Lenny muttered, "but sadly, yes, I can see how it wouldn't be followed up once Arnold and the girl had denied anything had happened. Of course, we all know Arnold could have threatened the kid to keep her mouth shut. I don't suppose there was anything in this statement that explained how the mother found out something was going on, was there?"

"Nothing," Oliver said. "But there's possibly no smoke without fire, not now we know Nancy Rawlings's feelings on Arnold's inappropriate behaviour towards women in the pub. Not to mention Shannon's views about Effie's affair with him. It all sounds like he's been allowed to continue in plain sight. Yes, Shannon is the most likely suspect for Effie, but there's no reason for her to have killed Mina. And why would she have left the body on her own property? It's like purposely getting herself in the shit."

Anna's head spun with information. "Let's move away from that for just a second. Has anybody found anything regarding Frank Quinlan, the farmer who lives to the rear of Shannon's property? We've heard a little bit about him from Steven Timpson. Basically, his cows and sheep are allowed to graze on the land belonging to Shannon Workington, Nancy Rawlings, and Yvette Danes. They've refused to sell it to him or anyone else because they don't want developers anywhere near their homes. Apparently, their gardens used to reach all the way down to the hedge that cuts off their grass from the farmer's field, which is quite a bit. He owns the grassy area either side of the lane, which then merges with his land on the other side of the hedge."

Rupert held his pencil up again. "That's just reminded me about the trampled grass. I had a quick scout through everything that's been uploaded so far from the various uniforms and whatnot, and the curved trail that was made by footprints to and from Shannon's starts and comes out by a parade of shops."

"Which one?" Anna asked. "There's two."

"The one with the little Tesco, the Chinese, and the newsagent's."

"We've not long been there talking to Molly Griffin. She's going to be doing us a favour and speaking to people in Mina's street to see if they'll open up a bit more to her instead of the police. Did you upload a map?"

Rupert nodded and switched the screen on the interactive board. The map showed an aerial view of the three properties at the end of the lane, all of the greenery, and the route taken to and from Rowan. A red circle indicated the entry and exit point at the row of shops.

"Tesco are bound to have CCTV," Anna said.

Rupert smiled. "I've already requested it."

Anna thanked him. "I don't want to burst anyone's bubble, but I will because I'm a realist." She smiled tightly. "I noticed when we were there today that the car park at the back of the shops has no CCTV. It would be easy enough for whoever it was to have nipped across that car park and dipped down the streets either side of the parade, and no one would be any the wiser in the dark. Still, we'll view the CCTV footage — Louise, you've got a better eye than anyone else."

Louise appeared shocked at the praise, which brought Anna up short. Had she been lacking in that department? She must make a bigger effort to appreciate her team verbally.

"I'd like to thank everybody for their hard work today. There's still an hour or two to get through. I need to go and see Isabella. On a brighter note, I'm nipping to the Hoof for a Coke afterwards if anyone would like to join me. Ah, before I forget, we popped over to see Candy Jacobs, who possibly spread the first rumour that Mina had died up the lane." She related the conversation. "So can one of you locate a blue Mini in that area, please. I'd like to find out how they heard about Mina's body. I'm spitting feathers that we might well have a leak."

CHAPTER TWENTY-ONE

To: carebear@worldnet.com
From: thecowcatcher@worldnet.com

It's taken me a while to calm down so I can formulate an appropriate response. Don't you ever, EVER talk to me like that again. All the shit I've been through, and yet you brought up Tanner when you knew I was spiralling because of him. You're not a Care Bear, not when it comes to me. You only care about the money and all those flowers and gifts that come your way. You of all people should understand how desperate someone can get when they just want to feel special. You feel that way when I send you things, and I felt that way with Tanner. If I were to remove the flowers and gifts you'd feel abandoned, just like I was abandoned by Tanner. Do you see now? Do you understand how being so used to receiving something then having it snatched away can upset someone, get right inside their mind, and make them do bad things?

* * *

To: thecowcatcher@worldnet.com
From: carebear@worldnet.com

Look, I'm sorry, okay? You just annoy me with the way you treat me, like you think I'm stupid enough to speak to the police. I know what my part was with Effie, I think about it every single day. And I know I risk going to prison, you don't have to keep reminding me. You must understand the pressure I'm under — again. I didn't sign up to be an accessory to murder, and yes, if I hadn't been so nosy then I wouldn't be, but I was, and there's nothing I can do to change that. I wish I didn't know you were a killer. All I ask is that if you do it again, don't tell me. I'm at my wits' end here trying to keep everything together, trying to act normal so I don't let anything slip. Please, get help. Talk to someone about what Tanner did to you. It's the only way you're going to fix yourself. I worry about you holding it all inside and how it affects you. I do care about you, no matter what you might think.

Catcher sat back and sighed. Maybe talking to Tanner would do the trick; it might stop the urges. Telling him how his treatment had had such an effect. How Catcher's life appeared good on the outside but a mess on the inside since being discarded.

Maybe I should have killed him instead of Effie and Mina.

Tanner didn't discriminate. He liked girls *and* boys, although he'd said he no longer indulged in those tendencies. Maybe having affairs with younger women had been his way of trying to forget about the children, but the fact that his ladies had been years his junior, and Mina could have been next on his list — in a way he was still acting the paedophile, an older man preying on the young.

Effie had died because Tanner had gone back to her. She'd been one of his children the same as Catcher, and he'd discarded them both, yet he'd chosen to start up again with Effie, who'd gloated to Catcher in private, saying she was the best and Tanner had wanted to come back to her for old times' sake. She was dead because of those horrible words, for being smug, and Mina was dead because Catcher had been transported to the past, reminded of Effie, and just . . . had . . . to . . . kill her. To make the feelings go away.

Tanner needed to know what it felt like to have a silk scarf wrapped around his scrawny neck. So yes, Catcher would talk, and then the liar would see what a mistake he'd made. Bastard.

CHAPTER TWENTY-TWO

Anna left the room to go and update the DCI, who'd sent several messages throughout the day asking how the case was going. They weren't intrusive queries, more like offers of help, but she was snowed under with paperwork today and couldn't join them out in the field. She'd done so many times in the past, partnering herself with Lenny, leaving Anna to investigate with Oliver. It wasn't like the days when Placket was there and Anna was left to her own devices, the one fully in charge. It felt like taking a step back in her career, but Isabella was only doing her job.

Anna knocked on the office door and, at the call to come in, she stepped inside. Isabella flapped a hand at the spare chair, and Anna sank onto it.

"That was a sigh and a half," Isabella said. "Has it been a tough day?"

"It's been a hell of a lot of talking." Anna gave a quick rundown of events and the suspicions so far.

"Okay, hear me out," Isabella said. "You said Mina laid her head on Arnold's shoulder and hugged him last night. Someone could have been watching that and got offended."

"That's plausible. There *has* been talk of him having affairs other than with Effie. Maybe one of those women held a grudge. She got rid of Effie and now Mina. What about the other women he's been with, though? Why aren't they dead?"

"Because their identities aren't known? Christ, what a can of worms. Regardless, concentrate some of your efforts on Arnold. Who he knows, who he's close to, who he sits with in the pub, who visits his house. Shannon killing Mina makes no sense to me. Shannon killing Effie makes no sense either — why would she want to off her cousin just because she was having sex with someone? Maybe someone else is out there who's linked to these two cases, and it's just a matter of finding out who it is. Could it be the alleged abused girl? She'd obviously be an adult now."

"Why would an abused person take it out on the two women and not Arnold?"

Isabella scratched her forehead. "It's still an avenue, though. You're better off sleeping on this and starting again tomorrow. More information will have come in from the uniforms by then. There's a hell of a lot of them out there asking questions. Until you've got all the data, you're not going to get a clear picture."

Obviously. Anna stood and stretched her back. "Thanks for the chat."

"I'd suggest having another talk with Arnold in the morning. Actually, what if *Shannon*'s the ten-year-old? What if that's why she told Effie not to have an affair with him? Is Arnold warped enough to choose Effie on purpose, to get at Shannon? Maybe she has an unhealthy attachment to him."

"I'll go and put all of your points to the team. They can percolate the information overnight. Perhaps more clarity will be forthcoming in the morning."

"Have you had the post-mortem results through yet?"

"No. There's so much ground to cover before that body gets moved. I wouldn't be surprised if it's only just happening now. Right, I'd best be off. I've got paperwork to look at and I haven't finished checking the post. I was interrupted when the call came in about Mina's body."

"Okay, have a good evening, and I'll see you tomorrow."

Anna left the office and returned to the team. She threw out Isabella's theories, writing them on the whiteboard as she spoke. "One, someone is upset at Arnold for being involved with Effie and Mina. Two, it could be another woman Arnold was seeing. Three, the ten-year-old he allegedly abused has a problem with Effie and Mina — the girl, now a woman, could well have been attached to Arnold despite what he did to her. We have far too many threads and far too many suspects, some known to us, some we have no clue about. I'll be completely honest, I'm not in the right headspace to chat through all of this now. There's something to be said about taking a step back. I think all of our brains are crammed and we need some space."

She sensed an avalanche of overwhelming emotions heading her way, and if she didn't take herself out of this room she'd likely scream. She dived into opening the post and dealing with emails that had come in regarding the previous case. There was still a lot of information to sort on it before it went to court. While it wasn't a murder, it did involve knives. She wanted the kids to pay for what they'd done. Fourteen was no age to be going round waving blades in elderly people's faces. Or anyone's faces, come to that.

An hour had passed, and she felt sufficiently detached from Mina's case, enough that she ventured back into the main office. Everyone sat at their desks, plugging away at their computers, so she made another round of hot drinks, passed them out, and then went downstairs to speak to Karen on the front desk before her shift ended.

Making sure no one in reception was around to hear her, Anna leaned over the desk and asked, "You sometimes go in the Dagger, don't you? Have you heard anything about Arnold Tanner, the older bloke who sits at the bar?"

"Can't say I have, no. That place is more the kind where I go in, have my dinner, then go home. Why, is he a wrong 'un?"

"Potentially." Anna explained about the statement that had mentioned no names, meaning there was no one they could go and question about the child abuse allegation. "It seems he's been allowed to go around doing whatever he wants and hasn't been held accountable for it. The creepy uncle everyone tolerates."

"With no proof, there's not much you can do."

"He claims he's not a pervert, but then he wouldn't exactly admit to it if he was, would he?"

"No. Change of subject. Are you going to the Hoof after work?"

"Yes, but only for a Coke. I have to drive back to the village, remember." Anna lived in Upton-cum-Studley, close enough to Marlford to get to work quickly but far enough away not to bump into colleagues if she ventured past her front door.

"I want to bend your ear about something," Karen said.

"It's not going to do my head in, is it? Today's almost done me in."

"I'm well aware of how you need to empty your brain every evening, so no, it's nothing too taxing. I just want some advice on this outfit I've seen. I didn't know whether it was a 'mutton dressed as lamb' situation, and I know damn well you'll tell me if it is."

"I'll be truthful if I think it isn't going to suit you, but I'd never tell you not to wear it, because, you know what, I'm actually *sick* of seeing those bloody articles that say women in their forties and fifties shouldn't do this or do that. *Why* shouldn't we?"

"Fucking hell, I didn't mean to set you off on your soapbox. It's only a skirt and jumper and a pair of bloody boots, nothing to get up in arms about, love."

Anna laughed, some of the tension leaving her. "Oh, you are funny. I know, I need to chill out."

Karen glanced at the clock. "Go and send that team of yours home, then come back for me. We'll trot down to the Hoof together."

"I did extend an invitation to them, so one or two might come along with us."

"That's all right. I'll get their opinion on the outfit as well."

"What's it for? Anything special?"

"No, I'm tired of feeling drab all the time. I thought a whole new wardrobe would make me feel better about myself."

"Bless you." Anna wasn't really bothered about what she looked like. She stuck some hair dye on when her grey roots came through and she wore whatever she was comfortable in. She had no one to impress, seeing as there was no future for her and Parole, but she'd felt nice those times she'd dressed up and gone out on fake dates with him. Not that he'd known they were fake at the time. Poor bastard. She'd used him for her job, and he knew it now yet didn't hold it against her. Or he hadn't the last time she'd seen him, anyway.

She trudged upstairs to power down her computer and collect her bag and coat. Everyone else did the same, and Oliver quickly attached his printout to the whiteboard using a magnet. Back downstairs, Karen was waiting for Anna, and they walked together, with Lenny and Louise tagging along behind.

They settled in their usual seats. Anna took their order and bought the drinks. While she waited for them to be poured, Karen popped up next to her and showed her a picture of the outfit on her phone.

"That's really bloody nice," Anna said. "Why would a knee-length skirt, boots, and a long cardigan make you mutton dressed as lamb? It's actually really classy."

"Aww, thanks, mate." Karen rested her head on Anna's shoulder.

And it got Anna thinking. Had that gesture from Mina to Arnold last night looked so much more to someone observing? Had she died for something innocent?

Anna shivered at the thought.

CHAPTER TWENTY-THREE

Molly had been waylaid by stopping to ask people questions, so it was half past five by the time she got to Cedar Avenue. She'd also had to nip to the school and pick Polly up, then drop her and Basil off with her niece and nephew. She'd bunged some chicken nuggets and smiley faces in the air fryer and left them all to it. The cold air had got worse, so she wrapped her scarf around the bottom half of her face and pulled up the hood of her puffa jacket. Two people were just arriving home in their cars, and she grabbed the chance to speak to them before they went indoors.

"Have you heard the news?" she asked Jack, someone she went to school with back in the day.

"What news?"

"About Mina Isherwood."

Jack glanced at his wife, Sheryl. "We've been away for a couple of days for work, so no. What's going on?"

"That's why there's a police car up the road a bit. I don't know all the facts, but Mina was killed after she came home from the pub last night and was dumped up the lane. I wondered if you knew anything."

"Bloody hell," Sheryl said. "She hasn't been living here long. What a shame. Have you spoken to the woman over the road dead opposite? I know she was helping Mina out on the day she moved in. Maybe she knows something?"

Molly nodded her thanks and marched up the pavement, eyeing the police car parked outside Mina's. An officer sat inside it, reading something on a laptop. A cordon stretched in front of Mina's garden gate, tied to the posts either side. The lights were off indoors, so the coppers had obviously finished in there now.

She rushed across the street, checking which house was "dead opposite", then knocked on the door. A sharp snap of breeze pushed into her left side, sending her off balance for a moment. She hugged herself, tucking her hands beneath her armpits in order to keep warm. Just as she was about to give up, the grumpy woman who worked down the Co-op opened the door. She stared over Molly's shoulder at the officer in the car and then gave Molly her attention. Molly lowered her scarf, realising she must look a bit menacing with it over her mouth.

"Oh God, what do *you* want?" Valerie said. "I've got to get to work. I've had enough of people asking me questions today, I don't need you adding to it."

"Have the police been here, then?"

"Yes, I told them what I know and don't need to repeat it to the likes of you."

"The likes of me? Fuck's sake, you're well rude. I'm actually talking to people for Mina's mum," Molly lied. "I want to help her get justice for her daughter. Is there anything you can tell me that you didn't tell the police?"

"What, and have you pass it on to her mum and her mum tell the Old Bill I was holding something back? No thanks." She slammed the door.

Fuming, Molly wandered down the garden path and onto the pavement.

An old woman shuffling by pushing a tartan shopping trolley stopped and said, "I heard Mina knocking on Valerie's door last night, but by the time I'd got up and looked out of the living room window she was staring down the street at that Effie ghost, then she went indoors. I went back to bed and didn't think anything else of it other than someone was playing silly buggers by dressing up."

"Did you tell the police?"

"I didn't want any hassle."

"What about other people down here? Have they got anything different to say?"

"How should I know? It's not like I've been out here gossiping with everybody, is it? I've only just got out to the shops, what with the street so full of police and neighbours all day."

Molly stomped off across the road to knock on one of the houses next to Mina's. A woman she didn't recognise opened the door and told Molly to fuck off and mind her own business. Molly moved to the house on the other side, and this time the resident was friendlier. Maybe she'd heard about Molly's reputation and decided not to give her any gyp. She asked her inside, and, while a couple of kids played with Lego on the dining room floor, Molly and the woman, Chardonnay, sat at the table with a cup of tea.

"I feel really bad," Chardonnay said, "but I heard the banging and didn't do anything about it. You know what it's like on this estate. People are noisy, and if you poke your head out of the windows and tell them to shut up you get threatened. I thought it was best to mind my own business, especially because Mike's away with work and it's just me and the kids on our own. Clearly it was the right thing to do because she was bloody killed."

"Do you know whether she was killed at home?"

"First off, there were some screams just after Mina got home, but they were muffled. Actually, it was more like shrieking. I heard something smash, and then there was the thundering of footsteps, like she was running upstairs."

Chills scooted down Molly's back. "Did you hear screaming or anything then?"

"I heard a shout. I think she said, 'Please don't!'"

"Jesus, did you tell the police?"

"No, because I don't want the bastard to come for me and the kids next. It wouldn't take him long to work out which neighbour was blabbing."

"There's rumours going round that it was Effie's ghost, or whoever it is who keeps dressing up as her."

"I didn't look out, so I wouldn't know."

"Was it all quiet, then, after the shout?"

"Yeah."

"I went round to the other neighbour, and she told me to fuck off."

"She's not the chatty type. She probably got scared as well. Doesn't want to be seen gossiping about it. Like me, she could be worrying the killer's going to come back."

Molly hadn't thought of that, how frightening it would be to live beside someone who'd been killed, possibly in her own house. "You'll double-lock the doors, won't you?"

"Yeah, I've got bolts and chains."

Molly took a couple of gulps of the hot tea and then stood. "Thanks for the drink, sorry I didn't finish it. I've got to get off. I've left my kids with sitters, and I want to be back for their bedtime."

She still had to go to the Plough. She was narked Harry hadn't sent any messages or phoned her to see where the hell she was, considering she was meant to be there around four o'clock. She left the house, her hood up and her scarf back around her mouth. She paused to stare up at Mina's place, at the window that might have been her bedroom. She imagined what had happened behind that pane of glass and how the rude neighbour must have slept exceptionally well to not have heard all that banging. Or maybe she had and she'd chosen not to do anything about it. Rowan was full of Chardonnays who were too afraid to stick their neck out and help.

***

Unsurprisingly, the Plough was busy. Molly, glad of the warmth, shoved her way through the dense crowd near the bar and caught Harry's attention. She couldn't remember where he'd told her to meet him, then a vague recollection came of it possibly being at the back in the car park. She shrugged. It was too late now, and besides, he'd seen her, and pointed to a door marked *private*. She pushed it open and leaned against the wall in a corridor. He came out of another door opposite that revealed the length of the bar and a few customers waiting to be served before it swung shut. He jerked his head at her, and she followed him to the next door along.

It was an office, but instead of sitting on a chair behind the desk he opted for one of two armchairs. "Take the files and shit off that one and have a sit-down." He reached across to pull open the bottom drawer of a grey metal filing cabinet and took out a bottle of gin and a can of tonic water. Next, he produced two glasses, and placed everything on top of an upside-down cardboard box. He poured a generous helping of gin into each glass. "Did you find anything out?"

"Yes, and I didn't ring because I was saving it all up to tell you in one go."

He added tonic water, then passed her a drink. "What kept you? You've been ages."

She took it from him and sipped. "First, those two coppers stopped me, Anna and Lenny. They wanted to know if I'd heard anything. Second, on the way to Mina's street, I got chatting to people, and then it was school pickup time. Jesus Christ, it feels like hours ago when I saw you last." She told him everything she'd discovered bar the fact that she'd be reporting to Anna and Lenny later regarding whatever Harry told her about Effie. She didn't think he'd appreciate her going behind his back. "So what do you think about that, then?"

"Which bit, Chardonnay not telling the police that she'd heard screams and a scuffle going on?"

"Yeah."

"I can't say I blame her, to be honest. I reckon everyone finds themselves in a particular position at some point in their lives where telling the truth is the right thing to do, but in order to save their arses they have to keep their gobs shut."

Why did he look shifty when he said that?

Harry went on, "For Chardonnay, this is one of those moments, but her keeping quiet isn't going to do the investigation any favours. And whoever killed Mina could stay out there, undiscovered for years, just like what's happened with Effie."

"Do you think I ought to get hold of Anna and tell her what Chardonnay said, but not tell her it was Chardonnay, like?"

"Depends if your conscience can handle Chardonnay working out it was you who said something. It's bound to come out in the news or whatever that somebody heard screams. If Chardonnay's only told you, it'll be obvious who opened their trap."

"But that's not fair to Mina's mum. She deserves to know what happened to her kid. I'm not saying if I was her I'd want to know whether my child screamed or not before she died, but . . ." Molly sighed. "Fucking Nora, you know what I mean. I'm between a rock and a hard place here. Oh, and you need to tell me about Effie because that old lady in Cedar told me the lookalike was there last night. I mean, what the hell?"

Harry knocked back his gin in one go and poured a fresh one, then fished out another can of tonic. "I know you're a fucking blabbermouth, and I know I shouldn't be telling you this, but at least try and keep this to yourself, eh?"

"But what if something you tell me helps with this shit about Mina?"

"Then you didn't hear this from me, got it?"

"Got it."

Harry launched into a story about the night Effie had disappeared. He and three other men had vouched for Arnold Tanner, saying he'd stayed behind after the pub had shut for a poker game and fallen asleep. Except he hadn't. He'd nipped out for at least an hour.

"Shit, so it could have been *him*?" Molly asked.

"I can't see it, honestly. He was here when the police came to ask questions about Effie's disappearance and it was all news to him — or it seemed to be anyway, going by the shock on his face. But I suppose he could have been acting."

"What about the other men?"

"A couple of them are dead and the other one lives in Spain. It feels like me and Arnold are the only ones left who know the secret. I'm just glad he drinks at the Dagger and has done ever since the shit hit the fan years ago. I see him sometimes in town or whatever, and I can't bear to look at him. What if he's the pervert people say he is? What if he went to Effie's flat, got her to come out for a walk with him, and then killed her?"

"What makes you think they went out for a walk?"

"Because there was no indication at her place that anything bad had happened there, so the papers said. I think we should both come clean. We go to the police and tell them what we know and let the chips fall where they may. Chardonnay could think you're a bitch, but you're doing this for Mina and no other reason. Maybe if you tell Anna that Chardonnay is worried about the killer coming for her, Anna will keep everything you told her quiet. No press release, nothing like that."

Molly slipped her hand in her pocket and closed her fingers around Anna's business card. "Look, I'll tell her, but I won't mention anyone's name. Anyway, I think all Anna's interested in is getting the information. It doesn't matter how she gets it."

Harry nodded. "I already feel like a weight's been lifted by telling you about Tanner. When are you going to talk to her?"

"There's something I need to do when I leave here, then I've got to get home and put the little ones to bed. And I want a bath to warm up. So probably about nine by the time I ring her. If it *was* Arnold who killed them both, it's not like he's about to do it again anytime soon, is he, because there's police all over the place. Why do you reckon he killed Effie?"

"Probably because she would have wanted more than just the affair. She was really struck on him, thought he was the bee's knees. Maybe he was angry about that argument between Shannon and Effie. They'd kept the affair secret until Shannon opened her mouth. Arnold could have panicked and killed Effie to shut her up or stop her begging him to leave his wife."

"That's stupid, because people would have heard the row and told his wife anyway. What about Mina?"

"She probably thought of him as a mate, not someone she should get into bed with."

Molly shuddered. "He's gross."

"Maybe he killed her because she wasn't interested in that way."

"Can you see it, though? *Really?* And where does the lookalike come into it? If last night's alibi is another lie, can you see Arnold prancing around in a white dress with a wig on, in *ballet* shoes, for fuck's sake?"

Harry laughed. "No. He probably wasn't anything to do with Mina's murder, but there's a good chance he did something to Effie. If he didn't, where did he go for that hour?"

Molly finished her drink and stood. "Right, I'm going. I've got one more person to see, then I'll go home. I'll message you as soon as Anna's in the know."

She left him pouring yet another gin, the alcohol swimming through her veins, warming her up nicely. At least she wouldn't be cold on her trek to Parole's posh pad.

CHAPTER TWENTY-FOUR

Nancy had suggested going to the Dagger for dinner. Shannon had planned to go there herself anyway, and they sat at a table that afforded her a view of the bar and the dining area. You could pick up lots of conversations there. She liked listening to gossip, it gave her something to think about on the lonely evenings. It stopped her from thinking about Effie.

Yvette had been acting strangely, jittery and ill at ease, some of her responses snappy. It was understandable, what with having a dead body so close to her property, but bloody hell, all three of them were dealing with it. Yvette acted like she was the only one going through any kind of trauma.

With their empty plates removed and their glasses refilled with wine, Shannon whispered what she'd just heard from the table behind them. "Those two back there are wondering if Effie going missing is linked to Mina, and they're saying Effie isn't really dead."

"Of course she is," Nancy said. "It's the obvious conclusion, for goodness' sake."

"But is she, though?" Shannon asked. "There was never a body." She held up her hand to stop their protests. "Yes, I know she didn't use her bank card or anything after that night, but what if she *did* run away and start again with a new name?"

"If she did, then she owes you an apology," Nancy said. "For a while there everyone thought you'd killed her. You went through hell."

Yvette stared at Nancy, a faraway look in her eye. "Shannon would have always been the first one accused because she was the last one to see her, and you know it."

"As far as the police know," Nancy said. "Someone else clearly turned up after Shannon left. Effie's probably buried on the moors."

"As I recall, none of the moors were disturbed," Shannon reminded her. "No one had dug anything up."

"They could have patched up the ground so it didn't look like anyone had dug there." Nancy sipped some wine. "It's not like the police had any equipment with them, those ground radar thingies, so they could have missed it."

"Police dogs were up there, though," Shannon said. "Those ones that smell dead bodies. I've imagined all sorts over the years, like she's been kept in one of those big chest freezers or buried in someone's back garden."

"Well, whatever happened, she's definitely dead," Nancy said. "Denying it only means you're not facing the truth. I know she was your cousin and you loved her, but don't you think it's time to accept that?"

Yvette shuddered.

Shannon sighed. "I just think it's weird that someone's running around looking like her. I mean, what's the point? What are they trying to achieve? Do they want us all to think she's still alive? Earlier I heard someone saying that they reckon Effie killed Mina. That doesn't make any sense to me. Mina would have been a little girl when Effie was still around. Why would she even *have* beef with her?"

Yvette opened her mouth as if to say something, then clamped it shut. Shannon eyed her, on the verge of asking her to spit it out, but Nancy downed the rest of her wine and announced she'd buy a bottle. She swanned off to the bar, and Yvette got up to go to the toilet.

Shannon tuned her ears to the conversations around her. One in particular caught her attention.

"There's a rumour that Mina was Effie's kid and there's a link between the murders," the woman behind said.

Shannon wasn't having any of that. There was gossip and then there was outright ludicrous bullshit. She turned to address the couple. "How the fucking hell do you work that one out? Do you think I wouldn't have known if Effie had been pregnant and gave a child away? I'm her *cousin*. And for your information, I remember Mina's mum being up the duff, so what you're saying is utter bollocks."

The young blonde woman turned her nose up. "I'm just saying what I heard, that's all."

"Well, don't. You're not even old enough to know what went on back then."

The woman sneered. "Why don't you sod off and stop being nosy?"

The blonde's fella, a scrawny type with black hair, laid his hand on her arm. "She's right, though, love."

Satisfied she'd made her point, Shannon faced the other way. Yvette came out of the door that led to the toilets, stared over at Shannon sitting alone, then went back inside. What was up with her, tummy troubles? Nancy reappeared with a bottle of white and plonked herself down on her seat.

"Yvette's acting well weird," Shannon said.

"She's always been weird, take no notice of her."

"I know, but . . ."

Yvette poked her head around the door again, spotted Nancy, and then walked over. She sat and accepted the wine refill Nancy had poured for her.

"Have you got the shits or something?" Shannon asked.

Yvette stared at her, blinking rapidly. "What?"

"You came out of the loo and then went back in again."

"Oh, I left my lipstick by the sink."

It was a plausible enough excuse, yet Yvette didn't have any lipstick on, so Shannon wasn't buying it. A horrible thought filtered into her head, an insidious snake that bared its fangs. Was Yvette so jittery because she had something to do with Mina's murder? That copper had questioned her earlier about why there were no fingerprints on her back door. Yvette had said she regularly washed it and the one out the front, and it was true she was obsessive about housework, but what if she'd washed it because someone had called round in the night and touched it? The someone who'd dumped the body?

Bloody hell. She wouldn't be involved, would she?

Now she'd had the thought, she knew she'd let it spiral into plausibility in her mind if she didn't put a stop to it. Over the years since Effie had gone missing, Shannon had entertained a number of scenarios. It was understandable considering she had no answers except those the police had given. Having someone in your family missing meant you filled in the blanks, and she tormented herself with everything to the point that sometimes she thought she was going mad.

"You must have been up early to wash your back door," she said.

Yvette jumped, and some of her wine sloshed over the rim of her glass and onto the back of her hand. She put the drink down and snatched at a napkin to clean herself up.

"What time did you get up?" Shannon pressed.

"I didn't look at the clock."

"So you could have been out there when Mina was being dumped." Shannon folded her arms. "Did you see or hear anything?"

"Of course I bloody didn't," Yvette snapped. "If I had, I would have told the police."

"You told them you slept right through when you didn't."

Yvette blushed.

"Pack it in now," Nancy said. "Yvette washed her back door, big deal. She cleans her house to within an inch of its life most days after work, so it's nothing unusual. Next you'll be saying she washes her hands too much and that's also a sign of guilt."

"She said that was her OCD." Shannon turned to Yvette. "Why didn't you do the front door after?"

"Because I got tired again and went back to bed." Yvette threw the napkin down, picked up her glass, and took a long swig. "You're talking to me like I'm a suspect, like I had something to do with Mina. I would *never* kill anyone." She looked at Nancy. "*You* don't think I had anything to do with it, do you?"

Nancy laughed. "You, kill someone? I don't think so. You don't have the balls for a start. Like I said, Shannon, pack it in now."

Shannon would do as she was told, but they couldn't stop her thoughts, and they couldn't stop her imagining Yvette outside, dumping the body. Deep down, she knew that wasn't true, but she'd contemplate it all the same.

"Sorry," Shannon mumbled.

"I should bloody think so," Yvette said.

It was all a bit awkward then, Shannon's cheeks growing hot, guilt giving her a mighty prod for even thinking such things. And Nancy was right, Yvette *did* clean a lot, so it *wasn't* anything unusual.

"Are you going into work tomorrow?" Nancy asked Yvette.

Yvette fiddled with her necklace. "I'll probably take the rest of the week off. It's all been such a shock."

Nancy nodded. "Not as shocking as it is for Shannon — she found the body."

Yvette glanced away.

"I think I'll have the rest of the week off, too," Nancy went on. "Maybe we should all go and do something to take our minds off it."

"Like what?" Shannon asked.

"I don't know, a spa day?"

"And who's shelling out for that?" Shannon huffed. "I haven't got money to burn."

"No need to be snippy," Nancy said. "*Now* who's acting weird?" She flipped her gaze towards Yvette, then back to Shannon.

"Um, what's going on?" Yvette asked.

Nancy twirled her wine glass. "Shannon said you're being weird."

"What?" Yvette's mouth dropped open, then she seemed to get some steel in her spine as she leaned forward and hissed, "You had a dead body in your garden, Shannon, so no wonder I'm acting weird. No matter what the police have said, we're all suspects. They've been through our houses, for God's sake, like we're criminals or something."

"We're all criminals in one form or another," Nancy said.

"What's that supposed to mean?" Shannon asked.

"Come on, everyone's nicked something at some point in their life. Stealing is a crime, therefore we're criminals. By the way, you're getting on my wick tonight, Shannon."

"What, because I think Yvette having no fingerprints on her door is suspicious? And now she's being all shifty? It's a rational conclusion to come to."

Nancy shook her head. "The police have accepted her version of events."

So you think. What if they don't believe her but they've got no proof so can't charge her with anything?

Bristling from being reprimanded, Shannon hit out, "You're always so sanctimonious, Nancy bloody Rawlings."

She got up and stormed out. She contemplated getting a taxi home but instead did what she always did when she was troubled and took the long route that would lead her through Cooper's Crossing.

By the time she got there, she was panting, hot, and sweaty, despite the chill in the air. She stood in the darkness, remembering that night so long ago. As usual, she spoke to Effie, grumbling at her for going missing, or, she had to finally admit now, dying, although that was hardly her cousin's fault.

"Where are you?" she whispered. "Why did you have to go and leave me? It's shit here without you."

She always expected Effie to emerge out of the blackness and answer her, and, as always, it didn't happen. She rushed towards the alley that led to street lamps and humanity, relief punching her in the gut that she wasn't alone now or a target like Effie had probably been. She *had* died. Shannon had been fooling herself with hope for two decades, and, much as she hated to acknowledge it, Nancy was right. The truth had stared her in the face for twenty years, and it was time to fully accept the grief.

Tears burned her eyes and trailed down her cheeks. She dashed them away, pushing on through the streets towards the lane. Stupid of her to have not got a taxi. The lane was secluded and scary, and she rushed up it, heading towards the lights of her house that she'd left on. They acted as a beacon, giving her a measure of peace, but then her mind piped up again about Yvette's back door.

She was in for a restless night.

CHAPTER TWENTY-FIVE

Colder than a witch's tit, Molly stood in front of the glass doors of Parole's apartment building. It seemed chillier here with the breeze skimming over Jubilee Lake. The water rippled, pretty with the stripes of light coming from the many windows. The trees to one side gave her the creeps, though, so she turned and pushed a door. It didn't budge. She peered in. A man sat behind a glass-topped desk, and she recognised him as Ken Marshall, one of the security guards. He was an all-right fella, and she got on okay with him. Once he saw it was her waiting to come inside, he waved and walked over, chest puffed out. Oh God, was he one of those people who were different at work, all cocksure of himself?

He buzzed open the door and pulled it wide. "Who has the pleasure of your company this evening, then?"

Is he taking the piss? He had to be. Or was that his way of finding out what she was doing in such a high-end place? Or worse, was he subtly pointing out that she didn't belong here because she was common as muck?

She straightened her spine and, as the meme said, remembered who the fuck she was and stuck her crown on. "I'm here to see Parole, but he doesn't know I'm coming. Can you do me a favour and give him a bell to see if we can talk?"

"Not a problem. Can I tell him what it's in relation to? Because he's going to ask me. You know that, don't you?"

Yeah, he's fishing. "Just tell him I need his help with something."

"Fair enough, but if it's something dodgy you may want to rethink it."

"I know. Fucking hell, can you just ring him?"

Ken appeared ruffled for a second, but he went behind the desk and lifted the phone, stabbing at one of the buttons. "Molly Griffin's here to talk to you. No idea, she just said she needs some help. Yeah, that'll be fine. See you in a minute." He placed the handset in the cradle. "He'll be down in a sec, and you can have a chat over there." He pointed to a sofa by the doors with a leafy potted plant next to it.

That was a bit of a bummer. Molly wanted to go into Parole's posh apartment to see if he was as rich as the rumours said he was. "Have you got anywhere more private? Only, it's sensitive information."

"Is it to do with the Kings?" Ken asked quietly. "If it is, Parole won't want to know. He's not in with them anymore."

"What are you, his keeper? It's nothing to do with the bloody Kings." Her frustration verged on bubbling over. Ken meant well, but my God was he being irritating.

She was saved from telling him to go and do one by the lift doors opening. Parole stepped out and, as always when she saw him, she sucked in a sharp breath. A man with a face full of tattoos shouldn't be so bloody gorgeous, but he was. Not that she stood a chance with him, but a girl could dream.

Ken must have picked up something in Parole's expression, because he said, "My office?"

Maybe Parole's also clocked that Ken's a nosy sod.

Parole gestured with his head for Molly to follow him. They sat in a small room that had CCTV monitors, a desk, and a couple of hard chairs plus a soft one that looked like it might pull out into a single bed. He didn't offer for her to sit, so she took the initiative and plonked herself down. It had been a long walk here, and she wanted to rest her legs for a minute.

"What do you need me for?" Parole asked.

Molly imagined he'd appreciate her coming straight to the point. "Did you hear about Mina Isherwood being found dead up the lane?"

"It wasn't up the lane, but yeah, I heard about it."

"Where was it then?"

"It was up that way, that's all I'm saying."

"Do you know anything so I can pass it on to the police?"

"If I did, I'd ring the police myself." He chuckled. "Have you appointed yourself as the pigs' little helper or something?"

Molly flushed, her cheeks growing hot. "Why be a wanker? I'm trying to *help*."

"I heard you like to hinder in certain situations, especially when it involves the police."

"Only when I'm protecting one of us. It's stupid sending people to prison for a bit of nicking."

"Fair point."

She plunged back in, annoyed they'd gone off topic. "Have you heard anything about Old Tanner? You know, Arnold, the old boy who props the bar up at the Dagger all day."

"Just that he's possibly a nonce and needs to be watched."

"You what? A nonce? An actual paedo?"

"So they say."

How come Molly hadn't heard about that? Or was he seen as a paedo because he was ancient and Mina was young? "Jesus Christ. That aside, what would you say if I told you the prick who goes round pretending to be Effie Workington was actually out in Mina's street last night?"

"I'd say it was bloody weird, but maybe not unusual because it happens regularly."

"What about if she was in Mina's street just before a neighbour heard someone scream?"

"I'd say maybe the Effie person had something to do with her murder. It's not rocket science. What is this, twenty questions?"

Molly told him everything she'd discovered. "I swear to you I'm not being a gossip this time. It's really bothered me that Mina's dead when she was such a nice person and didn't upset anybody. I want to find out who did it. Will you help me by keeping your ear to the ground? You're at the factory now, aren't you? Someone's bound to be talking up there."

"No one was talking today."

"How did *you* find out?"

"An old friend got hold of me, and if you repeat that to anybody, I'll come after you, all right?"

Molly's stomach rolled over. He shit the life out of her, yet at the same time she wished he'd ask her out and kiss her silly. She'd bet loads of people fancied him.

"Have you got a girlfriend?" she blurted.

"There was one who got away, and I'm still waiting for her."

"Who's that then?"

"None of your business." He moved towards the door. "Our conversation's over. Put your number on that pad and I'll give you a bell if I find anything out, but it won't be until *after* I've told the police. I'm not going to go around trying to solve this like the old days. My King life is over. Finished."

"You know people aren't swallowing that, don't you?"

"I don't care who's swallowing what, love. As long as me and the ex know what I'm about, that's all that matters. Now fuck off, you've outstayed your welcome."

Molly wrote down her number, left the office, and waved goodbye to Ken, who buzzed her back outside. The chill walloped her. "Oh my God, that's cold!"

"Fuck's sake, do you need a lift home?" Parole called from the lobby.

She turned and nodded.

"It's the red motor over there in the car park. Wait inside it while I get my coat."

The sound of the locks blipped, and she turned to find the indicators flashing, lighting up the night. Bloody hell, she was going to have a ride in a red Porsche, something she never thought she'd do in her lifetime. *And* she'd get to sit right next to Parole while she was at it.

***

Ten minutes later, Parole sped away from car park, and she told him her address.

"Did you think I wouldn't know something like that?" he asked.

She felt silly then. Of *course* the Kings would know where people like her lived. It was a bit disturbing, though, to realise that maybe they'd been keeping an eye on her. What had they seen her as, a liability? Someone who could cause trouble, maybe because she spent a lot of time out and about drumming up customers for stolen gear? Had they worried she'd stumble on some dodgy deal they were doing?

"Do you always make people feel like they're thick as shit?" she fired at him. "Is it something you do on purpose or does it just come naturally?" She'd pushed her luck, but fuck it, who did he think he was?

"It wasn't my intention, so I apologise. Who's your police contact? I assume you've got one, or were you just going to wing it and approach a plod on the street with whatever you found out?"

"You're doing it again, talking to me like I'm stupid. Of course I've got a contact. It's Anna James."

He cleared his throat. "And what will you be doing, phoning her?"

"That was the idea, yeah."

"You ought to tell her everything you told me face to face. I'll take you to her place." He'd said it like she had no choice.

Molly wasn't sure about this. If Anna ended up being a good revenue stream, she didn't want to piss her off. "Isn't that a bit rude? To just turn up?"

"Like it was rude when you turned up at mine?"

Molly sniffed. "Point taken. I should at least ring her and see if it's okay." She took the business card out of her pocket and used the light from her phone screen to illuminate it so she could see the numbers. She added Anna as a contact, then took a deep breath and connected the call on speakerphone, as she assumed that was what Parole would expect.

"DI Anna James speaking."

"It's me, Molly."

"Are you all right? You sound nervous."

"I've got some stuff to tell you. Is it okay to come to your house?"

"No, it isn't. I can meet you somewhere."

Molly glanced across at Parole, who shook his head. "I'm with someone, and they're bringing me to yours." She ended the call. "That sounded really weird, and she'll be worrying now."

"What do you care?"

"I heard she lives on her own. Yeah, she's a copper, but she must still get scared. Why couldn't we have just met her where she wanted?"

"Because I want to have a word with her, and I don't want anyone in Marlford seeing me."

"Bloody hell, are you a grass?"

"No."

She believed him and didn't bother pressing for more, suspecting she was getting on his wick. He drove out of the city, and she kept her mouth shut all along the dark winding road until she spotted a sign for Upton-cum-Studley. He sailed into the village and parked in what she assumed was Anna's street.

Parole shut the engine off. "I'll wait outside until you've said what you have to say, then you can sit out here and I'll go in."

Molly hesitated.

Parole sighed. "If you're worried about which cottage it is, don't bother. She's standing at the front door."

Molly turned her head.

Anna did *not* look happy.

CHAPTER TWENTY-SIX

Anna stared at the car Molly was getting out of. Parole's. *Shit! Of all the people.* Was Molly aware of Anna's previous relationship with him? Had he told her? Were these two in on something together?

Only Molly approached. Parole faced straight ahead, his silhouette black against the orange glow of a streetlight. Butterflies twisted in Anna's stomach, and she forced her gaze away from him to Molly.

"This is really inappropriate, coming to where I live," Anna said.

"I know. I was happy to ring you, but he said he'd bring me here because he needs to speak to you himself."

What? I really don't need this. "No idea what that's about. Anyway, come in."

Anna had never expected to have members of the public just turning up at her home. Thank God she kept things minimalistic so there was never any mad rush to tidy up if someone came round unexpectedly. Still, she glanced at her living room with the critical eye of a stranger, feeling like she might be judged, and not in a good way. Anna was single, had no children, and earned a good wage. Molly was single, had kids, and she was on benefits plus cash in hand for whatever hooky gear she sold on the side. There was a stark contrast in their lives and, Anna suspected, their homes. She felt guilty for having more.

"Would you like a cup of tea?" Anna thought she'd better offer in case Molly needed an excuse to stay in here for longer. For all Anna knew, Parole could have forced her to come here.

Molly appeared uncomfortable, shifting from foot to foot. "No, ta. I just need to say what I've got to say and get home. I wanted to put the kids to bed, I was supposed to be doing that first and then ringing you, but he brought me out here. Clearly he's got a habit of getting his own way."

"Has he threatened you?" Anna asked.

Molly laughed. "God, no, he doesn't need to. It's easy to pick up the gist of doing as you're told around him. Anyway, if I could just get on, because I really do want to go home."

They sat, and Anna listened to what Molly had discovered.

"That's brilliant information, but why can't you tell me who told you these things? Is Parole making you stay quiet? I'm telling you, I don't care who he is, I won't have him going round making threats."

"It isn't him. I only spoke to him to see if he'd found anything out. Some mate of his told him that Mina was dead, and he knew it wasn't up the lane. I mean, it was *me* assuming she was left on the side of the road there because of what Candy implied . . ."

Anna wasn't falling for that tactic. News would come out that Mina had been dumped in Shannon's garden, but Anna wasn't about to divulge that now. "Why do you need to protect the people who gave you the information? Have *they* threatened you?"

"No. There's just no reason for you to know who they are, that's all. All you need to know is that Arnold's alibi for Effie might be bullshit and you need to find out whether it's the same for Mina. Oh, and Parole said Arnold's a nonce."

Oh God, so the accusation from years ago could be true after all.

Molly stood. "If I find out anything else, I'll tell you, all right? Now, where's my fifty quid?"

"I don't have any cash on me. I'll give it to you tomorrow."

Molly huffed but walked out, and Anna followed and watched her get in Parole's car and him getting out. Her stomach clenched at the prospect of having a conversation with him. Yes, she could keep it professional on the outside, but she didn't like the way she crumbled on the inside when she saw him. The chemistry between them was something she could ignore when she wasn't with him, but in person it slapped her in the face. If she believed in soulmates, then in another life they'd have been together, but they lived *this* life, and it was impossible to shack up with him unless she left the police force.

Not happening.

He was rich enough to fund their life, his grandfather had founded the local chocolate factory, and Parole had said she'd never have to work another day in her life if they got together. She wasn't a sponger, she preferred to make her own money, but every so often she thought about it, leaving the force and starting a life with him. It could only be a dream, though.

She backed up down the hallway a bit. He came in and closed the door, his gaze wandering up and down her body, but not in a predatory way, more that he wanted to check she was okay. Did he think Molly had hurt her?

"What do you want?" She forced herself not to fold her arms, trying to play it casual.

"I used this as an excuse to see you."

"Right. Well, you've seen me, so off you trot."

"You haven't changed your mind, then?"

"I change it several times a day but always end up with the only answer I can live comfortably with, and that's us two not together."

"So you're still not someone who'd ditch her current life for love?"

"No."

"Shame. I'll still wait. For a little while, anyway."

"Is that supposed to make me panic and think you'll move on with someone else? Because believe me, that's the most sensible option. If you hang around for me, you're going to be wasting your time. Find a woman your own age."

He stepped forward and touched his lips to hers.

Anna brought her hands up and pressed them against his chest to push him away. The contact did things to her. "We are absolutely not going there. Get out of my house."

He smiled, the bastard. "See you around, Anna."

She hated the fact that as he walked towards his car she wanted to call him back, sod the neighbours or Molly watching. Having him inside her home for all of what, two minutes, had shaken her steely resolve to keep him out of her heart. She'd worked so hard to lock him away, and he'd ruined it. She shut the door quietly, throwing off those emotions and drawing on the professional ones. Better that she drowned in work than thoughts of him.

She picked up her phone and rang Lenny, and related to him what Molly had said.

"Bloody hell," he muttered. "So is this phone call about me being picked up so we can get back to work?"

"Shit, I've just remembered you're on a date. I am *so* sorry. I'll get hold of Ollie."

"No, no, it's fine."

"Is that your way of telling me you need saving or are you just trying to make me feel better?"

"The second one."

"Then bugger off and continue your evening. You'd only be note-taking and acting intimidating, so don't worry about it."

"Maybe take Louise instead of Ollie?"

"Err, I'm not in the mood for her tonight. See you in the morning."

She stuffed her phone in her pocket and cursed herself for interrupting Lenny's evening, especially when he rarely *got* to the three-date mark. This must be someone special, or at least someone he could tolerate. She'd had her mind solely on work, selfishly using her job as a way to avoid facing matters of her own heart. She rifled through the memories in her brain to recall whether Oliver had said he was busy this evening. Taking Louise was a fair shout from Lenny, so Anna could get closer to her and perhaps repair whatever awkward rift existed between them, but Anna was prickly because of Parole's visit, and Oliver was more used to her snippy responses whenever she felt overwhelmed. He seemed to understand her strange little ways. Louise would take offence.

Anna gave him a bell and agreed to pick him up in fifteen minutes. She slipped her shoes and coat on and drove to Marlford. Oliver was waiting for her on his doorstep, and he waved as she parked at the kerb.

He got in and buckled up. "What's happened?"

She told him about Molly's visit while she drove towards the Dagger. She'd chosen not to knock on the neighbours' doors by Mina's house because Molly was right, it didn't matter *how* she'd found out about the obvious noises of a scuffle and the screams, just that it had occurred, and it was clear Mina had likely been killed in her bedroom. As for the old lady who'd seen the lookalike, it wasn't especially important that Anna had her name either until it went to court. Knowing the lookalike had been in the street was enough information for now.

"So we think it's an imposter and not Effie herself?" Oliver said.

"Right, but she looks exactly the same, so is there a relation out there somewhere, even though Shannon said she's the only one left?"

"Not that I've found. And we're going to the Dagger to speak to Arnold?"

"We're going to double-check his alibi with Zoe but take Arnold to the station for a chat. He's not going to be arrested or anything, unless he confesses to something, but I want to see his reaction to being taken down there."

She parked and got out, standing in the dark like Mina may have, staring at the street the Dagger was on. Opposite, to the left across the road, houses, the alleyway that led to the park, and the ginnel. In the middle, the street that led to the park and Mina's address. To the right, a long row of houses.

Oliver got out and stood beside her. "To think that no one along here saw Mina at all when she left the pub."

"I know. It seems off, like it does with the residents of her street. I know people on Rowan are secretive, but bloody hell. Have we spoken to everyone around here, do you know?"

"I did a final check before I went home this evening and emailed you the main points, but only two people weren't in when the officers did door-to-door today."

"I haven't accessed my email. Do you remember the house numbers by any chance?"

"There's that one there with the SUV outside and then one halfway up the street that goes towards Cedar Avenue."

"Are you up for doing that one now and I'll do the one with the SUV?"

"Yep, not a problem."

They went their separate ways, Anna crossing the street and ringing the bell, pleased to see the lights were on in the room to her right. A man in a white polo shirt and blue joggers opened the door and inspected the ID she held up.

"Ah, I wondered if one of your lot would knock. Do you want to come in? It's right nippy out."

"No, I don't want to take up too much of your time, but thank you for the offer. I take it you've heard about Mina Isherwood's death?"

"Yeah, it's bloody awful. I don't know her personally, like, but I heard she's young."

"Were you across the road at the pub at all last night?"

"No, that place is the devil. It gets me in trouble with the missus. The problem is, I tend to go in absolutely fine and come out bladdered, and I have no idea how it happens, I really don't . . ."

"Oi!" a woman called from indoors. "You know damn well how it happens. You ask Zoe for a pint, and you put your hand in your pocket to pay for it, usually out of the sodding rent money."

Anna pulled an *eek* face. "Did you happen to be awake at around eleven when Mina left the pub?"

"Yep, we were in bed watching telly by ten. My wife's got a routine, and it's best we stick to it." He projected this loud enough for his wife to hear, clearly trying to wind the poor woman up, and scrunched up his face. "On a serious note, I was going to ring this in tomorrow, but maybe I should have done it at the time. There was a scream just after eleven. I got up to nose out of the window, both ways, and I saw what I suppose you'd call Effie's ghost running down the ginnel. There was someone else there, too, but I didn't recognise her. She had a light-coloured leather jacket on and high heels. She dithered about for a bit by the alley entrance, but then she took that road up the middle there. I got back into bed. Please tell me it wasn't her and if I'd gone out there she might still be alive . . ."

Anna wasn't about to heap guilt on him. "Thank you for that, it's really helpful. Is there a chance you can nip to the station to give a statement? It doesn't have to be tonight."

"I can pop in and do it in my lunch break tomorrow."

Anna took his name, noted down his address, and gave him her card. "I'll send a message to the station to let them know what you saw and heard."

"Glad to have helped, but I wish we weren't in the situation where I had to. You know, her being dead and everything. Is it something we need to worry about? Was it that Effie person who did it?"

"I wouldn't worry. Again, thanks, and have a good night."

She turned and walked towards the middle road, meeting Oliver. "Were they in?"

"Yes, and they saw a woman walking quickly towards Cedar. They gave a description that matches Mina's pub clothing."

Anna told him what her resident had said. "So the Effie person had perhaps scared Mina into screaming, Mina then rushed home, and the lookalike was waiting for her. Then she ran off after banging on the back door but must have returned a bit later, after the phone call to Elizabeth."

Oliver pinched the bridge of his nose. "The weirdest thing for me is her behaviour in the garden, pegging her hair on the washing line."

"Hmm. Come on, we'll go over and have a chat with Zoe, then deal with Arnold."

Anna stepped inside the Dagger and was assaulted by a wall of noise: chatter, laughter, music. It was almost too much, and she had to work hard to block it out and concentrate on why she was there. Zoe glanced over from behind the bar and rolled her eyes, then shook her head and made her way to the hatch. Anna nodded at Oliver to let him know they should follow her, and they ended up in the woman's office.

"What now?" Zoe jammed her hands on her hips.

"Can you reconfirm Arnold's alibi for last night, please? I just want to warn you that I'm giving you the chance to change your mind if your original statement isn't correct."

"What, you think I lied to you about where he was?"

"I'm just letting you know that, if your story is different, nothing more will be said about it."

"It's the same, so I'll get back to work now."

Zoe opened the door and gestured for them to leave. Anna and Oliver walked into the bar and headed straight for Arnold.

Anna leaned close to his ear and said, "We need you to come and have a chat with us somewhere quieter."

Arnold glanced from her to his beer. "But I've still got half a pint."

"I can see that, but I'll buy you another one when we drop you back, all right?" *If we drop you back* . . .

"Where are we going?"

"Down the station."

"What for? I never did anything to Mina."

"We just want to discuss your alibi."

"Right. Well, let's go and get this over and done with. I've got nothing to hide, Zoe will tell you that."

That wasn't the answer Anna had wanted. She'd been expecting a reaction of some kind, but, if he was genuinely innocent, she'd be setting her sights elsewhere as to who'd killed Effie Workington and letting him go.

Unless he admitted the child abuse allegation.

CHAPTER TWENTY-SEVEN

In interview room three, Arnold sat opposite Anna and Lenny. She'd cautioned him just to be on the safe side and offered him a solicitor, which he'd declined. She'd explained that the caution was in his best interests, and he'd seemed happy with that. Looking at him, Anna now wondered whether he *was* innocent and whoever had told Molly he'd left the Plough for an hour twenty years ago was actually a liar. This person could be trying to shift the investigation away from themselves and onto Arnold, an easy patsy.

Anna said the time and date for the video camera. "People present, Detective Inspector Anna James, Detective Constable Oliver Watson, and Arnold Tanner." She smiled at him. "Thank you for coming in to speak to us, Arnold. Someone has come forward to inform us that your alibi for the night Effie Workington went missing, Wednesday the second of June 2004, may now be in question."

"You bloody what? I was in the Plough that night playing poker during a lock-in. I fell asleep and I didn't leave there until six in the morning."

"We've been told you left for an hour and then came back. Could you please explain that?"

"Yeah, I can explain that — you've been lied to. Is this what you've got me all the way down here for? Some load of bullshit from someone trying to make trouble?"

"We have to follow things up. The person saw you leave the Plough and then come back."

"The blokes I was with at the time wouldn't lie, so it's got to be somebody who was outside and wants to pin this on me. I'm telling you, I didn't do anything to Effie, and I stand by my statement from all those years ago. She was special to me, so why would I hurt her?"

"If there was a reason you left the Plough that night and you're worried it may put you in a bad light, don't you think that with twenty years having passed you could perhaps admit to whatever you were doing? All I'm interested in is finding out whether Effie died or whether she literally took herself off, changed her name, and started a new life. But now, there's the link with Mina . . ."

Arnold frowned. "What do you mean, link?"

"Someone resembling Effie was near Mina on three occasions, that we are aware of, last night. The place where Mina was found also has a link to Effie. It's too big a coincidence for us to dismiss any connection. As you can imagine, we're looking into the past and who the key players were there. It's on file that you had an affair with Effie. Is that true?"

"Yeah, and the wife divorced me over it because some stupid copper went and told her what I'd been up to. If I'm honest, I was kind of glad it was all out in the open anyway. Helen, that was my wife, loved her job more than me and was bound to have found out in the end. She ranted and raved for a bit, told me I was a useless prick, and then filed for divorce. She got the big house, I got myself a poxy little council place. The end."

"Assuming it isn't possible Helen made Effie disappear herself — we were told she was away at a conference — is there any way she could have arranged something, staying away deliberately to give herself an alibi?"

Here was Arnold's chance to put the blame on his ex-wife. Would he take it?

"What, you're asking me if Helen did away with Effie? Don't make me laugh. She was on the right side of the law at all times. You've only got to look at her job to know that. There is *no way on this earth* Helen would have put a foot out of line. You're barking up the wrong tree. Before you say anything, it wasn't me either. I cared about Effie a lot but not enough to set up home with her. I'm not being big-headed or anything, but she was obsessed with me. Maybe some other woman I was seeing got the hump and did her in, I don't know, but it wasn't me and it wasn't my ex."

"Was there anyone else Effie may have been seeing? Anyone who would have been upset at her having an affair with you, offending them in some way. Enough that they'd either make her disappear or she'd disappear of her own volition. As you can probably understand, it's very difficult for us to know which direction to take when we don't even know whether Effie is alive. We can assume she's dead, given the time that has passed, but without a body we're stuck."

"This is going to make her sound like some slapper, but Effie liked men, so she might have run off with one. She liked the attention, the drinks, the adoration. Surely there must be a list of her fellas somewhere in a file. Your lot must have spoken to them. As for her being dead, it could be any number of people who offed her, even Shannon. They used to hang around together all the time unless Effie had a bloke on the go, then Shannon got shitty because she had no one to go to the pub with. That's why I reckon she kicked off that night, telling Effie to finish it with me. We'd lasted a long time and she was pissed off at being by herself. They left the Plough together. Shannon got home and Effie didn't. What does that tell you?"

"But what you're implying doesn't make sense. If Shannon was upset at being alone, killing Effie means she'd be *more* alone. At least with her alive she'd have seen her sometimes."

Arnold nodded. "Maybe. Or maybe they'd had another argument on the way home and things got out of hand."

"Can we switch topics for a second? There's something I'd like to clear up as it's pretty disturbing if true. In 1983—"

"Oh, for fuck's sake, I know what you're going to say."

"Let me just finish. In 1983, a young girl's mother made a statement saying you had touched her daughter's chest inappropriately. You and the child denied this. Why do you think the mother made such a claim?"

"I can tell you exactly why. Her mum — Diana, she was called — got all flirty with me one night down the Plough. She wasn't my type. She made it clear she wanted something to happen, but I turned her down, said I was married. She comes out with some guff, saying she'd heard I might be married but I liked a bit on the side. I told her she'd got it wrong, and the next thing I know I've got the coppers at my house."

"What's Diana's surname?"

"Blake, but it won't do you any good because she's snuffed it. I'll do you a favour, though, and tell you who the kid is. She's married now, so she isn't a Blake, obviously, but it's Nicola Perry. Lives in one of those fancy apartments by Jubilee Lake. She came into money by marrying some bloke who's into banking."

Arnold giving them that information had Anna thinking he must be telling the truth, but, on the other hand, what if he'd threatened Nicola when she was a child? The woman could still be afraid of him even now.

"Thanks very much for being honest with us."

She ended the recording with the usual verbiage and walked him out to her car. Arnold sat in the back with Oliver, and she dropped the old boy at the Dagger, and bought him half a pint. She was tempted to stay and ask questions of any woman who'd be willing to admit Arnold had inappropriately touched them, but she didn't want to do it in front of him. One of her DCs or uniforms could do it when he wasn't around, although by all accounts he spent a hell of a lot of time sitting at the bar.

She drove to the Plough on a whim. Was it because she suspected Harry Wells had told Molly that Arnold's alibi was fake? Actually, before she went in all guns blazing, she needed to read the old files from 2004 to see who Arnold was supposedly with when they'd played poker. She reversed out of the car park.

"Where are we going?" Oliver asked.

"Back to the station." She explained why.

"I can tell you exactly who he was with. Two of them are dead, that's Gary and Chris Farnley, and they were brothers. One of them, Mitchell Bennett, lives in Spain and the other one is Harry the landlord."

"Have you got a photographic memory or what?"

Oliver laughed. "Do you think Harry could be a suspect in Effie's case?"

"I don't know."

"Wouldn't we be better off looking at him in the background for now? If I can get hold of Mitchell Bennett tomorrow and get his side of things, we'll be better armed. For all we know, if he kept his mouth shut for whatever reason twenty years ago, he might be willing to open it now."

Anna couldn't fault his logic and appreciated him offering suggestions for a change. "Fair enough. I'll drop you home, then."

CHAPTER TWENTY-EIGHT

Shannon had picked up the sound of a taxi as Yvette and Nancy had come home. They'd arrived at just past eleven, and it had hurt that neither of them had gone after her when she'd stormed out of the pub. Typical, really. Shannon had always been on the periphery of their supposedly three-way friendship. It felt as though she was only indulged because she happened to live between their two houses.

Tears stung her eyes. She wouldn't have needed Yvette and Nancy if Effie was still here. They'd been best friends, and Shannon had never experienced another relationship like it. Her neighbours would never match up to Effie, and she was stupid to have thought they would. She'd tried so hard to replicate the bond she'd had with her cousin, but she was continually climbing up an ice-covered hill and slipping down. Maybe she should leave Yvette and Nancy to it, let them get on by themselves. But Shannon could admit she was so desperately lonely, even *with* them as her friends, so what on earth would it be like without them? Maybe she should get some self-respect and find someone else to spend her free time with instead of basically begging them for any crumb of time they deigned to give her.

"You're bloody pathetic," she whispered into the darkness.

She turned her pillow over to the cool side and willed herself to go to sleep, but it was pointless, her mind was too wired. She got up and walked into the bedroom at the back, staring out at where the body and tent had been. She shivered, imagining Mina's last moments. Shannon glanced left towards the edge of Rowan where the killer had supposedly come and gone. Had the police discovered any new information yet? Did they have a suspect in custody right this second? If they did, Shannon wished they'd informed her. It was unfair to keep that sort of stuff to themselves because she wouldn't be able to sleep properly until she knew someone had been apprehended.

So what's new? You haven't slept properly for twenty years.

A sudden smudge of white movement outside gave her a jolt, and she moved farther behind the open curtain to hide. She studied the trees behind the bottom fences, trying to make out what it was in the darkness. A figure appeared and stood looking at the houses.

Oh my God, the Effie ghost.

She hadn't brought her phone in here with her but would have to ring the police. As much as she didn't want to leave the window and lose sight of whoever was out there, she dashed back into her bedroom and took her phone off the charger dock. She returned to the back room and peered out. Effie had gone. Had she seen the curtain move in Shannon's rush to get her mobile? Would that even have been possible with no lights on in her house? Or was she hiding behind one of the tree trunks? Shannon glanced to the left to check whether Effie was running towards the estate, but nothing stood out.

Another shiver attacked her, and she lifted her phone, ready to bring it to life, but a tapping sound downstairs stopped her. God, had someone broken in? Effie? Or had Shannon forgotten to lock up? How stupid of her, considering what had gone on. Her breath was catching, and she held it in order to listen. The tapping came again — footsteps on her laminate floor? Her blood running cold, she tiptoed out onto the landing, skirting the creaky part, and peered over the banister rail. Effie walked along her hallway, then planted one ballet-slippered foot on the bottom stair. Shannon shrieked, almost dropping her phone, and ran into the bathroom and locked the door. She sat, leaning against it, and stuck her legs out to brace her feet on the toilet pedestal. If Effie tried to get in it would delay her enough so she could ring the police.

More footsteps, on the landing this time — the groan of the floor gave away the intruder's position. Shannon fumbled with her phone but managed to put in her code, then bring up the keypad.

"I just want to talk," a disarming voice said.

Shannon relaxed. "Fucking hell, what are you *doing* prowling around in the dark? Why didn't you just phone me? And what the hell? *You're* the Effie ghost? Why?" She got up and unlocked the door. "I'll stick the kettle on, then."

A fist came towards her and smacked into her face. The shock and unfairness of it sent her staggering backwards, colliding with the toilet. She toppled, whacking her temple on the edge of the sink, then her forehead on the side of the bath. Stunned, she waited for what came next.

CHAPTER TWENTY-NINE

Last night after dropping Oliver off, Anna had had to force herself not to turn up at Nicola Perry's apartment unannounced. She'd driven into work this morning and arranged a meeting with the woman at ten o'clock. She'd scanned Effie's file until the rest of the team had come in, and for now she awaited some feedback as she'd just told them about last night's events.

"So has Molly been doing a Miss Marple?" Rupert asked.

Louise tutted.

Anna wasn't going to pull her up on it or take her to one side and ask what her problem was. Mina was more important at present. "She sees the estate as hers. Now the Kings have supposedly disbanded, she probably feels she's got *carte blanche* to do what the hell she likes on Rowan. She's always seen herself as the queen bee there, but now she can fully believe it as there'll be no King interference. Saying that, I didn't get the impression she was doing this for any other reason than to gather information to help us find out who killed Mina. For once, she's not thinking about herself."

"Or maybe she is," Lenny said, "because if there's a killer on Rowan, she's going to be wondering if she's in danger, along with every other woman on the estate."

"Yes, there might well be that motive, too, but the fact that she had the brass balls to go to Parole's apartment tells me she's serious about lending us a hand. Okay, actions for today . . ."

Anna dished them out, then announced she and Lenny were going to see DI Keith Norton to get his take on Effie back then and what he thought about her strange ghostly appearances now. She drove to Southgate and into Charlton Mews, and left the car in a hidden area behind a row of shops containing seven houses built in an L shape. No front gardens, just cobblestones in a charming courtyard with trees in pots, ivy trailing out of them that appeared to be the plastic variety.

Lenny knocked on number three, and in her head Anna went through the information she'd found about Keith just before they'd left the station. Eighty-seven. He'd been a police officer since he was eighteen. Married for sixty years but now a widower. Two children, sons. One lived in Wales, the other in Bristol.

When he opened the door, her imagined version of him didn't match the reality. She thought he'd appear every bit his age, with liver spots on his face and thinning hair, but she couldn't have been more wrong. How it was possible without surgery, she didn't know, but he appeared to be in his late sixties, his white hair thick and luxurious, swept back with some kind of product. His trousers, shirt, and blue V-neck jumper spoke of someone who had a bit of pride in how they looked, as did the brown leather moccasin slippers.

She held her ID up and introduced them, then followed Keith into a lovely spacious kitchen with an island in the middle. Marble worktops, shiny-fronted cabinets that would be a bugger to keep clean of fingerprints. Keith made tea and chatted about the swift change in the weather and how he already had to pop the heating on every morning for an hour to take the chill off. He placed the cups on the island, and they all sat around it.

"You said you wanted to chat about Effie Workington," he said. "And I remember you." He pointed at Anna. "Very diligent PC, I'm not surprised you're now a DI."

"I don't remember doing anything much except searching the moors and asking questions during door-to-door," she said.

"Hmm. Modest, too."

Anna disliked this back-slapping nonsense. "What we're interested in is what you think really happened back then. I don't mean the usual stuff that you put in files, but your personal feelings."

"I remember thinking she must have been abducted, that you don't walk home on a night out and just disappear. Cooper's Crossing is dark, even on summer evenings, because of the surrounding trees and no lamp posts. It would be so easy for someone to have grabbed her there. I thought they'd killed her and then buried her. To me it just seemed the most logical thing, even above her running off and starting again elsewhere. I say that because we couldn't find any reason why she would have wanted to hide herself, other than that her affair with Arnold Tanner had become public knowledge. From the character reports we had of her, she didn't strike me as the type of woman who'd be unhappy if Helen Tanner found out what was going on. Effie did what she wanted, when she wanted. If she needed something, she took it. It made no sense to me that she would scuttle off and never show her face again."

"What do you think about the sightings of her?"

"It's someone dressing up."

"But to have the exact same face?"

"Maybe the person appears similar and people see what they want to see in the dark."

"I saw in the file that Arnold Tanner was a suspect up until he'd given his alibi. What were your thoughts?"

"That a group of mates had ensured none of them could get into trouble for anything because they were supposedly all together. They could well have been telling the truth — they were playing poker and Arnold fell asleep — but I just found it a little convenient. Sadly, I couldn't prove otherwise."

"And Shannon?" Anna had discovered something new while reading the files earlier and wanted to discuss it. "There was talk that she'd also been seeing Arnold behind Effie's back."

"She vehemently denied it. Maybe protested a bit too much, if you know what I mean. I questioned Arnold about it, and he said she'd 'fumbled' with his private parts over his jeans around the back of the Plough, but they hadn't had an affair or actual intercourse. What I gathered from Arnold was that Shannon was pissed off he'd chosen Effie over her, which is why I was convinced she was the one with the bigger motive, plus she kept cocking up her statements. The thing was, the timings worked out in her alibi. From when she'd have left Effie at Cooper's Crossing to when she got home was spot-on if she'd walked it. No one recalled her car leaving in order for her to go and collect Effie's body or whatever the rumours were at the time."

"Because Mina Isherwood's body was found in Shannon's garden, or should I say perhaps deliberately placed there, we're now having to chase up any links no matter how tenuous they may be."

"Hence why you're talking to me about Effie."

Anna nodded. "And the fact that the lookalike was seen on the night of her death, by Mina herself when she got home, and by a lady in Mina's street."

"Did Mina report it to the police?"

"No, she telephoned her mother. The lookalike had pegged her own hair to Mina's washing line, and then she banged on Mina's back door. To scare her, to be let in, we don't know. Mina then ran across to a neighbour over the road, and the lookalike left the street. We can only assume she returned and killed Mina. One of the Rowan residents reported the sounds of a scuffle and screams that night."

"So she was likely killed at home."

"Yes. We think she was carried to Shannon's garden. What we don't know is whether she was placed in a car prior to that or whether she was carried from her home to the garden, which is around half a mile."

"Has anybody given you any idea of the build of this lookalike? What I mean is, are they strong enough to carry a dead person for any length of time?"

"They must be strong, otherwise they wouldn't have been able to do it, but no description was given other than the white dress, blonde hair, and ballet shoes. One of my team is watching CCTV this morning regarding the vehicle angle. As I predicted, the CCTV from Tesco where the killer returned to Rowan showed nothing. Mina didn't own a car, no one in her street has reported hearing one, but then they've all been tight-lipped when it comes to speaking to the police. They did speak to my contact, though, but they'd never believe she'd pass the information on to me because she's known to dislike the authorities."

"What you've got to think about is *why* someone would want you to know Mina's death is linked to Effie. If, of course, it isn't just a coincidence that she was left in Shannon's garden."

"That's what we're trying to establish. So when Effie's case got put on the back burner, what did you walk away thinking?"

"That Arnold had done it, even though he had what appeared to be a solid alibi."

"My contact told me that Arnold apparently left the pub for an hour that night, so maybe Effie did make it home and Arnold met up with her there later on."

"No, she didn't. There's CCTV in the foyer of the flats where she lived, did you not see it in the file?"

"I haven't had a chance to view everything, so no."

"It showed her going out but not coming in. You'd need to find out exactly what time Arnold left the Plough in order to pin it on him."

Anna hadn't even thought about what time Arnold had left, just that he had, so she'd have to speak to him about that. She was going to have to pay Shannon a visit, too, and ask her about the fumble behind the pub, see if she was willing to admit it now.

"Did anyone else come up as a significant suspect?" Lenny asked.

Keith ran a finger over his top lip while he thought. "We did discuss whether another woman had got the hump with Effie. Arnold had apparently been a pro at having affairs, but unfortunately no women's names were given and none of them stepped forward to admit they'd ever been near him, so that could have been Chinese whispers."

"It must have been frustrating to know there were people out there who could have done it."

"You're telling me."

"What about other family members?"

"There was only Effie's and Shannon's parents, and they'd all been together that evening. They'd had an Indian meal in Southgate and stayed on until midnight drinking. The restaurant manager was questioned and said that at no point did the Workington parents leave the establishment before then."

"What's your opinion regarding a Diana Blake filing a complaint against Arnold for inappropriately touching her daughter's chest?"

"See, that's what put him at the top of my suspect list, that and the fact he couldn't seem to keep his hands to himself when it came to women in the pub — again, that's rumours and gossip, we had no actual proof of it. Unfortunately, the report on file was so vague that we had no idea who the woman or her child were. How did you find out?"

"Arnold told us. We're on our way to see Nicola, the daughter, after we leave here. Diana's dead, unfortunately."

"So why didn't he admit it to me at the time I questioned him? He just said it was all a load of nonsense and he wasn't prepared to talk about it."

"Time changes us," Anna said. "What was once majorly important becomes insignificant a few years down the line."

"Very true. Arnold may not have wanted to tell me anything because he may have found the abuse allegation a touchy subject back then."

"He still says he didn't do it."

"And maybe he didn't. What was his excuse for the mum coming forward?"

Anna told him. "And it could well be true. Some people think nothing of doing this kind of thing out of spite, regardless of how it could damage the person they've targeted."

"Hmm."

Anna slapped her hands on her knees and stood. "Right, we've taken up enough of your time. Thank you very much for speaking with us this morning. It's been a great help."

"Neither of you drank your drinks, look."

"Blimey, sorry." Anna picked her cup up and gulped several mouthfuls.

Kevin took it from her and waited for Lenny to drain his. "I know how it is, too many cuppas at people's houses and then you find yourself with nowhere to go for a pee. Do you want to use the toilet before you leave?"

"That's very kind of you. Thank you."

"Take a left out of here and it's down the hallway."

Anna followed his instructions, her mind on Shannon and why she hadn't mentioned that fumble.

CHAPTER THIRTY

Arnold sat at the bar in his usual spot nursing half a lager. Going to the police station last night had brought back a slew of memories, ones he'd tried hard to forget. Ever since he'd been a young man, he'd had a thing about children. Boys or girls, it didn't bother him which so long as he got what he wanted. He'd backed away from those dalliances years ago, though.

He hadn't actually touched Nicola, he'd told Anna the truth about that scenario, but the others she didn't know about, yeah, he'd done a few things. He'd asked the kids not to say a word, no need for threats or anything, and, as far as he knew, none of them had. Likely the shame had kept them silent, but he often worried they'd come forward like so many were doing lately.

He'd rather top himself than face time in the nick.

He'd wondered whether Effie had confided in Shannon regarding his time with her when she'd been little, but then, knowing Shannon's temperament, that woman wouldn't have kept that to herself. At the very least she'd have had a go at him and called him a pervert, and on the other end of the scale she'd have gone to the police. But did he really know her well enough to gauge her reaction to such information? She might have been sworn to secrecy.

All the disparaging stuff going around about homosexuals hadn't sat right with him either, which was another reason why he'd ditched the children. He didn't like the thought of people thinking he was gay.

He glanced to the right at the two windows and the door that led out to the smoking area at the back of the pub. Someone he knew stood there, face close to the glass, condensation clouding it from their breath. He'd seen them around over the years but hadn't particularly paid them any mind. They hadn't given him any trouble; they'd kept the secret.

At their beckoning hand, he got up to go out. It was obvious they wanted to talk. What about? He had no idea, unless rumours had already started spreading — had a copper leaked the fact he'd been taken to the station last night and questioned about Nicola?

Bloody hell.

He left his glass on the bar and dipped his hand in his pocket to take out his cigarettes and lighter. He may as well have a smoke while he was out there. He ambled over to the door, and the person from his past stepped back to let him out. He followed them around the corner where the empty beer barrels were stored, relieved they'd chosen a private spot so no questions would be asked.

"What's the matter?" He lit up a ciggie.

"I need to speak to you. About Effie and Mina."

He frowned. "What about them?"

"I also need to speak about me and you. What you did."

His stomach rolled over. "That was a long time ago. And you consented."

"I wasn't old enough to consent."

He'd have to nip this shit in the bud. "Come round mine this afternoon, but go down the back alley and in through my garden. There might still be police around near Mina's, plus the neighbours will be gawping. I don't need to tell you my address because I've seen you a few times over the years standing outside. What was that all about?"

"I just wanted to see you."

"Fair enough. Two o'clock. That's the time I usually go home for a nap."

"I might not be able to make it then. There are other things going on. What about five?"

"Whatever."

Annoyed he'd miss an hour or two in the pub — he usually went back there at four — Arnold stubbed his smoke out and returned to his seat. Uneasy, he lifted his glass, his hand shaking, and pondered on what needed to be discussed. As far as he was concerned, there was nothing to say, but it was best he indulged his recent visitor. If they were thinking about going to the police, forewarned was forearmed. Then he smiled. There was no proof he'd done anything, so what the bloody hell was he worrying about?

CHAPTER THIRTY-ONE

Nicola Perry appeared worn out with life, or at the very least needed a holiday. Grey threaded her brown hair, and, at the front door of her apartment beside Jubilee Lake, she shoved a hand through the strands at the side, her fingers snagging in it. "Sorry, but I've been so stressed about you coming. My husband doesn't know about what happened, and I'd prefer he didn't, if that's all right."

That sounded to Anna as if something inappropriate *had* happened, or was he the type who'd go off the handle if his precious wife was connected to anything remotely distasteful? Would it taint his reputation?

"You'd better come in," Nicola said.

Anna and Lenny had announced their arrival to the man behind the security desk in the lobby, and he'd phoned through to Nicola, who'd given them permission to come up in the lift. She lived on the second floor, and, even though none of her neighbours had poked their heads out to have a nose, it didn't mean they wouldn't see Anna and Lenny in their suits. Each front door had a camera above it.

Anna followed Nicola into the open-plan kitchen and living area, which was the same layout as Parole's. She shoved away the memories of being in his place — and the worry that they'd bump into him when they left if he happened to be having a day off work. She didn't need the emotional hassle of that. "Do you know your neighbours well?"

"Not really, we keep to ourselves. Why do you ask?"

"Because you mentioned your husband doesn't know anything. I wondered whether a neighbour you were friends with would unintentionally bring our visit to light, considering they may have spotted us on their CCTV."

"No, no, it should be fine, it's just he'd be upset that I've kept this from him all these years. I can't really tell you anything much about what went on because I wasn't there when my mother made the complaint. Would you like a drink?"

"We've not long had one, but thanks anyway," Anna said.

"Not for me, thank you." Lenny smiled.

Nicola indicated for them to sit on a cream U-shaped sofa facing the wall of windows that overlooked the lake. "Arnold didn't come anywhere near me. I didn't even know who he was at the time. My mother told me I had to say he touched my chest, and I was going to do it, too, until a policeman in uniform came to our house to speak to me. Of course, I got frightened because, you know, it's the police, and I blurted that he didn't do it. I remember my mother telling the officer that I'd clearly been frightened by Arnold, that he'd threatened me to keep my mouth shut. I opened it to tell the policeman that wasn't true, but Mum stared at me, and when she stared at me like that I did as I was told."

Anna nodded.

Nicola continued. "I've felt bad about this ever since. It pops up in my head every now and again, and I often wonder whether I should go and find him and tell him I know he didn't do anything to me. Which would be silly because he *knows* he didn't do anything, but it's the stigma, what people could be thinking of him, because my mother did have a big mouth and she told people she'd made a complaint. A lot of the kids in our street called him Pervert Tanner after that."

"Do you know why your mother made the report?"

"I do, unfortunately. I overheard her talking to one of her friends in our road, saying she'd warned him she wouldn't be rejected and that he ought to watch himself. They laughed about it, although her friend seemed a bit sad. Maybe because Arnold had been accused unfairly and everyone in our road thought he was a child molester."

As Anna didn't think Nicola was hiding anything or had made up this little story to keep Arnold safe, she didn't feel there was any need to hang around. "Thanks for your time today."

"Can I ask why you had to speak to me about this? Has he been inappropriate with someone else? Is he actually a pervert after all?"

"No such allegation has been brought to my attention. We wanted to clear up what happened in 1983 and see whether his story matched yours, which it does."

"But what I mean is, why are you even looking into Arnold? What's he done?"

"The current case we're working on has links to the past, and his name cropped up because of your mother's allegation, that's all."

"So that's it? Nothing else is happening? My husband won't find out about this conversation?"

"Not that I can foresee at the moment, no."

"Thank God for that."

Nicola showed them out. Anna and Lenny left the apartment building and got in the car. Anna thought about paying Harry Wells a visit, and explained her reasoning to Lenny.

"What do you think?"

He shrugged as he put his seat belt on. "He'll probably twig Molly told you about it — I mean, it's obvious it was him who passed on the information."

"Then I'll *say* it was obvious and that's how I worked it out. I don't feel like I can leave this one without questioning him about it, although I should probably wait until we have news from the fella who moved to Spain."

"But it might take a while to get information from him, so it's best to speak to Harry now. Why do you feel more inclined to speak to him rather than the old lady in Mina's street and the person who heard the screams?"

"I knew you were going to say something like that and you should know the answer anyway."

"Because the old lady and the neighbour are unlikely to have killed Mina, but Harry might have."

"Yep."

* * *

The Plough bustled with customers even at eleven o'clock in the morning — the tail end of the breakfast crowd and the beginning of brunch. The scent of fry-ups hung in the air along with coffee. Harry stood behind the bar with two members of staff, and he lifted his chin in a sort of nod when he clocked Anna and Lenny coming his way. They ended up in his office, and he let out a weary sigh.

"Let me guess, Molly Griffin got hold of you."

"She has, but she didn't mention any names. We realised part of the information came from you because the other players in the alibi are either dead or in Spain."

"The powers of deduction, eh?"

Anna sat on one of the chairs, leaving Lenny to take notes while he stood by the door. "Why did you give Arnold an alibi on the night of Effie's disappearance if you knew damn well you couldn't account for a missing hour?"

"Because, to be honest with you, he isn't a killer — or that's what I thought at the time anyway."

"He told us he had feelings for Effie, and, when emotions are involved, things can go tits up pretty quickly."

"But the reason it couldn't have been him is that he left the pub between three and four a.m."

"But no one knows exactly when Effie went missing."

"Where the bloody hell would she have been then, between Shannon leaving her at Cooper's Crossing and

Arnold leaving my pub? That's hours. No one saw her around. She didn't go home. Look, am I going to get in the shit for giving him an alibi? Because I didn't actually say that he was here all the time. What I said was we played poker, he fell asleep, and everyone left at six in the morning. I just happened to leave out that before he went to sleep he nipped out for an hour."

"It's lying by omission. I don't have any plans to get you in trouble for not telling the truth back then, but I'm going to ask you outright: did you have anything to do with Effie Workington going missing and Mina Isherwood's death?"

"You fucking what? Is this a piss-take? Where in all of this did my name come up as a suspect? Seriously?"

His reaction told her all she needed to know. "Thanks for your time, Harry."

"You need to brush up on your fucking policing skills. I've got sod all to do with any of it, and I was going to tell you about the alibi thing myself, but Molly said she'd do it, so don't go thinking I'm hiding anything else or I haven't got the balls to admit to lying, because I have."

"Like I said, thanks for your time."

They left the pub, and Anna drove them up the lane. Two SOCOs were still poking around the front of the houses, but she imagined their job here would be done soon. Yvette's car was parked outside her home, so maybe she'd decided not to go into work today. Nancy's bike had been propped up next to her living room window, so she'd either already been out or was just about to go. Anna led the way up Shannon's garden path, but Nancy's door opened before she had a chance to knock.

"Any news?" Nancy asked. "Do you want a cup of tea? The kettle's just boiled."

"We need a chat with Shannon, actually," Anna said.

"She'll be having a lie-in, always does if we've been out the night before. We went to the Dagger for dinner."

"Maybe you can help us with what we need to know, then," Anna said.

She and Lenny trailed Nancy into her kitchen and sat at the island while she made drinks and babbled on about Shannon asking to borrow her bike because it had a basket on the front and she could pop some of her beetroots in it to share them with Vaughn Bates. She brought the cups and some biscuits over on a tray and placed them down, then lowered herself into a seat, took off the tin lid and flapped her hand towards it. Lenny took a chocolate digestive and bit into it. Crumbs fell onto the top page of his notebook.

Anna popped a couple of sweeteners in her tea, then stirred. "I read some files this morning regarding Effie's case, and during our investigation it has come to light that Shannon may have been involved with Arnold Tanner. Did you know anything about that?"

"Oh, they had a 'moment' around the time of his affair with Effie."

"Are you happy to talk about that with us?"

Nancy nodded. "Oh God, she was such a *stupid* cow. Her and Effie hung around with each other all the time until *he* came along. When Effie was with her other boyfriends, she was still able to go out with Shannon, but when Arnold was in the picture she never wanted to. It was like she'd shoved Shannon out of her life and didn't need her anymore. Shannon thought if she could get Arnold to have sex with her, she could tell Effie what a bastard he was, how he was using her, and she'd finish it with him. But Effie wasn't having any of it, so Shannon called him out in front of everyone in the Plough. Not only did his and Effie's affair become public knowledge, but so did the suggestion about others. Shannon felt bad, but she was so desperate for Effie to see what was going on, she didn't even care that his poor wife would find out. It was like she had tunnel vision. She'll tell you all this herself, I'm sure."

"Why didn't you tell us about this yesterday?"

"I didn't think it was relevant to Mina dying. I mean, it isn't, is it?"

Anna ignored that.

Nancy went on. "Shannon's spoken to me a lot about that night in the Plough. She still believes Effie's alive, you know. Misguided hope, perhaps. I told her last night she needed to face the truth. Anyway, Effie said Shannon was clingy and she ought to find some new friends because the way she'd acted in the pub, Effie wasn't sure she wanted to have anything to do with her anymore. Shannon's told herself for twenty years that it was just a knee-jerk thing, what Effie said, something to hurt her, to get her back because she'd embarrassed her in the pub, but maybe Effie meant it. Shannon's version of events is that she left Effie at Cooper's, then locked herself in her flat and cried in bed. That Keith detective came the next day and asked her questions, saying Effie had gone missing. There'd been an anonymous phone call; someone had heard talking at Cooper's — they'd walked past the alley and picked up that someone sounded scared."

Anna recalled reading that in the file, and her first thought had been that the talk was between Shannon and Effie. Having spoken to Nancy now, she was inclined to believe that argument was Effie and someone else. Arnold was still in the pub at that point with Harry et al. Shannon was in bed. Helen was in Glasgow.

So who the hell was it?

CHAPTER THIRTY-TWO

Oliver put the phone down. The man from Spain, Mitchell Bennett, had admitted that Harry Wells had also left the Plough that night. Oliver put his coat on and messaged Anna to let her know he was going to have a chat with Harry, taking Rupert with him. He drove to the pub, and they found the man stacking clean glasses onto shelves beneath the bar. Oliver held up his ID and introduced himself.

"What the bloody hell do you lot want *now*?" Harry griped.

"Can we have a quick chat in private?" Oliver asked.

Harry sighed and led them to an office. He gestured for them to take a seat on the armchairs, then sat behind the desk. "Look, I don't know what happened to Effie and I don't know what happened to Mina. None of it is anything to do with me."

Oliver gave him a tight smile. "There's a discrepancy in your alibi regarding Effie Workington."

"If you're on about Arnold, I cleared that up with Anna."

"I'm talking about yourself, sir."

"What I said back then stands today."

"You might want to change your mind when you hear what I have to say. One of the men who was with you that night said you left the pub."

Harry closed his eyes, then ran his hands down his face. He placed them in his lap and sighed again. "You've been on the blower to Spain. Fine, I did nip out, I'll admit that, and the only reason I said I'd stayed in the pub was because I didn't want to be accused of having anything to do with Effie going missing."

"Is that the only reason?" Oliver thought about what else Mitchell had said. "I'm giving you a chance to give me the proper side of the story."

"Jesus Christ, why would I when I could get in the shit for something else?"

"Yet you admit you left the pub."

"Yeah, but I don't want to tell you why."

"Then that's going to put you in a bad light. You're hiding something, and conclusions could be drawn that you did have something to do with the disappearance."

Harry made an obvious show of mulling over his options. "All right, fine. I left the pub because I had to go and see a man about a dog."

"Could you be clearer, please?"

"Seriously, this is going to get me banged up for Effie. I know what the police are like and how they manipulate things so they fit whatever narrative they want to spew."

Frustrated by going around the houses, Oliver said, "We could always continue this conversation down at the station if you prefer."

"No, I don't fucking prefer. Okay, the reason I had to leave was because I was meeting someone to pay them some money."

"For . . . ?"

"Beer off the back of a lorry, all right? Some barrels had been nicked from another pub, and someone offered them to me. I took them off their hands. Didn't really have much choice about it either."

"Why not?"

"I really can't say."

"I think you should."

"Sodding hell! Are you going to offer me protection, because that's what I'm going to need if I open my gob."

"So you were involved in something big?"

"Not really, but it could end up being big if I grass on a certain person."

"And that is . . . ?"

Harry looked about ready to blow a gasket. "Christ. Right, if I end up hurt — or dead — this will be your fault. Paul Dickens had nicked the barrels."

And now Oliver understood why Harry hadn't wanted to give up that name. Paul Dickens was currently serving time for armed robbery, and, despite him being locked in a cell, rumour had it he still had a decent reach. If he found out Harry had grassed him up, the landlord might find himself in a bit of bother.

"Where was this meeting?" Oliver asked. "And was anyone else there who can back up your claim?"

Harry closed his eyes again and, when he opened them, tears welled —frustration or fear? "I'm saying for the record, yet again, I didn't have anything to do with Effie Workington going missing. I met Paul at Cooper's Crossing, and, before you jump the gun, it was way after Shannon and Effie had left the pub."

This married with what Mitchell had said.

Rupert shifted forward on his chair. "When you were at the Crossing, did you see or hear anything? Effie's body on the ground, her handbag, something like that?"

Harry scoffed. "Have you been there in the middle of the night, pal? It's fucking pitch black, so no, I didn't see anything."

Rupert didn't seem fazed by the outburst. "You didn't answer my colleague when he asked if anyone else was there with Paul."

Harry let out a growl of irritation. "If I tell you, that means I'm putting someone *else* in the shit and my life will definitely be on the line."

"Not if we make out someone else saw them," Rupert said. "What about when they left after you'd given Paul the money? Which direction did they go in?"

Harry appeared to have admitted defeat. "What the hell. In for a penny, in for a pound. They went down the alley and into the street."

"There you go, then," Rupert said. "We can just say someone's come forward. We don't have to tell either of them it was you. So who else was there?"

Harry puffed air out. "He was with Whitey Scranton."

Another name Oliver recognised. The man had gone down with Paul for the armed robbery. "All our boss wants to do is find out what happened to Effie and Mina. If you know something about either of them, then tell us. And you're going to have to give us a statement."

"Obviously. Do you want to do it now?"

"It's probably best you come down to the station, even though you're not keen."

"Fucking great, the one time I break the law and it comes back to bite me on the arse twenty years later. What if I'm seen going inside and those two bastards hear about it? Do I get protection? And I mean it — if I get accused of doing Effie in, I'll create merry hell."

CHAPTER THIRTY-THREE

Yvette had seen Anna and Lenny go into Nancy's earlier. What was going on? Had they discovered something? Yvette had waited for them to leave, then knocked at Shannon's, but with no response she'd gone home to do some cleaning. Two hours later, she dithered outside Shannon's front door again. Shannon not responding to her knock was a concern, although, now Yvette came to think about it, she may be having her lie-in or still be holding a grudge about the argument in the Dagger last night. She was good at that, giving them the silent treatment, and, even though Yvette was annoyed with her for suggesting she had something to do with Mina's death, she'd still come around here to see if she could smooth over any ruffles.

She bent and opened the letterbox flap. "Shannon, are you in there?"

No answer.

"Shannon? Come on now. Enough's enough. I'm sorry for snapping at you, okay? I can see how me cleaning my back door looks, but I swear to you I had nothing to do with that poor girl."

You had something to do with another poor person, though.

Yvette shoved that thought out of her head, shivering at the idea of being caught. Sometimes she pondered coming clean just so she wasn't riddled with insecurity, but the thought of spending years in prison was enough motivation to hide the truth.

She let the letterbox flap go, and it closed with a clatter. She may as well go home and leave Shannon to her sulk. She'd be okay in a couple of days, and everything would be fine again.

Yvette turned to walk down Shannon's path, but stopped as Nancy opened her front door.

"Everything all right?" Nancy asked.

"She's not answering me," Yvette said.

"Why are you here, being so forgiving, when she basically accused you of having something to do with Mina's death?"

"I don't like any ill feeling. Why don't you try and see if she'll come out for you?"

Nancy sighed. "Honestly, all this pandering to her, it annoys me. Go and get the spare key for her house. If she's not answering then we'll walk straight in."

"Nancy . . ."

"What?"

"If she doesn't want to talk to us, then that's her right." But still, Yvette collected the key from inside her house and returned, holding it up.

Nancy took it and let herself in. "She could do with your Miss Mop help in here. The place is a pigsty."

Yvette had asked to clean Shannon's home before, but the offer had been rejected. Shannon had even seemed offended that Yvette felt her home wasn't up to scratch. Which it wasn't, but Yvette should have just kept her feelings to herself. Not everyone understood that cleaning was a way to take your mind off the bad things you'd done.

She followed Nancy inside and closed the door.

"Shannon?" Nancy sing-songed up the stairs.

"Let's just leave it, shall we? I'm not comfortable with this at all."

Nancy paused with her hand on the newel post. "Have you tried phoning her, by any chance?"

"Yes, and I messaged a few times as well. She's ignoring me."

Nancy sighed. "You go upstairs, and I'll check down here. She might even be on her allotment." She waltzed off into the living room.

Yvette climbed the stairs, hating being here. It felt wrong and intrusive. She checked all the bedrooms and even the airing cupboard. She itched to tidy up the jumble of sheets and towels but forced the urge away by opening the bathroom door. The toilet stood directly ahead beside the sink, of which Yvette could only see half, so she moved further into the room.

"Shannon? Oh God, Shannon!"

Her friend lay in the empty bath, fully clothed in her pyjamas. She appeared to be asleep, but she was so white, and her lips were such a pale shade of purple. Her eyes, wide open, had red marks on the whites. A black bruise covered one of her temples, and another sat in the middle of her forehead. Shannon's phone rested on her stomach, screen down, and her arms were by her sides.

Yvette backed away. She bumped into the radiator behind her, then staggered out onto the landing.

"Nancy! Oh my bloody God, Nancy!"

Footsteps banged up the stairs, and Nancy rushed along the landing towards Yvette. She stepped closer and looked around the door, then came back out and took her phone from her jeans pocket. She phoned the police as Yvette backed away to the top of the stairs.

Nancy went back into the bathroom and placed her phone on the closed toilet seat. "Okay, so what do I do, put two fingers on the side of her neck?"

She disappeared from view, and Yvette imagined her kneeling beside the bath to check for signs of life.

Their trio had just become a duo.

CHAPTER THIRTY-FOUR

The last thing Anna had expected to do today was stand in Shannon's bathroom and stare at her dead body. There was no doubt in her mind that this death was connected to the other murders. The question was, how? Did Shannon know who'd killed Effie, and possibly Mina, and whoever it was had killed her to shut her up? Herman had already confirmed that Shannon had died at the hands of someone else. He'd pulled her pyjama top away from her neck and revealed a nasty line of bruising that indicated she'd been strangled. Like Mina. Had Effie been strangled, too?

Anna stepped out onto the landing, then dipped into the spare bedroom beside the bathroom so she was out of the way of the SOCOs, who'd already given this room the once-over. Lenny appeared from downstairs and joined her, then shook his head and moved to the window to stare outside.

"There's no sign of forced entry on the back door," he said. "Steven just told me."

"Okay, so we can presume she either let her killer in, someone has spare keys, or she didn't lock up. Did you have any luck with Nancy and Yvette?"

"Both said they hadn't seen or heard anything. They went out for dinner with Shannon at the Daggar last night, but Shannon left before them, at about nine o'clock. They assumed she'd walked home."

"Bloody hell," Anna said. "I'm buggered if I'd walk down the lane that late at night."

"They said Shannon does it every so often if she can't get a taxi or a bus."

"Surely she could have got one last night around nine. This is a city, for God's sake. It's not like the taxi ranks close up shop early, is it?"

Lenny shrugged. "Maybe she fancied a walk. Yvette said she sometimes goes to Cooper's Crossing to talk to Effie in the evenings."

That hit Anna in the heart. She'd probably do the same thing if she were in Shannon's position, visiting the last place her loved one had been, trying to find answers. The only loved ones Anna had were her mum and dad, who lived in Devon, and she couldn't imagine not having them on the end of the line or to visit when she got the chance. "Poor cow. Then she comes home and someone does this to her."

"I wonder if the bath's significant."

"I thought the same, but it could have just been a convenient place to dump her."

Lenny shivered and drew his forensic suit zip higher. "What's Herman said?"

"The whites of her eyes and the red spots on her face point to strangulation, not to mention the mark on her neck. I'm thinking there was a struggle, like what was reported with Mina."

Steven popped his head into the doorway. "There's a silk scarf on the chair beside the bed. Thought you'd want to know. It's not the same one as at Mina's house, so I'm wondering if the killer's using the victims' scarves to get the job done. It'll be tested for DNA, obviously."

Steven dipped back out again.

Anna turned to Lenny. "It's frustrating the hell out of me that we don't know what happened to Effie and whether it was the same thing as Mina and Shannon."

"What are your thoughts on Shannon copping it?"

"It's obvious, isn't it? She knew something."

"I didn't get the sense that she had any clue what happened to Effie *or* Mina, so, unless she's a bloody good liar, what on earth *could* she have known?"

"Maybe this is nothing to do with Effie. What if Shannon saw Mina's killer dropping the body off? What if she was too scared to tell us because *they* saw *her*, too? Someone might have threatened her to keep her mouth shut, thinking she'd let something slip. We need to find out who else she spoke to yesterday."

"She was with Jayla for most of the day and then the pub. Is her phone around? She could have sent messages to someone of interest."

"It's on her stomach. Herman will get it sent down to digi-forensics. They'll find out who she was chatting to, if anyone. Did Yvette or Nancy mention whether Shannon spoke to anyone in the Dagger last night?"

"Not that they're aware of. I questioned whether she'd been to the loo on her own, to see if someone had chatted to her in there, but they said she stayed at the table the whole time."

"Were they drinking alcohol?"

"They had a glass of wine with dinner, and then Nancy bought a bottle, although Shannon didn't drink any from that. She went home shortly after Nancy bought it."

Anna pictured their surroundings. The darkness, the remoteness, how black the sky was in October. "With all the crap going on around here, what kind of friends are they to have let a woman go home by herself when there's a killer still lurking around?"

"I asked them the same question, and they said it would have been pointless to tell her to get a taxi or whatever, because if she was determined to walk she wouldn't have listened to them. She was stubborn, apparently."

"Okay, there's nothing much we can do here other than send Rupert and Louise to the Dagger to ask a few questions. Not that I expect them to find anything out if Shannon didn't speak to anyone else, but we'll cover our backs there just the same. I was supposed to send officers there to discreetly ask about Arnold, but they can do it instead. Oliver can check the CCTV to see if Shannon was caught on camera during her walk home. He should just about be finished taking Harry's statement by now."

"That was a turn-up. Will he get done for buying the beer?"

"We can't prove it even happened. Can you see Paul Dickens and Whitey Scranton admitting they robbed a dray lorry? I don't think so. With nothing to give to the CPS, I think Harry's going to get away with it."

"But that means his alibi for leaving the pub isn't watertight. If no one's going to back him up that he bought the beer, there's still a big question mark as to what he was doing during that time."

"Oliver said he believes him, and, for what it's worth, Rupert does, too." She paused, could have kicked herself. "That sounded nasty. It's not that I don't trust Rupert's judgement, but . . ."

"I know what you mean. I'm trying to trust and like him, too, but it's hard because of what Peter did."

"I'm not even going there." She straightened her shoulders. "So, we'll keep an eye on Harry, but I honestly don't think he did anything other than buy some hooky gear and lie about it because, let's face it, he *would* have been a suspect with Effie then."

Shannon's death had done nothing but provide another dead end. Yes, Anna was convinced everything was linked, but, until she could find out what joined the dots, they'd just have to continue digging until the truth showed its ugly face.

CHAPTER THIRTY-FIVE

Louise drove towards the Dagger. "Do you think this is going to be a waste of time? Nancy and Yvette have said Shannon didn't speak to anyone else in the pub last night."

Rupert grabbed a mint from a bag in the glove box and offered it to her. At the shake of her head, he put the bag back. Then she changed her mind in case the garlic from yesterday's carbonara lingered. She popped a sweet in her mouth and tucked it inside her cheek.

"It's best to double-check," he said. "Anyway, Anna asked us to discreetly find out whether anyone's willing to pass on the names of women Arnold had affairs with, so there's that angle to get on with, too."

"That's going to be unlikely if he's sitting there propping up the bar. People won't want to say anything if he's right there, but you'd think he wouldn't be bothered about saying who he'd been with now he's divorced and he's so old."

Rupert tutted. "People still want to keep secrets when they're in their eighties, you know."

Louise pulled into the car park and got out to stretch her legs, shaking her aching arms out. She'd been doing a lot of typing and mouse scrolling to try to piece together this confusing jigsaw, mainly researching Mina's life online, then visiting a few of her old neighbours. Both had turned into dead ends. Mina was, as people said, happy, and nothing strange stood out.

Louise led the way into the Dagger, expecting to see an old man sitting at the bar, but there wasn't one. A woman behind it gave them a funny look. She'd probably guessed they were the police. Funny how some people could spot them a mile away, even though they weren't in uniform.

Louise approached the bar with her ID held up. "Is Arnold Tanner in?"

The woman glanced at the clock on a side wall. "He's usually back from his nap about now, but maybe he slept for longer today. Why?"

Louise smiled and opted not to answer that. "We're going to be having a little chat with your customers, but first can I ask if you were here last night?"

"I was, yes."

"Can I have your name, please?"

"Zoe, and, before you ask, landlady."

"Did you happen to see Shannon Workington, Nancy Rawlings, and Yvette Danes in here yesterday evening?"

"Well, yes, because I was at work. What are you asking about them for?"

"Did you notice whether anyone other than Nancy and Yvette spoke to Shannon?" Rupert asked.

"Yes."

"Can you elaborate?"

"Nancy got up and bought a bottle of wine, and I happened to see Yvette go to the toilet. While they were gone, Shannon turned to a couple behind her. No idea who they were, I've never seen them before."

"Do you have any CCTV?"

"I'd have thought your boss would have told you that answer already, or don't you lot share info? The answer's no."

She's got a chip on her shoulder. Did Louise come across like Zoe? It was alarming to note some similarities between them, the snapping answers being one. No wonder Anna hadn't particularly taken to Louise, but then her behaviour towards the DI was more to do with the way Anna was so abrupt and blunt. A defence mechanism. Give back what's being dished out.

"Did the conversation between the couple and Shannon appear amicable or heated?" Louise asked.

"No idea because I was serving someone. By all means chat to my customers, but can you get a move on because I really don't want the stench of bacon lingering."

"Is there any particular reason why?" Rupert asked. "Have you got something to hide?"

Zoe let out a spiteful laugh. "More like my customers do. We're on the Rowan estate, for God's sake. Think about it." She flounced away.

It frustrated Louise that a lot of these people in here could have broken the law and there was nothing she could do about it without any proof. She and Rupert divvied up the customers between them, Louise taking the ones in the dining area. She asked her questions quietly and, with no one having told her anything she was desperate to hear, she approached the last woman, who suggested, in a smoker's whisper, that they meet elsewhere for a chat. Meeting place arranged, Louise walked away as if the lady had been unhelpful.

She met up with Rupert.

"We need to leave," she muttered. "I'll tell you in the car."

She drove them to a small courtyard with a Portakabin. The sign beside the door offered services for doggy daycare, and, given that no lights were on and the blinds were down, she assumed the business was closed. Another car drew up, and the woman from the pub got out and sat in the back seat of Louise's.

"Sorry about that," she said.

Louise turned to look at her between the front seats. She appeared to be around fifty, her blonde hair done nicely as well as her nails. "It's fine, we understand. Do you mind if I record this conversation?"

"Of course not." She waited for Louise to set up the device, state the time, date, and the officers present, then she said, "That lot in the pub are like sharks the way they round on you, which is why I couldn't talk in there. Right, I'd better take a deep breath and dive in then, eh?"

This sounds serious. "Take your time."

"It's about Arnold."

Louise's stomach rolled over. Would she be the one to crack the case? God, she'd love to run into the incident room and announce it to Anna, show her she was *better* than Sally. She forced herself back into the present. "Did you have an affair with him or know someone else who did?"

"I don't know about any affairs other than the one he had with Effie, and only then because Shannon blurted it out that night in the pub. I was there at the time, see. I'm talking about something else Arnold's done, and loads of people know about it, they're just not saying anything. It's the shame. I should know because I feel it myself. That's why I've kept my mouth shut for so long."

Louise quickly glanced at Rupert then back to the woman. "If you feel comfortable talking about it, please do."

"Well, he's a kiddie fiddler. Or he was. I have no idea whether he's carried it on all these years after us lot. I just know all of us who went to ballet lessons at the community centre in the late seventies and early eighties were a part of his group."

Louise frowned. "What on earth did he have to do with ballet lessons?"

"It started when he dropped off his mate's little boy and he ended up staying to watch the whole lesson. Mrs Drummond used to run it, she's dead now. I think her first name was Margo. As he said he enjoyed the arts — a likely story, now I look back on it — and he offered a donation to the class, she asked him if he wanted to come back every week. I suppose it was weird for a man to sit there and watch kids prancing around, but it seemed so normal back then. And at first he never did anything wrong."

"Are you prepared to give us your name?"

"I suppose I should if I'm going to accuse someone of child abuse, even though there's nothing I can do to prove he did it. I'm Debbie, and that's all you're getting for now."

Louise wasn't about to tell her they could find out her surname easily enough just by googling who owned the doggy daycare, not to mention running her number plate through the system. Now wasn't the time to act smug.

"I can give you the names of all the kids who went to the ballet class, but I don't want them knowing it was me who passed them on. As kids, we all talked about Arnold and how he touched us. We made a joke of it, giggling and whatever. And it was weird because he never threatened us, he just calmly asked us not to tell anyone. He was kind and gentle, and we did what he said, like it was natural. I've been carrying it around with me for years as just something that happens, but, as more and more stuff has come out about men like him and there's all those documentaries that show you about grooming and whatever, I realised what he'd done wasn't right, even though he'd made it *seem* right. It was a bit confusing to get my head around that, but I got there eventually."

"I'm so sorry you went through that," Louise said. "You kept it from your parents?"

"Yes. They're the type to have told me not to be daft, that him helping me go to the toilet was what adults did, but . . ." A deep breath. "It's . . . it's bloody shocking is what it is."

Oh God. "So Mrs Drummond allowed him to take the children to the toilet?"

"Yes."

"Can I just ask why you go to a pub where you know your abuser is? Why put yourself through it?" Louise was after tripping Debbie up. She may have seen Mina with Tanner and got jealous.

"Just to watch him sometimes. After he'd stopped going to the ballet classes — no explanation for that either; at least *I* wasn't told anything — I rarely saw him. Until I was older and started going out drinking. He used to be in the Plough back then, and he never acknowledged me, not even a wave. Maybe he didn't recognise me, but I personally think I still looked the same as I had when I was younger. Not these days, though, wrinkles an' all that. Anyway, I've been trying to get up the courage to speak to him, to ask him why he thought he had the right to do what he did to me and the other kids, but I haven't managed it as yet."

"Did you keep in contact with the other children from the class?"

"Not intentionally, although I see a couple of them around every now and then. We stop and chat but never talk about what happened. It's as if there's a silent agreement that none of us will bring it up."

Debbie reeled off the names. Louise darted another quick glance at Rupert before she could stop herself, and he stared back at her, communicating that they really ought to get hold of Anna regarding what to do next.

"Would you mind coming down to the station to finish this interview?" Louise asked Debbie. "Will your car be all right left here?"

"Yes, that's my Portakabin. I didn't have any animals booked in for today."

"Is there anything you need to tell us regarding Mina?"

"Only that I felt sick when I saw her keep sitting with him in the pub. She was way too young for him, so in my eyes he was still a pervert. He touched her inappropriately. He does that to a lot of younger women, and I know I should have stepped forward and told him to stop it, and I know damn well what he's doing is wrong, but I couldn't bring myself to go closer to him. I wish I had because then Mina would still be alive. I'd have given her a lift home to get her away from him."

"Please don't feel any guilt for that. She might not have taken up your offer for a lift anyway and could have still ended up dead."

Debbie nodded. "Let's go and get this over with, then. I've got a lot to tell you."

CHAPTER THIRTY-SIX

Sitting in his armchair, it took a moment for Arnold to comprehend what he was staring at. Or *who* he was staring at. Effie had let herself in, like the old days, and stood in his living room as though she'd walked straight out of the past and into the present. The only difference to the last time he'd seen her was she had no handbag and no high heels. She turned and closed the curtains, then spun around in a half-pirouette to smile at him.

"Were you told to come here?" He squinted because her face wasn't quite right — he'd taken his glasses off when he'd come home for his nap — but it was definitely Effie.

She twirled and swooped around, then came closer.

"Was it you who sent me those emails?" he asked.

They informed him she'd be here or there at a particular time and for him to go and meet her. He never had. He'd thought it was a kid fucking him around, but then that night or the next day people would say they'd seen her or her ghost. Whoever wrote to him knew he'd been having an affair with Effie long before Shannon had announced it. Maybe it'd been her all along. He'd received one earlier, telling him Mina's death was his fault because, if he'd given one of his other children another chance instead, she'd still be alive.

It didn't make sense.

"Where have you been all this time?" He reached out to the side table for his glasses and slipped them on. And now it was clear this wasn't Effie. Her face was a mask, a very good likeness, but there was no mistaking the eye holes. "Who are you?"

Whoever they were, they had her dress on, and he'd swear it was the same one she'd worn on that night. It was slightly grubby and torn in a couple of places, which hadn't been the case in the pub.

She didn't answer but danced out of the room, returning with his tartan scarf that he'd draped over the newel post when he'd got home. She stood behind him and draped it around his neck, then around again, and yanked the ends towards her. The wool tightened around his throat, and, as he opened his mouth to tell her to let go, she pulled the ends even harder. His head filled up with pressure, his eyes bulged.

He wasn't going to see another sunrise.

* * *

It felt good to be Effie, taking the scarf off and laying it on the chair arm. Opening the curtains so the neighbours would be able to see him in all his dead glory, if they even bothered to glance inside. Dancing out of the house and down the alley.

Catcher hadn't wanted to talk in the end. There'd been no point. Tanner would have lied. Catcher had wanted to explain about those emails, to tell him they'd been a test to lure him out, to see if he still loved Effie more than the other dancers, if he was prepared to meet up with her. To see if, when the mask was removed, he'd want who'd really hidden beneath it.

But that might mean more heartbreak, more rejection, so Catcher had remained silent and killed the germ that had lingered for too many years to count.

It was over now. Time to move on.

CHAPTER THIRTY-SEVEN

Debbie sat in an interview room with Louise and Rupert, while Anna and Lenny watched on a monitor in a different room. Anna felt it was better for Louise and Debbie to keep up the rapport they'd already established. Anna stepping in could make Debbie clam up, and that was the last thing they needed. She didn't dare hope that Debbie was the killer and had come forward to confess — but those names on that list had certainly been an eye-opener, giving Anna pause for thought and other suspects to talk to.

A search had provided information about Debbie. Surname Lines. Single, never married — did her past have something to do with that? The poor woman had just been explaining her time as a child with Arnold.

Anna had heard enough, but she wasn't sure which route to take first. Go and get Arnold, who may or may not still pose a threat to children, or go and speak to the other people on the list?

"At least that explains the Effie person wearing ballet shoes now," she said. "But none of them look like Effie, so if they're dressing up as her then they're wearing a mask."

Lenny nodded. "I wonder why Arnold stopped going to the ballet class."

"Maybe his friend's son packed it in so he didn't bother anymore. That's something I plan to ask him. Or maybe one of the parents complained to Mrs Drummond after their child told them about him but they didn't bother going to the police. We might get lucky and find one or two mums and dads who're still alive. Or maybe one of the children will know. Sounds weird calling them that when they're adults now, but you know what I mean." Anna leaned against the wall to gather her thoughts. "Because a lot of people called him Pervert Tanner after the supposed false allegation from Nicola's mother, Arnold would have been watched more closely from 1983 onwards. Debbie said the ballet class was held late seventies to early eighties, so that makes sense, doesn't it? People start thinking he's a pervert, so he leaves the ballet class."

"The question is, did he continue abusing kids elsewhere? Surely his wife would have been watching him as well."

"That's another thing we'll ask him." Anna sighed. "We've got a lot going on but it's coming together. Okay, I've made my mind up. I'll ask Isabella to go with Oliver to collect Arnold. Me and you have something else to be getting on with." She left the room, made her way to Isabella's office and poked her head around the door. "Please don't tell me you're too busy to help me, ma'am."

"I can make time. What do you need?"

Anna told her about Debbie and her accusation against Arnold, then revealed who'd attended the ballet classes.

Isabella's eyebrows rose. "Oh bugger. Is that a surprise to you?"

"Yes. It was there in the police files all along that he's a pervert, and we'd already followed it up, but he denied it and gave us the name of the girl. We went to visit her, and she stated he hadn't touched her. I believed her. But now there's this with Debbie, then there's the connection to ballet. We can't really dismiss it, can we?"

"Absolutely not. I'll take him in for questioning. What are you and Lenny going to be doing?"

Anna explained.

"Right." Isabella blew her cheeks out. "Which one of them do you think did it, if at all?"

"I wouldn't like to say any of them, to be honest. None have given us any inkling they're guilty."

"Did you look into who Mrs Drummond was and whether she has any family members you can question about the class?"

"I left Ollie doing that and nabbed a PC to help him out. I'll pop along to him in a sec and grab any info."

"What sort of person is Arnold? Do I need to be wary?"

"I don't think he'll give you trouble. What I want to do is get some kind of yes or no from the other people on the list so that, by the time you've got him in an interview room, I can let you know how many of them have admitted to being abused. The more we have, the more chance he'll crack under pressure if he knows there are several against him."

"Okay, and you think he'll be at the Dagger?"

"Louise said he wasn't there when they went, and Zoe, the landlady, said he hadn't come back to the pub from his usual afternoon nap, so you might end up finding him at home." Anna went on to describe Zoe so her boss had a visual to go on.

"I was just about to say I'll ring her to ask if he's there, but I don't know whether she's going to tip him off. If he's into younger people, who knows whether he has a thing going with her." Isabella shuddered.

Anna said her goodbyes. She met Lenny in the corridor, and he followed her into the incident room. Anna collected the relevant information from Oliver, printed it out, and had a quick read. It had the names and addresses of the class attendees on it. One name was very interesting, coupled with who else was on there, plus some extra information.

Anna warned Oliver he'd be going out with Isabella soon, then she and Lenny jogged out to the car.

She popped the information sheet in the cup holder and buckled her seat belt. "The more I think about it, the more

I'm inclined to believe that Shannon must have seen something when Mina was dumped, which is why she was killed."

"Or did she know something about the kids in the ballet class because Effie went there? Maybe they *know* she knows and they don't want it to come out. They could have worried that Shannon would buckle and tell the police, which would then lead us to all those who went to the class. I mean, we got lucky with Debbie and found out anyway, but the killer doesn't know that."

"If the killer's even one of them." Anna drove away, wishing she had several clones of herself so she could speak to everyone on the list at the same time.

Debbie had said she hadn't kept in regular contact with any of the people from the class, but that didn't mean the others hadn't. But like Anna had said to Isabella, she couldn't see any of the three people who stood out the most murdering *anyone*. It may well be one of the others, or none of them at all.

She remained inside her head for the rest of the journey, before stopping outside a house and taking a moment. "There are three people I want to speak to. Uniforms can do the others." She rang Karen on the front desk.

"Good afternoon, and what can I do you for today?"

"Can you send uniforms around to eight people? I've got their names and addresses here." Anna told Karen the details and waited for her to write them down, then gave her a brief rundown of why they needed to be spoken to. "So if the PCs can go in gently, please, and, while we want as many victims as possible to say what went on, I don't want any coercion to try and get them to admit anything. If they're not comfortable, back off. They may change their minds and come into the station for a chat later. But these people may be traumatised now they understand exactly what they went through, and I don't want to heap any more hassle on them than is necessary."

"Right, I'll get that done now. Speak soon."

Anna swiped her screen and stared over at the house, thinking about the woman inside. "I honestly can't see it being her, can you?"

"No, but we need to speak to her regardless."

Anna got out of the car. She slipped her phone in her pocket and led the way up the path. Xavier must have been looking out of the window because he opened the door before she could knock. Anna couldn't believe she was about to dump more crap on Elizabeth Isherwood's shoulders, but if she didn't question her she wasn't doing her job properly. She found the woman in the kitchen doing some sewing.

She glanced up at Anna hopefully. "Is there more news? Have you found who did it?"

"Not yet, I'm afraid." Anna sat and waited for Lenny and Xavier to join them. "I really don't want to ask you this question, but I have to. What can you tell me about your relationship, as a child, with Arnold Tanner?"

"I didn't have a relationship with him. I saw him for a year every week when I went to dance class, but he just sat there watching or he took kids down to the toilet. Afterwards, he handed out orange squash that he made in the little kitchen in the community centre."

"Did he ever do anything inappropriate with you?"

Elizabeth put her sewing down. "What?"

"Someone's come forward and made an accusation."

"Oh God, so the Pervert Tanner nickname might be true?"

"Yes."

"I didn't believe he was a paedo. I always felt like an outcast at ballet. Maybe because I was a bit older than the others and they all knew each other before I started, but I never fitted in. The smaller ones used to huddle together and giggle, whisper, all that sort of thing, and I felt so left out."

"Did you ever go to the toilet alone with Arnold?"

Elizabeth paled. "Oh no. No. Please don't tell me . . . Oh, those poor kids."

"So none of them told you he touched them in the loos?" Anna confirmed.

"No." Tears fell. "This is awful. Do you think he might have tried it on with my Mina? That he dressed up as Effie? I'm so confused."

"No, we don't think Arnold killed her, love."

"Who, then?"

"That's what we're about to find out. We'll be in contact as soon as we know, all right?"

Elizabeth wiped her cheeks on her cardigan sleeve. "You've got an idea, haven't you? Oh God, please don't tell me it's someone I know."

Anna gave her a sad smile and left Xavier to comfort her. In the car with Lenny, she sighed and drove away. "Maybe Tanner didn't touch her because she was older. Maybe he knew he couldn't manipulate her into keeping quiet. With the smaller kiddies, they're more likely to think he's just helping them in the toilet. It could have seemed totally normal to those children."

"What I'm struggling with is, if these murders are all linked to Tanner, and one of the people on the list killed Effie and Mina, why go for the women and not the man who abused them? I don't get it."

"I'm struggling with the same thing." Anna put her foot down.

CHAPTER THIRTY-EIGHT

Catcher stood in the Cow Shed and stroked the mask of Effie's face. Now Tanner was dead, maybe the urges would go away. And maybe everything should be burned, all reminders of the crimes erased. The mask, the white dress, the high heels, the outfit Mina had worn at the pub. It was dangerous to keep them now, even though the Cow Shed may never be discovered, hidden as it was at the top of the house. It was never an actual cow shed, just kitted out to look like a barn with the wood-panelled walls and ceiling. The former attic only had one little window, and the door leading to the Shed, built into the landing ceiling, was only visible if you looked hard enough for it. That ceiling was also boarded, the sanded and polished slats in a staggered pattern, an easy disguise. A push-up motion released the lock and the door swung down, as did a set of stairs. Catcher supposed it would be found eventually, should any officers come to have a look. Some bright spark would realise there was no loft hatch and go snooping.

It was too risky to dispose of it all now, though. It would have to wait.

Catcher left the Shed and went downstairs to the sound of the doorbell ringing. What if they'd found the fingerprints on the pegs? Would they tell Catcher, "You have the right to remain silent?" Would there be any point in denying it when the evidence was in the Cow Shed? Catcher would die in prison. Such a shame that for twenty years there had been no deaths, but then, seeing Mina spend so much time with Tanner, something had broken again inside, and the terrible urges had returned.

You should never have acted on them.

Catcher took a deep breath and opened the front door, but no police officer stood there.

Relief.

For now.

CHAPTER THIRTY-NINE

DCI Isabella Edwards liked to get out from behind her desk, and the fact that Anna didn't seem to mind her joining in on the grunt work was half the battle won. Isabella had dreaded taking over from Placket and heading a team that had lost members and gained new ones, but that was better than walking into a job where everybody had been buddies for years and she was the cuckoo in the nest. At least this way she had something in common with Louise, Rupert, and Oliver.

She smiled across at the latter where he sat in the passenger seat. Before they'd left the station, he'd given her an update on what he'd discovered regarding the ballet class. Both of Mrs Drummond's daughters were still alive, and Isabella had arranged for Sergeant Tom Quant to go and speak to them. They'd resided together in an assisted-living flat for the past two years. Whether or not they had any stories to tell about the ballet classes remained to be seen. Their names weren't on the list of dancers, so perhaps they hadn't been the type of kids to want to participate, and it was refreshing that their mother hadn't forced them into it just because she was a dance teacher. Or so Isabella assumed.

"You've been reading up a lot on the Effie case, haven't you?" she said. "What are your thoughts on what went on back then, now that you know she could've possibly been abused by Arnold Tanner? I mean, she went back to him years later as an adult, so I'm wondering about her state of mind. Did she think that what he did to her as a kid was out of love?"

"On paper, it seems like he killed her. Perhaps she was going to expose him and he had to shut her up. But the times don't work — where was Effie from when she entered the Crossing to when Arnold left the Plough during the night? There's no way he has the strength to kill Mina, he's frail, and to be honest I can't see him being the lookalike. Anyway, it's already been established he was still in the pub when Mina left, so, unless Zoe's lying, then he's in the clear."

"What if the murders aren't linked?"

"To say they're not doesn't sit right with me, especially now Shannon's been added to the list. Shannon had a gripe about Effie being with Tanner. Was that because she'd found out what Tanner had been up to when Effie was a kid, or was it like she'd said in her statements, she was jealous of how much time her cousin spent with him? Okay, she might have only said that to the police so it kept Effie's secret safe, but surely if she knew her cousin had been abused she'd have wanted Tanner put away for it."

"Unless Shannon was abused by him herself."

"She's not on the class list, though."

"No, but he could have got hold of her at some other time."

Oliver's phone went off, and he read the screen. "Anna's just messaged me about Elizabeth Isherwood. Apparently she didn't know anything about what Tanner was doing."

"So she doesn't think Elizabeth had anything to do with this?"

"She said she believes her. She's had word from a couple of officers who've already spoken to two others on the list and they've admitted what went on and have agreed to come forward. One is a man."

Isabella slapped the steering wheel, a thrill going through her. "That's brilliant, just what we needed. Three people against Tanner will give us a good amount of ammunition when we speak to him at the station. Not that I'm happy those poor people have been through hell, but now we can really push forward, get them some justice." She parked outside the Dagger, got out and waited for Oliver by the main doors.

He walked over, texting. "Anna's just sent another message. They've arrived at the next address."

"Right then, let's go inside, see if Arnold's there, and, if not, we'll need to make it over to his gaff before word gets out we want to speak to him. We could do without him doing a runner."

They entered the pub side by side through the double doors, and Isabella glanced at the bar to check for any old men. All the stools were filled by younger people.

Isabella led the way to the bar. She eyed the young woman behind it. "Zoe?"

"Yep."

"DCI Edwards." She held up her ID. "Is Arnold Tanner about?"

"He's popular." Zoe rolled her eyes. "But nope. I haven't seen him since about two o'clock. Now will you *please* piss off out of my pub? I'm sick of the sight of coppers in here."

"No need to be rude." Isabella slung her a filthy glare and then exited and got into the car.

Oliver laughed as he joined her. "If looks could kill."

She smiled as both of them belted up, then checked Arnold's address on the notes app in her phone. She put the information into the satnav and drove away.

"He's five doors down from Mina," Oliver said.

"I didn't know that. Is it relevant?"

"He says not, that they never went to each other's houses, yet from what I've gathered from the uploaded PC reports she sat with him quite a few nights in the Dagger. Some said they thought she was using him to buy her drinks and that it was a bit creepy she'd let an old man put his hands on her, but others got the impression they were both lonely and just needed someone to talk to. Anyway, he's almost always at the pub. He goes home between two and four for a kip, then he's back at the bar till after closing time."

"Makes you wonder how he can afford to buy Mina all those drinks plus himself. He's over eighty, so where the hell is he getting his money from? What did he even do for a living?"

"Financial adviser. I poked into him today. I assume he had his head screwed on and knew how to use money to his advantage. Who knows, he might have stocks and shares, dividends, whatever. He could be living off the interest from the money he was left by his parents. Point is, he isn't short of a bob or two."

"Let's pick this up again after we've booked Arnold in." She parked and shut the engine off, glancing across at the house. A light glowed in the room beside the front door, the curtains open behind some grubby nets.

"Maybe he's still napping," Oliver said. "Must be all that lager he drinks."

Isabella chuckled and got out of the car, and they walked up the path together. She leaned across to peer through the window, the nets impeding her view a little. She squinted at the figure sitting in an armchair, a nasty bruise across his throat.

"Oh, Jesus bloody Christ," she muttered and stepped out of the way. "Come and see this while I call it in."

Oliver took her place. "Shit."

While she contacted the station, Oliver gained entry, and Isabella watched him through the window as he checked for signs of life. He glanced at her and shook his head, and her shoulders slumped.

She finished her call with the station and messaged Anna. Oliver met her on the path, closing the door.

"You stay here and mind the house," she said. "I'll start talking to the neighbours."

"Don't hold your breath, ma'am. No one round here wanted to speak about Mina."

"It's still got to be done." Isabella left the garden, opting for the house on the left first. With her expectations low, she raised her fist and knocked.

CHAPTER FORTY

Anna had been relieved to find Nancy and Yvette together. She could kill two birds with one stone and hopefully get one of them to confess. Unless, of course, it was someone else on the list. Or none of them. If that were the case, then they'd have to regroup in a debrief and discuss where to go next. Sadly, forensics took a while to come back, so the results of any DNA found at Mina's house or in Shannon's garden wasn't likely to appear this week.

She glanced at her phone screen.

> **Isabella:** *Tanner's dead in his house. Possible strangulation. Waiting here for officers and SOCOs. Whoever did this will have fluff on their shoes without a doubt. New grey carpet, and it's still shedding. Scarf left on the arm of the chair he's sitting in, but it isn't silk, it's wool.*

> **Anna:** *Thanks for the info. About to chat to Nancy and Yvette. Will ask for alibis. Do you have a timeframe?*

Isabella: *Tanner left Dagger at 2 p.m. and didn't return.*

Anna: *Thank you.*

Anna glanced around casually. The four of them sat in Nancy's kitchen, cups of tea in front of them, officers opposite suspects. Anna wanted to start the conversation off as if neither of them had anything to worry about so it gave them a false sense of security.

"What did you need to speak to us about?" Yvette asked.

She appeared as if she hadn't slept last night, dark circles beneath her eyes, the wrinkles on her face more pronounced. Nancy also seemed tired. She didn't appear as poised and put together as usual.

"It's come to our attention that both of you attended Mrs Drummond's ballet class in the late seventies, early eighties. Effie also attended, and the lookalike must be aware of that in order to have chosen ballet shoes when they took it upon themselves to go out and scare people at night."

"What are you suggesting?" Yvette asked.

"What I'd like to know is what those lessons were like once Arnold Tanner appeared on the scene."

Yvette paled. "He took us to the toilet and made orange squash. He helped Mrs Drummond. There was no *relationship* or anything like that."

"I didn't suggest there was," Anna said.

Nancy stirred a sweetener into her tea. "I see no reason why we shouldn't say something about him now," she said to Yvette. "It's not like anyone would call us dirty like they would have back then. We've got nothing to be ashamed of. Tanner was a pervert, and we were too small to realise it."

"Why didn't you do anything about it when you *did* realise?" Anna asked.

Nancy shrugged. "It didn't seem enough to make a complaint about because he didn't actually have sex with us. Well, he didn't with me, anyway."

Yvette played with her necklace. "I just wanted to put it behind me. I never understood why Effie went back to him later on, though. There's no way I'd want an abuser touching me again once I'd cottoned on to what he actually is."

"He told us he loved all of us, but he must have loved Effie the most." Nancy sighed. "I know he's old and everything, but I think he needs to be held to account."

"We've been told that as children you found the interactions with Mr Tanner something to be giggled about; none of you realised the seriousness of the situation. Was Shannon aware of what was going on?"

Nancy nodded. "After Effie had disappeared and Shannon kept going on and on about it being Arnold who'd made her run away, myself and Yvette made the decision to tell Shannon what the three of us had been through, but we didn't tell her it was Tanner who'd done it and we didn't say other kids were involved either. At the time we didn't want the hassle it would bring if we brought it up to the police, and, as it appeared that he'd switched from children to young women, we didn't feel there was any point in kicking up a fuss. I was married to George at the time."

"Yes, we noted George is also on the list. What was his take on Arnold and Effie being together years later?"

"He didn't have a problem with it," Nancy said.

Anna recalled some of the information about him on the printout. "He died shortly after Effie went missing."

"Yes."

"A heart attack."

"Yes."

"Unusual for someone so young."

Nancy shook her head. "Not when he had a heart defect from birth."

"Was he particularly stressed before he died?"

"No more than usual."

"I just wondered whether something set off the heart attack, that's all." Anna sipped her drink as though she hadn't just baited the woman. She placed the cup back down and adopted a sad face. "It must have been very difficult to lose a husband in your thirties."

"It would be difficult at any age."

"What were his thoughts on being abused by Tanner?"

"The same as all of us. We laughed it off."

"Except I've never found it funny," Yvette said. "Yes, I laughed along with everybody else, but what he did made me feel uncomfortable and sick, and I didn't want to go to the class anymore, but my mum made me so she could go to work while I was there. Mrs Drummond was our next-door neighbour, and I got my lessons for free. We weren't exactly well off."

"Have either of you ever wanted to get back at Tanner?"

Nancy shook her head. "Honestly, it wasn't anything to write home about."

"I disagree," Yvette said. "There have been times I've wanted to walk up to him and ask him what he thought he was playing at. Whenever we go to the pub and I see him, I shudder. Everyone seems to accept he's got wandering hands with the young girls."

"I see him differently," Nancy said. "I probably need therapy because all I can think about is how loved by him I felt as a child, how wanted, when at home my parents were indifferent to my presence. I was sent off to several different after-school classes every week so they didn't have to deal with me. Tanner was the only one who showed he cared. Of course I understand, now that I've had time to think about it, that viewpoint isn't healthy. He didn't love or care about me, he used me. But that said, there's still a bond there. I can't explain it and I don't expect you to understand."

Anna prepared herself for the next question. She nudged Lenny with her knee to let him know she needed him to watch their reactions. "Did either of you go out earlier after Lenny spoke to you regarding Shannon's body? Obviously I can check that with police officers who were here at the time, but it's easier if you tell me."

In other words, you'll have been seen leaving, so don't even think of lying about it.

Yvette pushed her cup away. "I went out for a drive. I ended up at work to make sure things were going smoothly and to tell the other manager I wouldn't be going back in until Monday, then I came back here and had a nap."

"Can you give me times?"

"I'd say between two and four?"

Arnold left the Dagger at two . . . She'd have had enough time to kill him, then nip to work. Anna made a mental note to obtain the CCTV footage to check exactly when Yvette had arrived at Sainsbury's.

Nancy stared down at her cup. "I went for a bike ride just as Yvette came home."

"So, to confirm, four o'clock."

"Yes, about then."

"Where did you go?" Anna asked.

"Down the lane and to the right along the country road there, then I turned around and came back."

No CCTV on that road. Convenient. "How far along did you go?"

"Quite a way. My legs were hurting, which is why I ended up coming home."

"Do you often go out on your bike in a remote area when it's getting dark?"

"I needed time to process Shannon's death. Being out in the fresh air clears my mind."

"What time did you get back from the pub last night?"

"We got a taxi," Yvette said. "I'm sure I got into bed not long after eleven."

Lenny tapped a pen on his notepad, and Anna paused to let him speak.

"When did you get your garden done, Nancy?" he asked.

Her eyebrows lifted. "Excuse me?"

"I thought I'd made myself quite clear enough."

"Years ago," she said.

"Yes, but how many years ago?"

"Twenty?"

"Before or after Effie went missing?"

"I don't remember, I just know it was something George wanted."

Yvette glanced at Nancy as though in shock, then she composed herself.

"Something the matter, Yvette?" Anna asked.

"No, no, I just wasn't aware George wanted the garden. I thought it was Nancy."

"Does it matter who wanted the bloody thing?" Nancy snapped. "I don't see what my garden has got to do with anything anyway."

Ah, the cracks are showing. Anna levelled a stare at Nancy. "Why did what Yvette just said make you prickly?"

"It wasn't what she said, it's this whole situation. I mean, let me think. A body was put in my friend's garden, then that friend is killed in her bath."

"Tanner's been murdered," Anna said.

Nancy remained calm, but her stare chilled Anna.

"You said earlier that he needs to be held to account for what he did to you, but you can't hold a dead person to account for anything." Anna glanced at Yvette. "Are you all right?"

The woman flapped a hand in front of her face, her cheeks red. "I'm fine, it's just all been a bit of a shock, that's all."

Anna returned her attention to Nancy. "Is there anywhere else you went that we should know about other than the bike ride and Tesco? Cedar Avenue perhaps? Forensics will have arrived there by now, and if either of you were in Arnold's house they will find evidence of that — unless, of course, you're extremely forensically aware."

"I've never been to his house, ever!" Yvette all but shrieked. "If he's dead then it's nothing to do with me. It's nothing to do with me that *any* of them are dead. I just want all this to stop. It's getting out of control. After Effie and George died, it was fine for years, and then . . ."

"Carry on," Anna urged.

"I have nothing else to say."

"I think you do, but maybe you're too afraid to say it." Anna smiled at Yvette and then flicked her gaze to Nancy. "Would you have a problem with us looking at your shoes?"

Nancy blinked a few times. "Pardon?"

"Your shoes," Anna said. "I'd like to look at them."

"They're on the rack in the cupboard under the stairs."

Anna left Lenny with the women. The cupboard wasn't the usual type where she'd have to ferret about in the dark. A light sprang on as soon as she opened the door, and the racks were fixed to the wall, the shoes in perfect lines. She took gloves from her pocket and inspected each pair, but they were pristine. No grey fluff in sight. That could have come off on the bike ride back from Cedar Avenue, but, unless one of the residents put Nancy in that street or she was seen by someone else or captured on CCTV, there was no proof the woman had even been there.

Anna returned to her seat. "I see you have ballet shoes on one of the shelves."

Nancy shrugged. "I still dance from time to time."

"Do you do that dancing while dressed as Effie Workington?"

"Very funny."

"I wasn't joking. I genuinely want to know the answer to that question."

"Don't be so ridiculous." Nancy got up and moved to the window to gaze out at her garden lit up by artfully placed spotlights in the trees.

Anna took the opportunity to stare across at Yvette, who shook her head and quickly pointed at the hallway behind them, then made a motion as if using a knife, and finished off with miming having a drink.

Anna mouthed, "The Dagger?" and Yvette nodded. Anna would go with her gut and do what she wanted. She'd leave Nancy thinking she wasn't a suspect, but she'd make sure she understood she was going to be watched.

"Okay, thank you very much for your time, ladies."

Nancy spun round from the window. "Oh. Right."

"I apologise for having to ask such intrusive questions but, as you can understand, another person has been killed in the vicinity of your houses and someone you both knew has also been murdered in his home this afternoon. We'll check your alibis, but I'm sure there's nothing to worry about. In the meantime, if you get spooked or anything, the officers are bound to be in Shannon's house into the late evening, maybe overnight, so just pop there. Thank you for the drink."

She led the way out of the house and got into the car that she'd had to park a short way down the lane due to the police vehicles still there. She waited a few metres from the end with her hazard lights on, and watched in the rear-view mirror.

"She's going to drop Nancy in the shit, isn't she?" Lenny said.

"I hope so. Hang on while I message Steven to get him to put PCs out the front and back to watch for Nancy making a run for it. If she's sensible, she'll stay put, but people in a panic do things they wouldn't ordinarily do."

Anna did that and let Steven know that Yvette would likely be leaving in her car soon but to let her go. Steven responded that officers were in the back garden anyway, working under halogen lights, and SOCOs who needed a break would take it in turns to watch the front.

Anna checked her mirror. Headlights appeared coming down the lane, and Anna switched her hazards off. A car pulled up beside her, and Yvette glanced across. She then overtook Anna's vehicle and drove off onto Rowan. Anna followed. Yvette parked behind the pub under the dark cover of a massive tree, and Anna slid in beside it.

"Let's see what she has to say, shall we?"

CHAPTER FORTY-ONE

2004

Yvette couldn't sleep. She got up for a look out of her front bedroom window and glanced across at Nancy and George's house. The couple stood on the garden path. Nancy gesticulated, her dark-red jumper tinted on one sleeve by the light coming from their hallway. George raised his hands and linked them at the back of his head.

Yvette pushed the window a bit wider, letting in the night air. George and Nancy whispered, and she had to strain to pick up what they were saying.

"I can't believe you've done this," George said. "She's your *friend*."

"It was an accident."

"How can *that* be an accident?"

"Shut up and get her out of the car."

"I'm surprised you were strong enough to put her in it on your own."

That didn't make sense. Didn't he know Nancy had joined the gym a while back? Hadn't he even noticed the muscles in her arms and legs these days? Maybe Nancy had told Yvette the truth after all, that sex was no longer on the table and George had no interest in seeing his wife undressed.

They moved to Nancy's car, and she opened the boot. The little light in there splashed on, and Yvette squinted in order to get a good view, but Nancy and George stood in the way.

"Oh God, I actually thought you were joking," George said. "One of your silly roleplaying games, but she's actually in the *boot*. Shit!"

"I wouldn't joke about something like this."

"You said you were going to the shop for milk."

"I lied. Take her through to the garden."

"The garden?"

"You'll have to dig a fucking hole and bury her."

"What? No! I think we ought to phone the police."

"I'll be arrested."

"You should have thought of that before you did this. Let me check whether she's still breathing. If she is, then you can make out you found her unconscious and brought her home." George bent over and held still for a moment. "There's nothing."

"Of course there isn't, I strangled the silly bitch."

"Why?"

"To stop her from seeing Tanner, that's why. Why the hell did he start having an affair with one of us when he told us all it was over?"

"Because he loved some of us more than others."

"What do you mean by that?"

"Nothing. I need to get her out of this car."

George scooped whoever it was out and turned towards their path. He glanced at Shannon's parents' house, and Yvette dodged behind the curtain just in time as his gaze swept her top windows, too. He walked up the path, and she switched her attention to Nancy, who took out a handbag and then shut the boot quietly and followed him indoors. Legs wobbly with fear, Yvette went downstairs with a view to going around there. Judging by the clothes the person had on, George had carried Effie Workington indoors.

Yvette needed a moment to process this. Had Nancy become jealous that Effie had been given a second chance with Tanner? Had she gone back to the pub to have a word with her instead of buying milk, and things had got out of hand? She'd said it was an accident, but, knowing Nancy, how vindictive she could be, Yvette wasn't so sure about that. Nancy had a sneaky side to her that George didn't seem to notice. Or if he did, he didn't pick her up on it in front of anyone. The fact that he was carrying a dead body for his wife came as no surprise.

Yvette slipped on her flip-flops and went outside. The lights had been switched off at the front of Nancy's house, but the one in the kitchen was on, glowing down the hallway and through the two glass panels. The front door stood ajar, and Yvette pushed it open. She wasn't stupid enough to call out, just in case the Workingtons heard her, so she stepped inside and used her bum to close the door. The click of the lock going into place sounded loud, as did the thud of her heartbeat in her ears.

Yvette moved forward into the kitchen. The back door stood open, and to the left of it, standing against the high fence, was Nancy. She stared at where the patio lay beneath the kitchen window on the right, one hand to her lips, the other tucked under the opposing armpit. She must have glimpsed Yvette from the corner of her eye because she whipped her attention that way, then came indoors and closed the door.

"What the hell are you doing creeping into my house? You don't just walk in like that," Nancy said.

"I saw George taking Effie out of the boot. What the fucking hell's going on?"

"She pissed me off, and I walloped her one. I strangled her, and she's dead, but I've told George it was an accident."

Yvette stared at her for a moment, trying to take that in. "You can't accidentally strangle someone. You must have had the intention of doing it, otherwise it wouldn't have happened. Did you even go and get milk?"

"Of course not."

"So going after Effie was intentional? What did you do, go back to the pub? Where did this happen?"

"If you remember, Shannon wouldn't come with us after the row. So I went back and waited just before Cooper's Crossing behind some trees because I knew Shannon and Effie would walk that way. After Shannon went off, I saw to Effie."

Cold fear swept through Yvette. "Why kill her?"

"You know how I feel about Tanner. When he stopped seeing all of us, that was okay because it meant he hadn't picked anyone else, and then we find out Effie had been seeing him. She never said a word to us. I couldn't stand it."

"Should he be doing that?"

"What? Who?"

"George. The heavy work. With his heart."

"I don't give a bloody *shit* whether he should or he shouldn't."

"Why not? I thought you loved him?"

"Things change."

"There's something wrong with you if you've killed Effie over some old pervert who touched children when you've got a lovely husband like George."

"Tanner isn't a pervert, he loved us."

"No, he didn't. He used us to get off, nothing more. He probably realised it was dangerous to fiddle with children so he moved on to young women. Who knows whether Effie was the first. Someone already suggested tonight that he has a few on the go."

"I had no idea he'd been cheating on Helen, and the shock of it, especially it being Effie — I saw red."

"What you should be seeing is a fucking counsellor. To get so upset that your abuser didn't pick you? You need help."

George's face popped up at the kitchen window, and Yvette jumped. He spotted her, his eyes going wide, then he glanced at Nancy.

"Why did you have to come here and be nosy?" she whispered at Yvette. "You're involved now. You saw him carry the body and you didn't do anything about it except come here and ask questions. The least you can do is help us."

"I don't want to go near a dead body!"

"She doesn't look dead, she just looks asleep."

"I think you should phone the police and say it was self-defence. Tell them about Tanner and say she punched you or something so you strangled her to try and get it to stop. You put your hands around her throat to push her off you and it killed her."

"I don't have any defensive wounds. And they're going to know I used a scarf. I can hardly be defending myself then, can I? No, we're going to bury her."

"In your garden, with her aunt and uncle living next door? And how are we going to keep this from Shannon?"

"She's the last person we need to tell. She's obsessed with Effie and will go to the police if she finds out what I did."

"And what about George? You know what he's like, he's got a conscience on him." Yvette was desperate to show Nancy the pitfalls of going ahead with the burial. It was better to confess now. "What if he feels guilty later down the line and tells the police?"

"He won't have the chance to."

Nancy pointed a creepy stare at Yvette, who backed away and then turned to run down the hallway. Nancy caught up with her and gripped her hair, yanking her back into the kitchen and twisting her around so she faced the window, where George looked through at her. He pleaded with his eyes for her to do what Nancy said — was he afraid of her? — but could she live with herself for hiding such a bloody scary secret? The police were bound to speak to everyone who'd been in the Plough tonight. Could she act calm and lie, saying she'd gone to bed as soon as she'd got home and slept straight through?

"You're going to do as you're told, and you're going to keep your mouth shut," Nancy snarled in her ear from behind, sounding unhinged. "You haven't got a pot to piss in, so I'm going to do you a favour. I'm going to give you some money, I've got a wedge coming my way, and it's going to pay for you to pretend you didn't see a thing here. There'll be enough to clear your debts and buy yourself some of those rings you keep gawping at in the jeweller's shop. Maybe even a necklace or two. You'd have no worries apart from this secret then."

Yvette was tempted to take the offer. She'd been struggling on her wages as a cashier in Sainsbury's. Her aim was to become a manager one day, but she had to work her way up the ladder first. She didn't have a mortgage, thank goodness, as her parents had let her live here rent-free, but she *had* got behind on the electric bill and a couple of her credit cards. What Nancy offered might end her sleepless nights, but then she might exchange those she spent worrying about her debt for ones where she'd worry about the body in the garden. She could go to prison just for knowing what had gone on here and not informing the police.

"And if you still don't think you can do it," Nancy hissed, "then I'll have no trouble strangling *you* either."

Nancy meant it, too, and it hurt that her friend could be so resolute about killing her. Nancy had always been somewhat emotionally removed, a strange little girl who'd grown up into a strange thirty-something woman, although she did a good job of pretending to be normal.

But she wasn't.

Yvette glanced outside at George, who wiped his forehead with the back of his gloved hand. He shook his head sadly, then bent to continue digging, or so Yvette assumed.

"I mean it," Nancy said. "I'll take you upstairs right now and strangle the fuck out of you and then we'll dump *your* body in the same hole with Effie. It's no skin off my nose. We go back a long way, me and you. We're tight. We promised to have each other's backs."

"Okay, *okay*."

Nancy let her hair go and took hold of Yvette's arm to guide her towards the back door, and shoved her outside. Yvette turned and stared, first at George standing in the light coming from the kitchen window, then down at the patio, where he'd removed eight slabs and placed them in a pile beside the waste-water pipe. Then she flipped her attention to the body lying behind him, the front facing the fence. If the Workingtons got out of bed and looked outside, they wouldn't be able to see Effie, just the slab removal. They'd think George had begun work on their Japanese garden that Nancy kept banging on about.

They'd think it was odd at this time of night, though. When it comes out that Effie's missing, they'll remember him digging a grave-shaped hole. They'll tell the police. Oh God.

The whole idea of the three of them being spotted frightened Yvette to death. The alternative was for her to run, to get in her car and go to a police station, because, much as she wasn't that fond of Effie and her tarty ways, she hadn't deserved this. She shouldn't be shoved underground and covered over.

Yvette didn't pick up another shovel and help George. Instead, she left that to Nancy and moved to sit by Effie and hold her hand. She cried quietly for a long time.

Unable to stand being here any longer, Yvette stood. "I-I'll just go home and pretend I never saw anything."

"That's fine by me," Nancy said. "But remember what I said."

Yvette staggered past George and Nancy, scooted into the house and opened the front door. She ran home, wanting to ring her parents to ask them if she could go to Spain for a while, but wouldn't it look suspicious if she disappeared the day after Effie was reported missing? Like *she'd* killed her?

She was going to have to stay home for at least a week, but after that she was flying to Mum and Dad's. They'd pop the fare in her bank.

CHAPTER FORTY-TWO

"So do you understand why I never said anything?" Yvette asked in the back seat, glad of the darkness in the car park. "The emails started a little while after that — she'd created an account for me, then gave me the log-in details. And once, we had a horrible conversation where Nancy took the piss out me for caring about what Effie's parents and Shannon were going through. She said I cared too much about things I shouldn't give a shit about, like little slappers who'd tarted themselves out to Tanner. And that's when she started calling me Care Bear, whispering it when we were in company. It got me so angry because she was mocking me. We had another row, and I started crying, so she took this white fabric out of a bag and wiped my face with it, the tears and snot, and she laughed and told me it was Effie's dress and, if I thought I could get her into trouble by grassing on her, I'd be implicated because a part of me was on the material. She brought it up regularly on other emails after that. About three weeks after Effie was buried, George was rushed to hospital. They said he died of a heart attack. It must have been all the stress. *She* did that to him."

"Did you end up visiting your parents?"

"No, Nancy threatened me, said if I went I might not come back, so if I was thinking about doing that I'd better think again."

"What threat did she make?"

"To kill me next. I honestly believe she'd have put a hit out on me."

"We're going to have to ask you to go over this again at the station," Anna said. "You'll be arrested, you know that, don't you?"

Yvette nodded, frightened by the future but so tired of the past being brought up by Nancy in the present. She'd needed to come clean and, now she had, a weight lifted. "I've had enough. As soon as I got the email saying she'd killed Mina, when I saw Nancy, that mad look in her eye, I realised she was spiralling again. She has serious mental health issues but she's able to disguise it. She's very good at masking. And that reminds me, there's something else you need to know."

"What is it?"

"She calls herself the Cow Catcher and named this creepy little room the Cow Shed. She thought Effie was a cow for being with Tanner again, and over the years she kept telling me she'd made this shed. Then she admitted she was Effie's ghost, but the ballet shoes you saw in her cupboard under the stairs, they're not the ones she uses when she goes out as Effie."

"She must wear a wig then, because Nancy's got short black hair."

"She actually wears *Effie's* hair. It's attached to a woolly hat that has been glued to a cast of Effie's face and then her skin was put over it. Her skin. Her face. *Her actual face.* She must have created the mask before they buried her."

Anna recoiled but recovered quickly. "Good God."

* * *

Anna would have to find out from Nancy why she'd left her in Shannon's garden instead of burying her. It had become obvious partway through Yvette's story as to why Nancy had gone after Mina. The poor girl had accepted drinks from Tanner and paid a hefty price. She was dead because of Nancy's jealousy.

"Where's the shed?" Anna asked.

"In her loft. She forced me up there once. She hangs the dress in a wardrobe." Yvette explained how to gain access to it. "Underneath the dress on this weird podium are the high-heeled shoes Effie had on that night. On the floor next to it are the other ballet shoes. She hung Effie's face mask on the wall. I have no idea why she kept going out and pretending to be her. I think her mind's broken." She wiped her cheeks with her palms. "And I think Tanner's death might be my fault. I told Nancy to get help and talk about what he'd done. She must have gone over there to talk to *him*."

"Do you know if there's any reason why she used a scarf to kill them all?"

Yvette shook her head. "I just know that I've kept this to myself for twenty years and it's time I paid for my part in it."

"Do you still have the emails?"

"I delete them after reading, but I expect you could find them somewhere. I'll give you the address and the log-in details." She appeared so tired, yet at the same time relieved to have got this off her chest. "Even living in prison having told the truth will be better than living in this house and keeping secrets." She nodded as if to confirm that to herself. "It won't stop the guilt or the nightmares, but I've got used to those."

"Nancy won't have a hold over you now."

"I hate that Japanese garden," Yvette said. "Because all that prettiness hides something so horrific under that pea shingle. Nancy and George got the garden done after Effie had gone missing, and, now I come to think about it, she kept talking about getting that bloody thing done for weeks before that night. She'd spoken to Shannon's mum and dad about it out the front, and I've got to wonder whether she planned to kill Effie all along." She sighed. "I'm just glad it's all over."

"In some ways it's over, love, but in others this is only the beginning for you."

Anna meant the constant interviews, being remanded or bailed, whichever she was granted, and the court case if Nancy pleaded not guilty. Yvette had concealed knowledge of a crime, and a jury may even see her as an accessory to one because she'd sat there while George and Nancy had dug the hole. But she might get lucky and twelve compassionate people may understand her fear and why she'd kept it quiet, despite taking the hush money and gifts.

But there was time enough to discuss that later. For now, they'd wait for a couple of PCs to come and collect Yvette. After that, they'd go back to the lane, along with backup, and speak to Nancy.

CHAPTER FORTY-THREE

She'd expected the knock on the front door, although she thought it would've been Yvette coming to discuss the latest visit after Anna and Lenny had gone. But the officers themselves stood on the doorstep with two men in uniform. She knew then that Yvette had finally caved in. It was obvious because of the amount of time that had passed since the detectives had left and then reappeared. Enough time for Care Bear to tell a little story. The one person Nancy had governed for years had now taken the controller and played the game on her own terms. Even if it meant going to prison.

In a way, Nancy was glad it was all over.

No more pretending.

She turned her back on the people at the door and walked through to her kitchen. Sat at the island and waited for them to join her.

"We have reason to believe that there's a body in your back garden and you have something called a Cow Shed in your loft," Anna said. "We're happy to wait for a warrant."

Nancy could make them wait. Mess them about. Continue to take the reins. But she wouldn't. "You may as well look now. You're going to see it in the end anyway." There was no point in being obstructive, not when she planned to plead insanity. She'd need Anna's sympathy now, not her disdain. From here on out, she needed all the help she could get. "I did it because the voices told me to."

There had been no voices, just the urges, but that was the route she was going to take.

Anna sighed and signalled for the uniforms to go upstairs, then she turned back and faced Nancy. "Well?"

CHAPTER FORTY-FOUR

2004

If George hadn't stopped having sex with her, she would never have followed him, but she had, and what she saw through a crack in Tanner's bedroom doorway not only sickened her to her stomach but scored a deep ache of hurt in her heart.

When Tanner had stopped coming to the dance classes, as far as she knew, none of them had been close enough to the man for him to touch them again. Nancy would go out with her mum and dad and see him in the supermarket or in town, and as she'd grown older she'd seen him in the pub, but he'd never acknowledged her. And, so George had said, he'd never acknowledged him either.

He'd lied.

George, naked, on all fours with Tanner behind him on the double bed, also naked. Beneath George lay Effie, her legs spread wide, her fingertips between them. The treasonous part of Nancy was turned on, but the other part couldn't comprehend what she was seeing. It was the betrayal from all three of them. Tanner had promised them he'd never touch any of them again, that they were all special, and then he'd left the class for good. George had promised to be loyal to her till death do they part, and at this second he was being the most disloyal he could ever be. And Effie had said that, if Tanner ever approached her, she'd tell him where to sling his hook.

Nancy backed away slowly, quietly, retreating down the stairs to the unlocked back door. She'd entered that way via an alley after seeing George go in through the front door. She'd stupidly thought he'd gone there to talk. But this? *This* . . . ?

She stumbled along the alley and back round into the street to get in her car. Her mind spun with scenarios of revenge, and they grew and grew until the urge to act them out was so strong she wasn't going to be able to ignore them if she stayed put. She drove home and, to calm herself, got ready to go out that night.

George was supposed to be at the supermarket picking up a few bits for breakfast in the morning, a hangover fry-up. He'd likely tell her the shop was packed, there was a queue, and he got caught in a traffic snarl-up on the way home. All plausible reasons why he'd been gone for over an hour.

How long had he been doing this? How many lies had he told her? How many traffic jams had he supposedly sat in?

She showered, dressed, styled her hair, and put on her make-up, and he *still* wasn't back. Then the sound of his key going in the lock churned her stomach, but she smiled at him as he entered the bedroom, kissing her on the cheek with the lips that he'd likely kissed Tanner and Effie with, the foulness of that making her want to scream. He blamed the traffic, then he was gone, into the bathroom, the shower water tinkling. A hard ball of hurt unfurled and spread through her body until all of her skin was hot with it. Her cheeks burned the most, humiliation living there. She used a tissue from the box on her vanity table to catch the tears before they fell and ruined her mascara.

They were going to pay for this, George and Effie, but Tanner held such a big place in her affections she couldn't bring herself to teach him a lesson. That may change in the years to come, but for now she'd go downstairs and wait for her husband, and then for the taxi that was coming to pick them and Yvette up to take them to the Plough. After that, she'd see how the night unfolded, and, if she could put at least one of her plans in place, if it was safe to do it, then she would.

* * *

She confronted George on an extremely balmy day when the temperature had risen along with most people's tempers. The end of June was far too warm compared to the cooler and more showery start to the month, and Nancy believed that heat was one of the factors sending her into the living room to let him know she was aware of what had been going on. She couldn't keep it to herself any longer. She'd used him to bury the body and revamp the garden, and now he was surplus to requirements.

"I suppose you deciding to help hide Effie's body and lie to the police about my alibi, saying I was home, was because you felt guilty about what you've been doing with Tanner and Effie." She held a hand up to stop him from opening his mouth and spewing out a big fat lie. She couldn't bear to hear it. "Don't. Just let me speak. I saw all three of you. At Tanner's. And then Effie died, so that was one of your lovers out of the equation, and I thought it would make you stop and think, but *no*, I saw you and Tanner, several times in the past fortnight, actually, when you were supposed to be going to work or to collect stuff for the garden, but you stopped off at Tanner's first. What's it like to have an old man's cock in your arse?"

"Don't make it sound disgusting."

"You didn't think to ask me to join in your sex games, you chose Effie instead."

"I didn't *choose* her."

"So how did it even come about?"

"She turned up when I was there one day. He leaves the back door open for her so she can just walk in."

"That explains how *I* could just walk in, then." Tears stung, but she was damned if she'd let them fall. "It was vile."

"I didn't mean—"

"Of course you meant it, otherwise you wouldn't have done it."

He shook his head, one of his little admonishments that she always had to get her words in first. "That wasn't what I was going to say."

"What was it then, that you didn't mean for me to find out?"

"Yes."

"So you were going to keep on behind my back for as long as you could?"

"I'm sorry, I love him."

"What about me?"

"I love you, too, just not in that way anymore."

She was going to have to get him riled up. Panic him. There was no way she could kill him because the spouse was always under the spotlight. She had to remain as clean as a whistle because of Effie. Any poking around this house might mean the police found certain things. "You're fucking gross. A filthy gay bastard."

"Now hang on a minute . . ."

"Or what? Are you going to tell me off for gay-bashing? Are you going to raise your fist to me like your dad does to your mum, so I'll be scared and keep my mouth shut? Because believe me, that's not going to work. I've got no problem with going outside right now and knocking on those doors and telling our neighbours you're bent, then getting in the car and going to the Plough and telling everyone there, and then the Dagger, and then all the pubs in the city . . ."

He took a deep breath, his cheeks flushing. "Stop it."

"No, I won't stop it. What will Mummy and Daddy say when they find out what their son does with his dick? God, your mum's going to have a bloody fit when she finds out, and your dad's not going to be able to show his face in the Conservative Club again, is he? You'll be their nasty disgrace; they may even move away because of the shame of it. That's why you didn't tell them about Tanner as a kid, isn't it? You don't want them looking down on you. Being ashamed. Disappointed. Ah, they're going to be disappointed now, all right, the homophobic bastards."

She moved towards the small table as if to pick up the phone. He clutched his neck, then gripped one of his wrists as though the pain was there instead of his chest. She didn't understand how heart attacks worked, just that she so desperately wanted one to happen. He closed his eyes, pain etched on his face, and she watched him struggling to breathe through the agony. When his eyes snapped open and he wheezed out the word "help", she walked into the kitchen and made herself a nice cup of tea.

* * *

She'd phoned for an ambulance half an hour later when he was a bit green and his lips had turned purple. Oh, and he'd gone unconscious. She claimed to have been sitting in the kitchen doing a crossword and happened to find him collapsed on the living room floor. If he came round and said she'd just left him there, she'd convince him he'd imagined it. All that trauma of his chest hurting, he'd have panicked. Anyway, these thoughts could all be moot. Hopefully it would be too late to save him, and, if it wasn't, she could always try again.

She paced the corridor outside the ward George had been assigned to, except he wasn't there. He was having an operation. One of the nurses came towards her with a clipboard, and imparted the wonderful news that George was dead. Nancy went down to her knees, her face in her hands, and screamed.

She was now a wealthy woman, his life insurance would see to that.

CHAPTER FORTY-FIVE

Nancy had been taken down to the station, leaving Anna and Lenny and the two PCs in the house. A cadaver dog had been brought in and had barked to alert that a body was below the ground. Steven had arrived, and he was in the loft and his team in the back garden, removing the pea shingle layer by layer. They'd do the same with the earth beneath, a painstaking job, until they reached Effie's skeleton. The dig team worked under halogen lights, a tent erected over where the old patio used to be, the flaps parted so the goings-on could be viewed from the back door.

Anna would speak to Nancy tomorrow. Of course, overtime had been on the cards for herself and Lenny as soon as they'd gone out to speak to Nancy and Yvette, but the others in her team had gone home. Anna envied them their relaxation time. She'd really had enough of people today and needed to be alone.

On the landing, she stared up and could see how well the Cow Shed door had been disguised. No wonder the officers who'd gone through this house had missed it on the day Shannon had discovered Mina's body. A set of retractable wooden steps with handrails either side led up there, and, while they appeared sturdy enough, she was still reticent about being in a loft. She'd never liked them. Still, she wanted to see this Cow Shed for herself.

Her forensic suit and booties rustled as she climbed, her hands already sweating beneath her gloves. She poked her head through the hatch, amazed at how this area had been made to look like the interior of a barn. It even smelled like one. Anna went the rest of the way up and made her way over three evidence steps.

Steven stood nearby, swabbing a small windowsill. "That mask is a bit creepy, isn't it?"

Anna glanced to the left, where Effie Workington's face stared back at her, but without eyes. "You can see why people thought it was really Effie, can't you?"

"Yep."

Anna opened the cupboard. Steven came over to stand beside her. They stared at a white dress hanging from a metal pole, and beneath it, on a podium in a glass case, a pair of high-heeled shoes. On the floor beside it, ballet shoes with long ribbons, and next to that, a neat pile of clothing.

A pink leather jacket. Dark-blue skirt. White blouse.

"Makes me wonder why Mina's shoes aren't here, the red heels, when Effie's are," Anna said.

"Hmm. Has Nancy not gone into detail yet about how she got the body from Mina's house to Shannon's garden?"

"No, that's to come in the interview tomorrow, if she deigns to tell us. She had a car in the past, which she used to transport Effie, but switched to a pushbike at some point."

"She likely had her hands full with Mina and couldn't carry the shoes. Or maybe she just didn't want them."

"Her hands weren't too full to carry the clothes, though." Anna recalled what Yvette had said. "She brought Effie here as well as her handbag but left Mina's behind in Cedar Avenue, so she's clearly not the type to follow the same pattern with each murder."

"Well, that's obvious because she killed her husband in a roundabout way, and she didn't take any of Tanner's possessions. It seems to me she killed who she needed to kill. Maybe she took Mina's clothes to make it look like she'd gone missing on the way home from the pub, to throw us off the scent. Did you ask her why she pegged her hair to the line?"

"No, that's another one for tomorrow. I'm actually wondering whether she's all there up top, so I asked for a mental health assessment this evening. I don't want to risk interviewing someone who needs to be handled by a different professional."

"You wouldn't be as gentle."

"No."

Anna glanced around. "This can't be the only part of the loft — the roof is so much bigger from the outside. It's like she sectioned this bit off so it's the size of a large garden shed."

Steven moved along a little and pressed the wall at various intervals. A thin, narrow door opened. Anna scooted over. Beyond, a normal loft stuffed with boxes, furniture, black bags, and the usual paraphernalia humans stored and didn't look at again for years. There was no system to the way it had been packed together. In fact, it was pretty chaotic.

"That's all going to have to be gone through just in case," Anna said. "Weird how her house is so clean and tidy, the same with the Cow Shed, and yet this area's a nightmare."

Steven nodded. "I could be airy-fairy and say the tidiness is the side of herself she presents to the world and the chaos is what's inside her head, but then you'd laugh and say I'm a dickhead, so I won't bother."

"I haven't got the energy to laugh at you, and I'd bet a therapist would say you're right anyway. It's sad, really, how the abuse affected her." Anna walked backwards down the first few steps. "I'll leave you to it."

"Cheers. Can you send Marty up to give me a hand? Now the loft's been opened up, there's a lot more work to do up here than I thought."

She nodded and went downstairs, where she found Marty standing at the back doorway, observing what was going on in the tent.

"You're wanted in the Cow Shed," she said.

Marty frowned. "The what?"

Anna smiled. "The loft. It isn't just a small one anymore."

CHAPTER FORTY-SIX

The next morning, Anna had chosen the soft interview room in order to put Nancy more at ease. She felt she'd get further with the woman if they sat on comfy sofas rather than the hard chairs with a table between them. Unobtrusive cameras flashed red in the corners by the ceiling. Nancy knew she was being recorded and didn't seem fazed. She'd mentioned being disappointed by the mental health assessment results as she'd been declared fit to interview. Apparently, the voices had been talking to her again and she really thought she should be sent to a hospital for proper checks. The psychologist who'd assessed Nancy had suggested she was using the voices as a means to get a more lenient sentence because she showed no signs of delusion or obvious auditory issues. No pauses to listen to those so-called voices. Of course, it couldn't be proved that she *wasn't* hearing things in her head, but for now Anna had the green light to go ahead.

Nancy's solicitor, Dick Warburton, a nice bloke Anna got along with, sat behind Nancy's sofa out of the way, as per his client's instructions. Maybe she wanted to create the illusion that she, Anna, and Lenny were having a friendly chat rather than her being interviewed about murder. Anna was inclined to let the woman have her own way for now.

So far, she'd gone back over what she'd done to Effie, George, Shannon, and then Tanner, but she hadn't touched on Mina. Maybe because she felt guilty about that one? She'd opened up about how she'd manipulated Yvette, sending emails over the years to always remind her of what she'd been a part of. To give Nancy her due, she'd said Yvette had never wanted to be a part of this. She was someone Nancy enjoyed playing around with and controlling. She'd enjoying watching her childhood friend being so frightened and nervous around her. While it was commendable that Nancy had tried to help get Yvette less prison time with that statement, what she didn't know was that Yvette had already admitted to taking the money and the gifts, and that her greed and desperation for cash had played a big part in her decision-making, not just the fear Nancy had inspired.

But she wasn't willing to take the second payment for Mina.

This morning, the fingerprint analysis had come back from the pegs in Mina's garden. They matched Nancy's, so, even if she wasn't being forthcoming and spewing all the beans, there would have been some questions to answer as to how her prints had come to be there. Why she herself had been there.

"Why did you peg your hair up on Mina's washing line? Or should that be Effie's hair?" Anna asked.

Nancy leaned back a bit and smiled, cradling her cup in her lap. It really was as if she was sitting in her living room entertaining friends. That in itself was strange. Most people, even though they'd confessed to murder, were still jittery and uneasy at being in a police station, even if it was the soft interview room, but maybe Nancy did have a serious mental condition, after all, and so she truly believed there was nothing to worry about here.

"The voices told me they were sick of me always being hung out to dry. They made me peg the hair on the line to prove their point, to hammer home what they were saying."

"Okay . . ." Anna wasn't quite sure how to answer that. It sounded reasonable enough, but she was more inclined to believe it wasn't symbolism Nancy was trying to get across to Mina but pure weirdness to frighten her when she'd parted the curtains. "I'd like to touch on a few points regarding Mina. We know you were sitting by the jukebox and you saw her speaking to Tanner on the night of her death and putting her head on his shoulder. Is that what set you off?"

"Of course it was. Not her, exactly, because it wasn't her fault, it was him. I was sitting there, ready to be with him, yet he'd chosen her over me. He'd done that with Effie and George, so doing it again right in front of me drove me mad. He must have been trying to get in Mina's knickers. Why else would he have plied her with drinks? The voices said if I got rid of her then he wouldn't be able to have sex with her and he'd finally pick me."

This was a very childlike way of looking at it, but Anna supposed Nancy *was* locked in childhood in some respects. Her thought processes had been shaped from such a young age with regards to relationships, and to her it was simple. If she was available, then why would Tanner want anybody else? What she probably didn't want to face was that he didn't fancy her now she was older. Nancy struck Anna as the vain type, someone who felt she was highly attractive. Tanner's behaviour had dented her ego.

"So what did you do after you finished your dinner in the Dagger on Monday night?"

"I got my bike and went home. I put the bike in the garden and watched telly for a bit, trying to take my mind off everything, but the urge was really bad and so I went into the Cow Shed and got Effie's stuff on."

"Are those her ballet shoes?"

"No, they're my old ones."

"Carry on."

"I went out via the back. Walked across the grass to Rowan. Then I ran through the estate, taking the alleys until I got to the one opposite the Dagger. I didn't know whether Mina would still be in the pub or not, but I waited anyway. It was about eleven when she came out. She saw me in the alley and screeched a bit, and I ran past her, banged into her with my elbow — I wanted to hurt her, shit her up. I went down the ginnel, across the park, and stood outside Tanner's house. It was dark in there, and I knew he'd be at the pub until the last knockings anyway. I was going to go in through the back door and wait for him, ask him to love me, but then one of the neighbours came back in their car. They told me to fuck off or they'd call the police."

"What did you do then?"

"I waited for them to go back indoors and then legged it down the side of Mina's house. It was like I knew what I was going to do to her, even though I hadn't planned it. Like the plan was already in my head but I don't remember making it. I think it was the voices that planned it all."

Anna resisted rolling her eyes and looking at Lenny. "You say voices. How many are there?"

"Two. One sounds like me, but I don't know who the other one is. It's a woman, though."

"What happened then?"

Nancy went through her story, which corroborated the one Molly Griffin had heard.

"When you ran off, Mina went back home and phoned her mother," Anna said. "What were you doing at this point?"

"I was going to wait for Tanner. I was going to leave her alone and speak to him instead. But the voice, the one that doesn't sound like me, he said Tanner would never want me even if I got rid of Mina."

"He?" Anna queried. "But you said the second voice is a woman's."

"I meant to say *she*."

"Right . . ." *What a load of crap.* "How did you feel about the voice saying that?"

"It made me upset, and I wanted to prove a point that the voice was wrong, so I marched up Mina's front garden path and I leaned close to the front door so she could see me through the glass. And then I went to stand in front of her living room window. She stared out and saw me there, and I could see by her face that she was angry and not scared anymore. I climbed over the little fence between the gardens and hid behind it. I watched her through a gap in the slats, and she came out and looked around, and then she went down the side of her house, probably to see if I was in the back garden again. I jumped over the fence and waited inside her house for her come back in."

So that explained why there was no forced entry, plus it answered the question of whether Mina had let her killer in. She had in a way, but not intentionally, poor girl.

Nancy drank some of her coffee, draping one leg over her knee. She leaned her head back on the sofa and closed her eyes, both hands wrapped around her cup. "She saw me there and screeched, rushing towards me. I ducked and ran for the front door, but she grabbed the back of the dress and pulled me. I spun round and punched her, and she lifted her arms to take my mask off. Her elbow caught a vase of flowers, and it smashed on the floor. I was worried about the noise carrying, so I used my foot to close the door behind me. I told her I was going to kill her. I was that angry and I knew I was going to do it. She ran upstairs, shouted something like, 'Please don't!' but I was past it. I didn't care anymore."

"Officers have been able to guess what went on in the bedroom based on the state it was left in, but a guess isn't as good as having the facts, so could you please talk us through it?"

Nancy opened her eyes and stared at nothing. "She was just closing the door as I got to the landing, so I pushed it and shoved her backwards. She fell on the bed. There were clothes all around, on the floor, everywhere, such a bloody mess, like she'd changed a few times before deciding what to wear earlier on. There's no need for it. I grabbed a scarf and wrapped it around her neck, pinned her arms down with my knees because she tried to slap me and scratch me. I wrapped the scarf round a couple of times really tight and then I flipped her over like I did with Effie, put my knee in her back. I tied a knot at the bottom of her neck, then pulled so it strangled her. It was the scarf, not me."

Lenny frowned. "But the scarf couldn't have killed her on its own, Nancy. You're saying it as if you're not to blame, when if you weren't pulling the scarf it wouldn't have cut off her air supply. Why did you choose a scarf?"

"Because it worked with Effie, I didn't see any reason to use anything else. I mean, I couldn't do it with George because I couldn't let anybody know that I'd basically killed him. There's no dark menace in my childhood that relates to scarves if that's what you're thinking."

Anna flexed her fingers. "What clothes was Mina wearing when you entered her home?"

"The ones she had on in the pub, except she'd taken her leather jacket off and her shoes, so she just had the blouse and skirt."

"Did you change her outfit after she was dead?"

"No, I stopped strangling her and made her dress herself. The voices told me I couldn't carry her over my shoulder in the clothes she'd had on in the Dagger because someone might recognise them, so it was better that she had dark stuff on."

"Someone seeing you carry her would have been cause for concern full stop, never mind what clothes she had on."

Nancy ignored that. "She was crying and kept whispering, begging me to leave her alone, but it was too late by that point. And besides, I couldn't breathe under the mask and I'd taken it off for a minute and she saw who I was."

"So you killed her after she'd got dressed."

"Yes."

"And then what did you do?"

"I made sure she wasn't breathing. And I folded up the pub clothes. I thought if they weren't left behind, the police would think she'd gone missing when she walked home. That had worked with Effie."

"But they'd know she got home because her red shoes were downstairs."

Nancy didn't appear to want to acknowledge she'd made a mistake. "I found the leather jacket and put the pub clothes in the bag, put a black coat on Mina, and carried her out the back way down the alley. In the end I popped out behind the shops. She was getting heavy by that point, think it was about a quarter of a mile, but I stopped a few times to catch my breath and managed to get her into Shannon's garden."

"Why did you once give us the impression that you didn't really know Effie? You said you'd known her as a child, and you mentioned seeing her in the pub, but you knew her much more than how you portrayed it. Surely when I said that we were looking into her case you'd realise we'd find out you went to ballet together."

"If you remember, I asked you whether you should be concentrating on Mina instead."

"And you thought that would be enough to make me do that? For me to drop the Effie connection?"

Nancy shrugged.

"I'm sure you said similar to us when we asked about Elizabeth Isherwood, that you only knew her because she ran a fabric stall, yet she'd also been in the ballet class."

"But she wasn't part of our group, she wasn't one of us. She never went to the toilet with Tanner."

"Do you have any remorse for what you've done?"

Nancy shook her head. "Tanner hurt me so much. When I found George and Effie with him, something broke. It was awful, like everything I'd ever known had been a lie. Even though I was married, I'd always thought about Tanner. When Shannon blurted out in the pub that he was seeing Effie, I had to act shocked, like I didn't already know what had been going on. George acted the same way, and I remember looking at him and thinking, *You absolute bastard, you're pretending you haven't been fucking them.* I had so much hate for them, and I had to get out of there. We'd got a taxi into Rowan with Yvette, and I said to them I wanted to go home. The argument was still going on, Tanner was denying everything, and Effie was upset because he wouldn't publicly admit he was seeing her. Shannon was shouting that he was a user and his wife was going to find out and he'd probably split up with Effie anyway. It was all so much noise. We got a taxi and left Effie and Shannon there. And then when I was at home the anger got worse, and I wanted to tell George then that I knew what he'd done, but I didn't, I waited. You know the rest."

"How do you feel now Tanner's gone?"

"I should have killed him right at the start. Everything felt better after he died."

"So why didn't you just go for him?"

"Because I wanted him to love me again."

Anna sighed. She had one more query she wanted to make, then she'd put in a request for Nancy to be placed on remand as she felt she was a danger to the public. She could go after the other people in the ballet class, and Anna didn't want that on her conscience.

"Do you know anyone who drives a blue Mini?" Anna already knew the answer. Oliver had found a link between a Mini and someone who worked at the same newspaper as Nancy. It was hardly a coincidence, but Anna wanted Nancy to admit to what she'd done.

"Barry Hardy at the newspaper. I sent him an anonymous tip about Mina. I wanted to make sure Tanner heard about her dying and then he'd remember Effie had died, too, and he'd been involved with both of them, so he'd finally realise he was upsetting me."

Anna didn't understand how he was supposed to have known that; he wasn't bloody psychic. "Why did you kill Shannon?"

"She saw me outside."

"When?"

"The night she died. I was Effie. I was dancing out the back by the oak trees, and I spotted her at the window. I got scared she'd phone the police."

"How did you get into her house?"

"We all have each other's spare keys."

"I'm going to finish the interview for now," Anna said.

She said what she needed to for the recording, stood, and went through the motions of getting Nancy back to her holding cell. The woman swanned off with her solicitor and a uniform as if she were going home instead.

Anna smiled at Lenny, needing just a moment to forget all this and talk about something else. "I didn't ask you how that third date went."

"Ah, it went better than dates one and two."

"Did you get dessert?"

"I did."

"And will you be going back for seconds?"

"I will."

Anna laughed and led the way to the incident room. She had interviews to read through. Yvette's official one from last night, and Nancy's. Then there was making sure they had all their ducks in a row with regards to the investigation, and that would take a good couple of days to get through. Oliver had left some notes out for her regarding Mrs Drummond's daughters, although he'd said they didn't recall anything sinister about Arnold, so the interview was a bust. She also wanted to get hold of digi-forensics to see if any of those emails from Nancy to Yvette had been found. They'd make interesting reading. Then there was a courtesy visit to Elizabeth to let her know who'd killed Mina, not something Anna was looking forward to, but it had to be done.

There was one loose end bugging her, and she'd likely never know the answer now: Why had Arnold left the Plough for an hour that night in 2004? Did he have some of his child victims on the go as adults? Did they meet for sex? Was one a man, and that's why he wouldn't admit to it?

She boiled the kettle and made coffee for the rest of the team, handing the cups out and letting them know what Nancy had said during her interview. They discussed her mental state for a while, and all concluded there was something wrong and that she ought to be assessed again.

"That Cow Shed sounds a bit creepy," Louise said.

"Thank God Yvette decided to open her mouth, eh?" Anna said.

"It took her long enough," Rupert grumbled. "If she hadn't been so nosy, going out to see what they'd been doing that night Effie was in the boot, no one else would have died. Nancy would have been arrested, and George wouldn't have had a heart attack."

"I expect Yvette will live with the guilt of that for the rest of her life," Anna said. "She's already tormented herself for twenty years."

"What's happening about Harry Wells?" Oliver asked.

"It doesn't sit comfortably with me to not mention it to the CPS, so I'll tell them he's admitted to buying stolen goods, explain there's no proof he bought the beer from Scranton and Dickens, and they can do what they will with that. As long as I've done the right thing, then I'll sleep at night."

What a hypocrite she was. She harboured secret feelings for a former member of the Kings, and a part of her admired them for the way they'd dealt with criminals, getting stuck in and issuing threats, shutting shit down with menace, something as a police officer she couldn't do.

So she didn't allow herself to dwell on that. Instead she grabbed Lenny's attention and asked him to go to see Elizabeth with her. It was a sad visit — the poor woman was confused as to why Nancy had murdered her daughter, but, like she'd said, she now had some form of closure.

Back at the station, Anna glanced at the clock. It was almost lunchtime. "Sod it. Shall we go down the Hoof for some food? The paperwork's still going to be here when we get back. I'll ask Isabella if she wants to come with us."

Anna nipped to the DCI's office and made her offer.

"Don't mind if I do," Isabella said. "Thank you for including me."

The team left the building, some of the weight of the case lifting from Anna's shoulders, making her steps lighter. Just a few more hours to get through today, then she could have a seriously introverted evening. Pyjamas and slippers. The fire on. A ready meal, a glass of wine, a book.

Sounds good to me.

* * *

At the end of the day, Anna remembered she hadn't given Molly her fifty quid. Sighing that she wouldn't get her peace and quiet as quickly as she'd thought, she dropped Lenny off at home — he was having a fourth date at his lady friend's house — and drove to a cashpoint. She drew the money out, got back in the car, and headed towards Molly's street. She wasn't about to park up there and alert anyone that Molly had passed information to the police, so she stopped down a lane that led to some private garages and sent the Queen of Northgate a message.

Anna: *Sorry, I've been tied up. I've got your £50.*

Molly: *I'm a bit busy at the moment.*

Anna: *When should I give it to you, then?*

Molly: *Actually, can you come to Jubilee Lake?*

Anna didn't like the sound of that. Jubilee Lake meant the possibility of bumping into Parole. Had Molly lied to her and she was in with the ex-gangster after all? Or was she there for another reason entirely? The coincidence was a bit much for Anna, so she worded her response carefully.

Anna: *Make sure you're alone because I don't want anyone seeing me handing this cash over.*

Molly: *Okay. I'll wait outside by the red Porsche.*

Was that Molly's way of letting her know she *was* with Parole without actually saying it outright? Was he looking over her shoulder at what she was typing? Much as Molly was a little bugger for fencing stolen goods, Anna didn't like the idea of her being controlled by a man like Parole, for whatever reason.

Anna: *Are you okay?*

Molly: *Yes.*

Instead of having a back-and-forth conversation to determine whether Molly had told the truth there, Anna drove over to find out for herself. Molly was indeed standing by the Porsche, but then so was Parole and someone else Anna hadn't expected to see.

She got out of her car and approached. "What's going on?"

Harry Wells folded his arms and tucked his hands under his armpits. "I didn't want to tell you any of this, but these two have taken it out of my hands by getting you here. Parole's guffing on about turning over a new leaf and going straight so he can't help, and it seems Molly thinks I'm in danger and I'm going to get murdered in my bed tonight."

Anna hadn't checked social media to see whether Shannon's and Tanner's deaths had been reported yet. If they had and this lot had seen it, had Molly got it into her head that Harry was next?

"Firstly, Shannon and Tanner being dead is nothing whatsoever to do with any of you," Anna said. "You don't need to worry about it at all. The person who did it has been arrested."

"Shannon? Tanner?" Molly said. "How the fucking hell did you keep *that* quiet?"

Anna couldn't help but smile. "Well, it isn't going to be kept quiet for long now that *you* know, is it?"

"Who did it?" Molly said.

She may as well tell them. It would be on the news soon. "Nancy Rawlings."

"Never!" Harry said.

"Effie and Mina as well?" Molly asked.

Anna nodded. "Yes. Anyway, what's the problem? What's going on here?"

"I've had a message," Harry said.

"Which was?"

"From inside, if you know what I mean."

"Scranton and Dickens?" Anna confirmed.

"Sounds like a fucking solicitor's outfit," Parole muttered.

Anna ignored him. She refused to even look at him in the light coming from the apartment block's foyer. "What was it? An email? A bit of paper sent in the post?"

Harry shook his head. "No, someone came in the pub. They said if it was me who'd told the police about buying the beer, I'd better start watching my back."

"Hang on a minute, how did they find out about that? My lot haven't done anything with the info yet, as far as I know." *There's definitely a leak at the station.*

"No idea. I made out I didn't know what they were on about. I said, 'What beer?' and they said, 'You know what beer!' and I said, 'Fucking hell, that was years ago and I'd forgotten all about it.'"

"Do you think they believed you?" Anna asked.

"I don't know."

Anna glanced from Harry to Molly. "What are you three playing at?"

Molly let out a cloud of breath. "Me and Harry, we've become friends. We're going to trade estate information instead of being arseholes to each other and butting heads. Anyway, I was there with my Basil earlier when that bloke came and visited. Don't ask me who he is because I've never seen him before in my life. I can give you a description, and he'll show up on Harry's CCTV anyway, but he sounded like he was from farther up north. So I suggested to Harry we come and speak to Parole, because he knows people inside who might be able to have a word with Scranton and Dickens."

"Molly, are you suggesting what I think you're suggesting?" Anna asked. "Because if you are, I'm going to walk away now and pretend we didn't have this conversation."

"Then pretend," Parole said.

"So much for you going straight," Anna clapped back. Her stomach rolled over, and she continued to look at Molly. "The reason I've actually come here in the first place — am I doing it out in the open or . . . ?"

"Yeah, out in the open. I let them know that I lent you the money and you were going to pay me back."

If Molly wanted to play this little game, that was up to her. Money handed over, Anna retreated to her car, but then her conscience got the better of her. Harry had just admitted he'd been threatened and his life may be in danger. She shouldn't walk away and leave it for an ex-gang member and a nosy parker to deal with. What would that make her?

A bent copper, that's what.

She struggled with her conscience. Her feelings, her morals. And glanced back at the trio who still stood by that Porsche.

"For fuck's sake," she whispered, then called out louder, "Do you want to officially report this?"

"No, we're fine," Harry said. "Nothing to see here."

Now she'd offered her help and it had been refused, she'd done her duty, although she still felt bad. She got in her car and drove away, hoping to God nothing happened to Harry, because, if it did, she was only going to blame herself.

THE END

THE JOFFE BOOKS STORY

We began in 2014 when Jasper agreed to publish his mum's much-rejected romance novel and it became a bestseller.

Since then we've grown into the largest independent publisher in the UK. We're extremely proud to publish some of the very best writers in the world, including Joy Ellis, Faith Martin, Caro Ramsay, Helen Forrester, Simon Brett and Robert Goddard. Everyone at Joffe Books loves reading and we never forget that it all begins with the magic of an author telling a story.

We are proud to publish talented first-time authors, as well as established writers whose books we love introducing to a new generation of readers.

We won Trade Publisher of the Year at the Independent Publishing Awards in 2023 and Best Publisher Award in 2024 at the People's Book Prize. We have been shortlisted for Independent Publisher of the Year at the British Book Awards for the last five years, and were shortlisted for the Diversity and Inclusivity Award at the 2022 Independent Publishing Awards. In 2023 we were shortlisted for Publisher of the Year at the RNA Industry Awards, and in 2024 we were shortlisted at the CWA Daggers for the Best Crime and Mystery Publisher.

We built this company with your help, and we love to hear from you, so please email us about absolutely anything bookish at feedback@joffebooks.com.

If you want to receive free books every Friday and hear about all our new releases, join our mailing list here: www.joffebooks.com/freebooks.

And when you tell your friends about us, just remember: it's pronounced Joffe as in coffee or toffee!

www.ingramcontent.com/pod-product-compliance
Ingram Content Group UK Ltd.
Pitfield, Milton Keynes, MK11 3LW, UK
UKHW021310190825
7460UKWH00009BA/121

9 781805 732181